"I feel obliged to let you know that you have once again caught me skulking about." The familiar voice sent shivers up her spine. Shivers that had nothing to do with the inclement weather.

"Your grace?" Vivian turned to see the duke standing in front of a settee that boasted plump cushions and an unobstructed view of the summer rain on the lake. The sky crackled as a streak of lightning blazed through the clouds. The answering thunder came only seconds later.

"Like you, I am a refugee seeking shelter from the storm," he said. "Please join me. I promise not to pry into your business unless asked."

"Your grace, I apologize for my behavior earlier. I have *such* a temper, and it sometimes gets the best of me, no matter how I try. Please accept my apologies."

"I will accept yours if you will accept mine. You were right. I have no business interfering in your affairs. I was simply reacting to your distress without thinking."

She smiled up at him, her attention held once again by cornflower-blue eyes that made her feel so…wanted. "A truce, then?" She extended her hand.

He raised his eyebrows.

"At least until the storm is over?"

The blue eyes twinkled. "Agreed."

He took her hand, marveling at how perfectly it fit in his own. And then he noticed her gown.

"Uh…may I offer you my coat? Your dress seems to be rather…ah…damp." In fact, what her dress seemed to be was the most erotic piece of clothing he had ever seen, and on a woman who already dangerously intrigued

Praise for Carolina Prescott

THE DUKE'S DECISION was a winner in the Historical Romance category in the 2019 Fiction From the Heartland contest of the Mid America Romance Authors in Kansas City.

The Duke's Decision

by

Carolina Prescott

Dukes in Danger:
A Haversham House Romance

The Duke's Decision

Cover Art by *Debbie Taylor*

The Wild Rose Press, Inc.
PO Box 708
Adams Basin, NY 14410-0708
Visit us at www.thewildrosepress.com

Publishing History
First Tea Rose Edition, 2021
Trade Paperback ISBN 978-1-5092-3396-0
Digital ISBN 978-1-5092-3397-7

Dukes in Danger: A Haversham House Romance
Published in the United States of America

To WPG, with thanks

Chapter 1

London, May 1815

"Did you say the third shelf, Mr. Alexander? I don't see it."

Vivian, Viscountess Rowden, ran a gloved finger over the spines of the books in front of her, happily examining the myriad titles. Generally speaking, ladies visiting Alexander's Books, Newspapers, Magazines, and Engravings sought out the recently published works of Maria Edgeworth or Mrs. Radcliffe, currently elegantly displayed atop tables on the right-hand side of Mr. Alexander's bookstore.

Generally speaking, however, the interests of Lady Rowden were not the same as those of most other ladies.

Vivian spent her time in Alexander's bookstore on the left-hand side of the shop—the general knowledge section in front of her was a particular favorite, even if it did want for a bit of a dusting. For her, Alexander's was a sort of Mecca, Xanadu, and the Promised Land all rolled into one convenient location. Every time she stepped through the door, she was transported by the smell of fresh ink and old paper—more pleasing to her than the most exotic perfume.

"It must be on one of the upper shelves, my lady. A moment and I will fetch it for you."

1

The murmur of voices at the front of the store reminded Vivian she was not Mr. Alexander's only customer this morning.

"No need to bother, Mr. Alexander. The ladder is just here. I'll have a look myself."

That was one of the many lovely things about Mr. Alexander and his shop. He never made one feel hurried or out of place. In fact, he encouraged browsing in all corners of his well-stocked store—even if not at all levels.

"Oh, no, my lady, please don't..." Vivian looked down to see Mr. Alexander shaking his head as he steadied the precariously perched ladder and watched Vivian make her way up to the tallest shelf.

"You know, dear lady," he scolded half-heartedly, "there really is no need for you to do *everything* yourself."

"It's no trouble at all, Mr. Alexander. Oh, I think I see it." Holding on with only one gloved hand, Vivian leaned over to examine the titles more closely as Mr. Alexander clucked in dismay.

"No, that's not it after all, although that one looks quite interesting as well."

With one hand still securing the ladder, Mr. Alexander bent slightly and pulled a volume from a lower shelf. "Lady Rowden? I believe this is the title you seek, is it not?"

"Oh, yes, Mr. Alexander. That *is* it. Thank you."

Mr. Alexander held the book, the ladder, and his breath while Vivian climbed nimbly down and back to *terra firma*.

"And now, if you don't mind, Mr. Alexander, I should also like to look at your astronomy books."

"Is there a particular volume I might locate for you, my lady?"

"I think I will just browse for a bit, if you will permit me?"

"Certainly, my lady. I'll take this one to the front for you, but please let me know if you need any assistance."

Vivian's beaming smile was just the right combination of contriteness and appreciation. "I promise, Mr. Alexander. Thank you."

She watched the proprietor trot down the center aisle before she turned back to her browsing.

The tall shelves made the most of every nook and cranny in the small but respected shop that held its own in the heart of Bond Street's fashionable traffic, and Mr. Alexander's well-earned reputation for being able to track down any book in print made it a popular spot—especially among the more literary members of the *ton*.

Only last week Vivian had asked Mr. Alexander to find her a book explaining Leonardo Fibonacci's sequence of numbers as they related to naturally occurring events, such as pinecones and daisies. She had asked for Fibonacci's work in the original Italian, and Mr. Alexander never batted an eye. On occasion, he would even discuss her selections with her as if she were a scholar, not just a woman. And only last week he had conceded a rather spirited debate about which of Shakespeare's plays was the most politically charged.

Vivian pulled out a book by Galileo Galilei and then reshelved it with a sigh. It was the same title she had purchased on her last visit.

Perhaps Mr. Alexander's most endearing trait was

that he was either oblivious to, or not interested in, the gossip that surrounded the death of Vivian's husband two years past. After a whirlwind courtship and fairy-tale wedding, her vision of living happily ever after with Henry, Viscount Rowden was soon dimmed by the viscount's unmitigated excesses and his careless indifference. That vision was shattered entirely with the news of her husband's untimely death in a high-priced brothel where he and several ladies of the demimonde were engaged in...group activities.

The dreadful scandal had made it impossible for Vivian to remain in London, where even the rituals of mourning triggered wide speculation behind open fans and closed doors. So, rather than pretend she didn't notice the curious glances and the whispers that cloaked themselves as condolences, Vivian fled London and the *ton.*

At the time, she was sure her life was over.

Henry's title and estate had gone to a distant cousin, but the shame of a failed marriage and the specter of her husband's depraved demise was his legacy to her. Confronting the circumstances of his death was *almost* as painful as admitting her own naiveté and acknowledging that the man she thought she loved—the man she trusted—had made a mockery of his wedding vows from the very start.

As a result of her husband's treachery, Vivian had made new vows—this time to herself. Never again would she allow herself to believe in all those silly notions of falling in love, and never again would she be susceptible to romantic words and promises from any man. She'd had her chance with Henry and had failed miserably. There was no need for a repeat performance.

But to be fair, things were not all bad.

At least Henry had the decency to die before he squandered *all* his money. His death left Vivian a widow of independent means, making it possible for her to live comfortably for the rest of her life—without the expectations and restrictions forced upon unmarried ladies and without the trouble and heartbreak of a husband.

The only real difficulty she faced was finding a place that would accept her…and her scandalous past.

The cottage near the ocean came to Vivian's attention quite by accident. Thinking the waters at Bath would provide a much needed respite, she traveled there, only to find that—although news *did* travel more slowly to Bath—the gossip of her husband's sensational demise still preceded her. Only by traveling farther toward the coast had she found the little village of Burnham-on-Sea and, on its outskirts, the vacant house that was now her home and sanctuary. It was here that Vivian found the scattered pieces of her former self and slowly started putting them back together again.

Vivian had always loved puzzles. At school, she delighted in creating enigmas and ciphers for the other girls to solve, and back in London, she was a devoted follower of the weekly puzzle page published by the *Mail Observer*, the city's most popular newspaper.

When they were courting, Henry ridiculed Vivian's passion for puzzles, making fun of her efforts to be the first of her friends to solve the weekly offerings. After their wedding, however, Henry suddenly stopped teasing her about her pastime and actually encouraged her puzzle making. He even went so far as to convince the editor of the local gazette to include one of her ciphers in the weekly newssheet—under a male pseudonym, of course.

After Henry's death, Vivian again sought distraction in the weekly puzzle challenges published by the *London Mail Observer*. Losing herself in the patterns of words and numbers kept the waves of loneliness and sadness at bay—at least for a few hours every week. Once, she found an error in one of the ciphers and wrote to the paper's editor pointing out the mistake. He responded by asking if she might be interested in creating some new puzzles for him to publish, and she happily agreed.

Of course, it was possible that the editor of the esteemed *Mail Observer* might be under the impression that the V. I. Burningham with whom he corresponded was an Oxford-educated, somewhat impoverished gentleman tutoring the eldest son of the local squire. But that same editor thought the puzzles of V. I. Burningham "brilliant" and the work of a "true genius," so who was she to contradict?

Not to mention that the income she derived from her creations was growing into quite the tidy nest egg, making the whole venture a most satisfying endeavor.

In a way, it was that same editor who brought her here today and had her browsing through the astronomy section of Mr. Alexander's bookstore. Vivian lacked only the right bit of information to complete one last puzzle, and then she would be ready to present her brand-new idea—a variety of puzzles with a common theme—to the editor at the *Mail Observer*. Exactly how *she* was going to present the puzzles to an editor who thought her to be a male tutor in Somerset was one enigma she had yet to solve.

But that was a problem for tomorrow.

Today's problem was finishing the cryptogram for her astronomy series. Vivian had studied the writings of Copernicus and Newton at school—usually when she was supposed to be memorizing Debrett's—but the information she needed for this particular word puzzle was outside the scope of her knowledge and her library. Reading her way around to the other side of the shelf, Vivian stood on tiptoe, reaching for a fat volume entitled *Des Mouvements Celestes, a l'usage Des Astronomes et Des Navigateurs* when a larger, gloved hand covered hers. Startled, she followed the hand's arm to its source and found herself looking up into the face of a very tall gentleman with very broad shoulders.

"Do allow me, my lady."

The annoyed look on the man's face did nothing to mar his extraordinarily handsome visage. His height eclipsed the light from the store's front windows, adding an air of mystery to his sudden appearance, but even in the dim light of the shop Vivian could see that his features were strong under the brim of his top hat—even a bit angular—and his eyes were a brilliant cornflower blue. The faint, fresh scent of balsam fir surrounding him made her yearn for a walk in the forest.

"I...ah...thank you, sir," she stammered, not quite able to catch her breath for some reason. "I thought Mr. Alexander's customer had departed. I assumed I was alone."

The gentleman easily lifted the book from the shelf and opened it. He was so...big. His presence made Vivian feel small, and at the same time, strangely protected—even though he exuded a masculine energy that was in itself rather threatening.

"I generally find it wise to assume nothing, madam," continued the gentleman, glancing down his nose at her before he returned to leafing leisurely through the pages of her book. "That way, I am seldom surprised."

The man's condescension was palpable and, all of a sudden, it was entirely too much for Vivian.

Resisting the urge to stamp her foot, she closed her eyes and took a deep breath before exhaling loudly. Then she slowly shook her head. *This* was the type of man she normally encountered in bookstores—the type that would kindly, but firmly, steer her to the artfully arranged tables displaying a popular volume of verse or the latest novel. Or—even more likely—the type that would pompously direct her out the door and down the street to the closest modiste.

"What a pity," she replied, looking up at the gentleman in mock sympathy. "No surprises must make for a very dull existence. If it is not too much trouble, sir, may I have *my* book?"

Raising his eyebrows, the man looked down at the heavy tome. "You are actually purchasing *this* book? On astronomy?"

"Actually purchasing and actually reading it," she said holding out her hands and smiling brightly as he slowly relinquished the item. "See how delightful surprises can be?"

Before he could respond, Vivian turned on her heel and marched to the front of the store.

"If you would be so kind as to add this to my account, Mr. Alexander, I'm afraid I'm late for an appointment."

"Certainly, Lady Rowden. It would be my pleasure."

"Thank you, Mr. Alexander. Good day!"

****

The door closed smartly, leaving behind a most pleasant scent of lavender with a slightly spicier scent that was more difficult to identify. As he emerged from the shadowed stacks, Whitaker Graham, the eleventh Duke of Whitley, known as "Whit" to the favored few who called him friend, looked toward the now-closed door and furrowed his brow. He glanced around the store to confirm there were no other customers—the very popularity that made Alexander's an excellent drop location was also, at times, a great inconvenience. Assured of their privacy, he turned to scowl at the smiling proprietor—a veritable emotional outburst for the painstakingly dignified and proper peer who was called the "Ice Duke" by more than one debutante's mother.

"Who the devil was that?"

The shop's bell still quivered from the lady's dramatic exit.

"That, your grace, was Lady Rowden, widow of the late and unlamented Viscount Rowden."

"The one who died *in flagrante delicto* several years back?"

"The very one. Remember how everyone thought the marriage such a love match? The lady and her viscount were touted as *la grande passion* of the season. As it turns out, it *was* a love match—she loved him and he loved his mistresses."

Whit looked out toward the street where the lady had vanished. "Why would anyone who had *her* ever want anyone else?"

"I beg your pardon, your grace?"

"Never mind. There was an inquiry into the viscount's death, was there not?"

"Yes, of course. He was a peer, after all, and a relatively young one, at that. As I recall, there was even a French connection, which fueled rumors of foreign intrigue—one of his many paramours, I believe. Nothing came of it, as far as I know, but the scandal was the first topic of conversation in every drawing room for quite some time."

"Yes, now I remember. The papers said his mistress was a spy. Did they say anything about the viscountess? I don't remember reading anything about her."

"The mistress was a spy, the viscountess was a spy, the valet was a spy, the butler was a spy—everyone was a spy. Like most scandals, without fuel it eventually died down and the next one took over." Mr. Alexander shrugged. "The whole incident happened more than two years ago, but this is the first time Lady Rowden has been back to London since her husband's death. She's here for her cousin's first season. Lady Rowden told me she was in need of additional resources for solving a puzzle. She said my bookstore was the very first shop she visited upon her return to London. Such a lovely lady."

"How charming. I am delighted that you and she have become such fast friends. Perhaps she will invite you to tea and then she can explain why she purchased the book containing *my* message."

"Really? I had no idea which book it was in—I only knew which shelf it was on. I'm sure it was just a coincidence. Lady Rowden comes in quite often and is interested in many different topics, so she goes all over the store."

"If she is constantly in your shop, then she would be familiar with your stock and would know, for example, when there was a new book on a shelf. I don't believe in coincidences, Mr. Alexander, and, as I told the lady, I don't care for surprises. I barely managed to retrieve the message before I handed the book over to her. You're to put it on her account, I believe."

"And the message? I assume it was what you expected?"

"Never assume anything, Alexander. I'll bring a reply tomorrow. In the meantime, keep your eyes open. If someone has learned that the Home Office is using your store as a drop, then the entire plan will need to change. I'll set my men to watch as well."

"Certainly, your grace. Good day."

Chapter 2

How typical of a man to imply she was in the wrong place just because she was looking at books on astronomy rather than poetry.

How arrogant of him to presume she couldn't lift a heavy book just because he was bigger and taller and had incredibly broad shoulders.

How rude for him to monopolize Mr. Alexander's attention in the first place with his cornflower-blue eyes—although, Vivian grudgingly admitted to herself, Mr. Alexander may not have noticed the color of his eyes, as such.

But that wasn't the point.

Mr. Alexander never treated her as if she were some helpless female. He never held one of her books hostage simply because he found it hard to believe she could be interested in it.

Yes, the book was heavy, and yes, she *had* dropped the previous one on her toes—which still hurt, by the way—but that was no reason for him to be so condescending or so…so…attractive.

And it was certainly no reason for him to assume— oh, but wait, she corrected herself—he *never* assumed. She smiled. Maybe not, but she did give him a bit of a surprise.

After her dramatic exit from the bookseller's, Vivian almost forgot her errand to stop by the haberdashery to pick up a length of violet ribbon to wear in her hair at Lady Calloway's ball tomorrow night. The jewels she might have worn as Viscountess Rowden were locked up under the eye of the new viscount, and to be honest, she was much happier with a plain ribbon than she would have been with all of Henry's family jewels.

With her purchase tucked securely in her reticule, she smiled at the street sweeper motioning for her to cross and quickened her pace. Her aunt and uncle's Mayfair house was just a few blocks away. With any luck, she'd be in time for tea.

****

Thomson opened the door before she could even touch the handle.

"Good afternoon, Lady Rowden. Miss Braddock was just inquiring as to your whereabouts. I believe she and Lady Thea are having tea sent up to the family parlor. May I take your package?"

"Yes, thank you, Thomson. Mind you, it's rather heavy. If you will have it sent up to my room along with my things, I'll join my aunt and cousin."

Vivian patted her hair and confirmed her appearance with a quick glance into the looking glass in the foyer. Her new topaz walking dress was one of the first items she'd ordered upon her arrival in London almost four weeks ago. She still smiled every time she saw how the rich color set off her chestnut hair.

When her cousin Linea sent the first note begging Vivian to come to London to participate in Linea's debut, Vivian had declined. Courteously, but adamantly. The last thing Linney needed was a widowed cousin who added, not respectability, but the specter of an old scandal.

When Linney's mother, Vivian's favorite aunt, added her pleas in a second note, pointing out that Vivian's period of mourning was up and no one would remember anything about the viscount anyway in light of the news that Napoleon had escaped his island prison and was regrouping on the continent, Vivian demurred. Graciously, but firmly.

But then, in a third missive, when Linney cunningly mentioned how Vivian—now with the freedom afforded a widow in society—could go all over the city to museums and bookstores without worrying about the proprieties that burdened unmarried women, Vivian finally acquiesced.

Truth be told, she missed London and its connections with the outside world. She also missed Linney, who was really more like a sister than a cousin. Their mothers had been sisters who shared everything, and when a fever took Vivian's mother and father within weeks of each other, Aunt Thea and Uncle Will had insisted on raising Vivian as their own along with their own daughter.

Being back in London at the familiar address would be a welcome homecoming, but Vivian was all too aware that her very presence could spell catastrophe for Linney's coming out—something she was determined would not happen.

Linney, you must understand the precarious position I would put you in, wrote Vivian to her cousin in her last letter on the subject. *As Aunt Thea well knows, your whole season could end before it even gets started if the ton decides to refocus on the scandal surrounding Henry's death. My condition for coming to*

London is that if there is any hint—even a whiff—of gossip, or if there are any comments that take hold or cause any slight to you, I must be allowed to leave immediately, with no further discussion. It is simply too important that this season be about your future—not about my past. You must promise me this.

Linney seemed to understand Vivian's determination and promised to comply in an oddly submissive note. *Whatever you say, Vivian. I'm just so happy that you'll be here to share it with me. Do let me tell you about the invitations we've accepted so far...*

Knowing her stubborn and headstrong cousin, Vivian suspiciously read and re-read the letter for loopholes but could find none. The reply from Aunt Thea was almost as bad. *We all agree with what you are saying, Vivian, but darling, there will be some gossip simply because you are who you are and have come to town.*

Vivian agreed but still wanted to make her position clear. *Tidbits of gossip are fine, Aunt Thea—as long as the gossip does not stick, or in any way affect Linney's season. I will have your and Uncle Will's word on it, otherwise I'll not stay one night. I will not have my scandal ruin Linney's debut.*

And so, with everyone in agreement, Vivian had arrived almost a month ago to an enthusiasm not usually displayed so openly in polite society.

"Here you are at last, Vivian," Linney had exclaimed as she tumbled out onto the front stoop to welcome her cousin. Her greeting made up in unbridled joy what it lacked in correctness.

Vivian smiled at the butler who held the door open with nary a disapproving sniff. "Thank you, Thomson. I see that the prospect of being presented to the Queen has not dampened Miss Braddock's overall *joie de vivre*."

"No, my lady. Indeed, if I might be allowed to venture an observation, it has served to do the exact opposite."

Vivian laughed. "That is rather frightening, Thomson. Thank you for the warning."

Vivian had also cautioned Linney and Aunt Thea that her wardrobe included only mourning clothes, so the weeks following her arrival were quickly eaten up with countless trips to the incomparable Madame Augustine, who all but gushed over Vivian's coloring—so different from her cousin's white-blonde hair and green eyes. The supremely talented modiste constantly reminded Vivian how fortunate she was now that she was no longer restricted to wearing the pastels of an unmarried ingénue and could *luxuriate*—Madame Augustine's word—in the vibrant gemstone colors that flattered her hair and her dark brown eyes. "And of course you still have your youthful figure, but," the modiste added knowingly, "with the voluptuous curves that come with maturity."

"We've both had voluptuous curves of maturity since the age of thirteen," whispered Vivian to Linney, who broke into peals of laughter.

"Yes, *cherie*," whispered Mme. Augustine, who missed absolutely nothing, "but unlike when you were thirteen, you can now show them off." She then proceeded to do just that, causing even Aunt Thea to gasp when Vivian emerged from the dressing room.

"Oh, my dear, you look stunning! That amethyst sarsnet simply glows. And the cut…Madame

Augustine, you have outdone yourself."

"Oh, Vivian," said Linney in a hushed whisper. "You are so lovely. That color is gorgeous on you—oh, look how it changes and shimmers when you walk."

Linney stood up suddenly. "Vivian, you will *not* wear that gown to my coming-out ball. I forbid it! Papa can pay for another gown to be finished in time. I refuse to compete with you in that. Oh, Viv, promise me you'll wait until the end of the season to accept any of the gaggle of suitors who will be hounding your every step."

The amethyst ball gown would make its debut tomorrow at Lady Calloway's ball—safely *after* Linney's spectacularly successful presentation ball. The topaz walking dress, however, had arrived two days later, and by the end of the next week Vivian had collected a long list of wardrobe items that featured a midnight-blue riding habit, three evening gowns, two ball gowns—not counting the amethyst creation— several walking dresses, four day dresses, and various and sundry other items, including matching shoes, headdresses, fans, parasols, reticules, gloves, and any number of undergarments and nightgowns.

In his generosity, Uncle Will had insisted upon paying for Vivian's entire wardrobe and accessories because—as he put it—Vivian was the one doing *him* a favor by ensuring the successful launch of his daughter. It was his honor, he insisted, to be escorting three such lovely ladies about town.

Pausing at the door to the family parlor, Vivian smiled at the picture her cousin made, sitting on the floor at her mother's feet. Aunt Thea looked up at her niece and motioned her in.

"Oh, Vivian. There you are, dear. We just rang for tea. I was asking Linney if she had decided what she was wearing to Larette's recital tonight."

Linney jumped up and came over to place a kiss on Vivian's cheek. "I asked Mary to press the rose muslin, Mother. I don't want to wear the blue because Lady Evenstone just had blue watered silk hung in the music room, and I would blend right in with the walls."

"She did tell me she was thinking about making a change," said Lady Thea. "The watered silk sounds lovely. Oh, good, Nancy, you brought up a cup for Lady Rowden."

"Yes, madam," said the maid, setting down the tray. "And this letter just arrived for you, my lady."

"Thank you, Nancy," said Vivian, taking the folded paper to open.

"You must let me know how it looks when you girls get home. I was thinking about doing something similar in our dining room." Aunt Thea handed her daughter a cup of tea and then poured one for Vivian.

"How about you, Vivian?" asked Linney. "Have you decided what you'll be wearing tonight?"

"Oh, no!"

"Whatever is the matter, dear?" asked Aunt Thea.

"It's Annie, my maid. She was to meet me here in London when she returned from her visit with her family in the North. But her mother has fallen ill, and she wants to stay a while longer to take care of her father and her brothers and sisters. I must write to her immediately—I'm sure she's beside herself with concern about disappointing me, but right now she just needs to attend to her own family. Maybe I should take a trip up there and see if I can be of assistance."

Linney took Vivian's cup of tea from her mother and held it out to her cousin. "Sit here, Vivian. That is a lovely thought, and you are the most goodhearted person I know, but I'm sure Annie would rather have you here so she doesn't have to worry about taking care of you as well as taking care of her family."

"You're right, of course, Linney. I wasn't thinking. I'll send books and treats for the children and maybe a tonic for her mother. I hope it's nothing too serious. Poor Annie—she's such a wonder. I'm always so lost without her, but I'm glad she's there for her family."

"Margie can act as your maid until Annie returns, Vivian. Or maybe the new maid, Estelle. Mrs. Jacobs hired her for the upstairs, but she has experience as a lady's maid. I'll talk with Mrs. Jacobs in the morning, but Margie can help you get dressed tonight."

As usual, Aunt Thea had the household well in hand.

"Thank you, Aunt Thea, but that's what I came up to tell you both. I don't think I can go tonight, after all. I'm so sorry, Linney, but I must finish this last puzzle for the paper before I meet with the editor tomorrow morning. Maybe Uncle Will and Aunt Thea can go with you."

"Are you sure, Viv?" Linney put down her cup. "I did so want you to hear Larette play. She is such a talented pianist. And I wanted to introduce you to…ah…to some of my friends."

"I would really love to go, Linney, but I just don't see any way around it. I have to get this puzzle to the offices of the *Mail Observer* by tomorrow morning, and it's proving more contrary than the other ones. I bought a new book at Mr. Alexander's that I hope will give me the information I need to finish."

"Mama, do you and Papa want to go? I know Larette would love for you to hear her play."

"Well, I can certainly see if your father would be willing to go out this evening. I *would* like to see that watered silk…"

"Good, then it's all settled," said Vivian. "I feel so much better knowing you're going with Linney. Thank you, Aunt Thea."

"Linney, pass Vivian a biscuit. I'll go and check with your father to make sure he's amenable to our plans." Aunt Thea left the room, but immediately popped her head back in with a smile. "And just so you know, I'm going to wear my azure taffeta with the pearls—I don't mind blending in with the background." She left her daughter and niece laughing.

Waiting until she heard Aunt Thea's footsteps on the stairs, Vivian took a teacake and smiled at Linney. "*I* know why you're wearing the rose muslin, and it has nothing to do with watered blue silk on the walls."

"Why, whatever do you mean, cousin?"

"Which gentleman are you thinking to snag with that dress that shows your every curve?"

"I don't know what you're talking about, Vivian. The rose muslin is very…comfortable."

"What is his name?"

"Well, if you must know, I am hoping to cross paths with the Earl of Hammond at some point this evening. He is the Duke of Easton's heir."

"And exactly where did you meet this Lord Hammond?"

"I've told you about him. He's the gentleman from the park who was so rude to Allyce."

"And *he's* the one you want to impress?"

"Yes. Ever since he apologized. Are you sure you won't go with us, Viv? I do so want you to meet him."

"I'm sorry, Linney. I'm sure there will be another opportunity for me to meet your earl."

"You'll miss Larette's new piece. She really is quite brilliant, and her sisters are doing only one piece each at the very beginning."

"It's not about the quality of the event, Linney. I simply must finish this word graph. I cannot believe how long it has already taken me." She smiled at her cousin. "I have neglected my work since coming to London, and I blame you. I don't know when I've had so much fun."

"I know, me too! When all the other girls talk about their day, I feel so smug. I know I shouldn't, but if I had to spend an entire day selecting a pair of gloves or listening to a gentleman wax on about his selection of waistcoats, I would never leave my bedroom. We have been all over the city—I could spend a lifetime just at the British Museum. Having a married cousin is wonderful, and having a widowed cousin is even better. No, don't bother looking at me that way. I won't apologize. Maybe I shouldn't have said it the way I did, but I won't take it back. I'm glad he's gone. You're obviously so much happier as a widow than you were as his wife." Linney took a defiant sip of tea, daring Vivian to contradict her.

"I won't make you apologize because you're right—I am happier. Honestly, I like to think of the whole affair as a nightmare from which I have finally awoken."

"And your reward for putting up with that horrible

man is the freedom you're so generously sharing with me. How much more do you have to do on the—what did you call it? A wordgram?"

"A word graph. It's something I created, and I want to show it to Mr. Davis when I deliver my regular cipher tomorrow."

"And are you going to tell him that *you* are the mysterious V. I. Burningham?"

"I haven't decided yet. He doesn't seem to be the type of man who thinks very highly of educated women. I don't know what his reaction will be if he finds out he's been dealing with a woman all these past months."

"I think it's too bad you don't get any of the credit. The *Mail Observer*'s puzzle page is all the rage. Everyone looks forward to the new puzzles on Tuesdays and Thursdays, and they all try to be the first to solve them. I'm dying to tell everyone that V. I. Burningham is my cousin."

"Well, for right now it needs to be our secret. I don't know whether I'll tell Mr. Davis tomorrow or not. I'll just have to play it by ear. Speaking of playing by ear, shouldn't you be getting dressed?"

"Not yet. Mama will take forever. She knows the younger girls are playing first, and she's terribly picky about the music she listens to. How about you? Shall I go so you can get started on your work? I'll leave you alone if you say so, because I want to make absolutely sure you'll be able to attend Lady Calloway's ball tomorrow night."

"I'm going to finish my tea and then go up. Don't worry about Lady Calloway's ball. My puzzle must be completed tonight. I think I'll ask for a dinner tray to be sent up so I can keep working. I did get the ribbon for my hair while I was out this morning. I found the velvet, and it's just a shade or two lighter than my gown. Have you decided what you'll wear tomorrow?"

"My new yellow silk, I think. At Nadine's mother's garden party, when my hair was all curly because it was getting ready to rain, Avery said my curls made him think of a downy chick. Isn't that lovely?"

"Avery?"

"Lord Hammond. He said I must call him Avery. We've seen each other six times now—seven if you count our first encounter in the park—and each time I find myself more in lov—I mean growing fonder and fonder of him. At Nadine's mother's we strolled for miles and miles, just the two of us."

"You strolled for miles at a garden party?"

"Very well, maybe not miles, but we strolled along the garden paths for quite some time. He says talking with me is like nothing he has ever experienced before." Linney's eyes had taken on a decidedly dreamy quality. "He listens to every word I say, which is one of the many reasons I lov—I esteem him so greatly."

"Linney, I'm sorry to be the one to break this to you, dear, but *nobody* listens to every word you say— mainly because you say so many. How is a person to keep up?"

"Well, Avery—Lord Hammond—does. He says listening to me makes him smile, and he says I make some very intriguing points in our discussions."

"Are you sure it's not just his attraction to your adorable, downy self that colors his opinion?"

"I certainly *hope* that's part of it." Linney batted her eyes at Vivian. "Otherwise a lot of people have gone to a lot of trouble for naught. Just think of tomorrow night. With you wearing your amethyst sarsnet and me in my primrose silk, we'll be opposites in every way. Your dark hair and dark eyes gowned in purple and, on the other side of the coin, I with my blonde hair and green eyes in yellow. We will draw everyone's attention when we arrive. I simply cannot wait!"

"I thought artists were supposed to be shy and reclusive. You *do* understand that not everyone is as keen as you are to be the center of attention," said Vivian, thinking specifically of herself. "Some of us are happy to remain on the sidelines."

"Well, I am here to tell you that *I* am not that kind of artist. I enjoy the limelight, and I am very much looking forward to *not* blending in with the wall coverings tonight—during the interlude, of course, because, after all, it is Larette's night."

"And if I changed my mind and pleaded for you to stay home tonight and help me with my puzzle, would you?"

"Not unless you were deathly ill. Then I would most assuredly *consider* it."

Vivian laughed at her cousin's brutal honesty. "I'm glad you have your priorities in good order, and I do look forward to meeting this paragon of a gentleman who has captured your attention. But for now, I'm away. I believe I have just had a thought that will solve my puzzle problems."

Chapter 3

In fact, the message the Duke of Whitley had taken right out from under Lady Rowden's freckled nose was *not* what he expected.

Whit nodded slightly at a passing acquaintance and stopped briefly to consult his pocket watch before continuing on his way at a slightly faster pace.

The message he *expected*, the message he hoped for, was one saying they had discovered the source of the leak—the breach, the weak link in his chain, the rotten apple in his barrel.

What he *expected* was to hear that the leak had been eliminated, damn it!

What he *expected* was to learn that his extensive network of men and women, carefully cultivated over time, whose job it was to gather information for the Crown, need not be hastily dismantled.

But that was not the message he had received. He knew no more now than he had this morning. If drastic measures had to be taken, then so be it—that was part of his job. But until he knew for sure the identity of the person—or persons—behind the leaks, he could not afford to let anyone else know what he knew.

He hated this aspect of the job...the waiting. The other aspects—the planning, the complicated schemes, the danger, the risk—those he loved, but the waiting... The waiting was beyond his control, which made it totally unacceptable.

Knowing he was being betrayed by someone he trusted made it all the worse. It was a personal affront. He had recruited the leaders for this operation himself. He oversaw their activities, and he made the life-and-death decisions that affected them. He was responsible, and someone was betraying him. And because of that, his entire organization was in jeopardy—scores of individuals, who daily put themselves in danger simply because they loved their country, were at risk because he could not find one villainous traitor. The only thing he knew for sure was that until he found the source of the leak—and until that source was neutralized—*everyone* was a suspect.

Including the lovely Lady Rowden.

Whit climbed the steps to his club and left his hat and gloves with the doorman. It was still early for most members. Afternoon papers and tea time usually signaled the exit of the daytime patrons and the lull that preceded the evening arrivals. It was the perfect time for a public private meeting.

"Good afternoon, your grace. May I bring you some refreshment?"

"My whiskey, please, Alfred. Is Lord Edgewood about?"

"In the back room, your grace. He claims he cannot feel any heat coming from the fire here in the library."

Whit chuckled. For a man who spent a great deal of his time in the cold, wet environs of Scotland, the Earl of Edgewood could be something of a namby-pamby. He was also the only man whom Whit trusted completely.

"You're late." Edgewood squatted before a roaring

fire, thrusting at it with a poker.

"You're early," countered Whit.

"No, we agreed on tea time. Tea time is three o'clock sharp."

"Yes, we agreed on tea time, but tea is properly taken from three o'clock to five o'clock. When split evenly, that is four o'clock. And, if you listen carefully, you can hear the clocks chiming the four o'clock hour just now."

"Humph." Edgewood moved to sit in a leather chair that had been pulled as close as possible to the hearth. "Did you get your answer?"

Whit sat heavily in the chair's twin. "I got a response, but it was not what I wanted to hear—just another possibility and more speculation. Another nail in the coffin, but nothing definitive. I'm beginning to think we won't be able to isolate the leak in time. We may have to make our move without confirmation."

Anyone observing the conversation between the two gentlemen might think they were discussing crops or the weather. Nothing about them betrayed the seriousness of their words or the grave consequences of their decisions.

"If that's the case, then the extraction will have to be bigger so we can be sure the guilty party is caught up in the net."

"Agreed." Whit nodded at the steward who placed a glass of his favorite Scotch whiskey on the table beside him.

"Innocents may be caught as well," said Edgewood, his face convincingly void of concern. There was no need for him to tell Whit what they both already knew. Unless they started the mission as scheduled, more British soldiers would die. But unless they were certain about the identity of the traitor, some of their own operatives would end up being sacrificed.

"That may be unavoidable." Whit stared at the fire through the amber liquid in his glass.

"How long can you wait?"

"I can stall for another week, but we must have a plan in place before *Masquerade* begins."

"And if we don't?"

Both men sat quietly for several moments before Edgewood rose to take up the poker again. "Do you plan to attend the Calloway ball tomorrow night?"

Whit took a sip and leaned back, still holding the heavy glass. "Tomorrow night I am attending the theatre with my family. It is my brother Avery's birthday, and we are taking our sisters and our aunt to hear Mozart. *The Magic Flute.*"

"Might there be room for one more in your party?"

Whit laughed. "What? You don't relish navigating the dance floor at Lady Calloway's? I hear this year's crop of debutantes is quite stunning."

"It's neither the dance floor nor the debutantes I fear. It's the mothers. I have only recently recovered from a bullet wound. I'm not at all prepared for so strenuous an evening."

"Get married, then. I hear it is the only way to successfully avoid the mamas."

"Or I suppose I could take my half-brother, my half-sisters, and my aunt to the theatre and avoid the whole scene, as some cowards do."

"You don't have any sisters, half or otherwise and, God rest her sainted soul, your aunt has been gone these many years. I'll thank you not to call me a coward to my face. I would hate to have to kill you. I dislike replacing operatives in the middle of a mission."

Edgewood laughed. "I like my chances, your grace. My second would have you begging for mercy in less than a minute. His biting sarcasm would force you to retract every slight and confess to all manner of things, and his obsession with duty would have you doing penance for the rest of your life."

"Who is this paragon of strength, cunning, and loyalty? I should see about recruiting him to the cause."

Edgewood laughed again. "You, of course. You are my most stalwart defender and your own worst enemy. In a battle between you and yourself, all bets are off. The only thing certain is that *I* would be the victor."

The two friends were silent for a moment until Edgewood picked up one of the previous threads of conversation. "What about you, your grace? When will you set the hearts of mothers and daughters aflutter and turn to the business of choosing a duchess to set up your nursery?"

An almost imperceptible shudder went through Whit. "Thankfully, my cousin Anthony has had the decency to see to the succession. He will fill the shoes of the Duke of Whitley admirably upon my departure from this realm. Fortunately, he is enamored of his lady wife and that blessed union has already produced two sons. I am free to spend my life in the service of the Crown with no untoward pressure to marry."

"Do you truly believe you can escape the mamas as easily as that?"

"I do if I continue to play my cards right. I am, after all, the Ice Duke—have you forgotten? The ladies suffer the vapors just anticipating a smile from my cold lips. The thought of sharing a bed with me would more than likely send them into a dead faint or fits of apoplexy."

Edgewood snorted and poked more vigorously at the coals. "Not all of them. I could give you quite a long list of females who would be delighted to be your duchess and your bedmate—and not necessarily in that order. Don't you have some business you could do at the Callaway ball?"

"It's beneath the dignity of a peer to pout, Edgewood. You should simply accept the fact that this is not the first time—nor will it be the last—that my strategy proves superior to yours."

"How about the Evenstone musicale tonight?"

Whit took another sip of the excellent whiskey. "What about it?"

"Will you be attending? I understand the oldest daughter is quite accomplished on the pianoforte."

"You know that I seldom attend amateur performances. Why would I make an exception tonight?"

"I just assumed you would be there, since rumor has it that Lady Ferrington will be in attendance and the two of you have...things...in common. It's been months since you dismissed Claire."

"Never assume anything, Edgewood. Not about me and most especially not about my amatory arrangements."

"I don't know what you're waiting for, Whit. It's high time you found a new mistress. Celibacy is making you difficult to deal with."

Whit raised an eyebrow.

"I stand corrected. Celibacy is making you *more*

difficult to deal with. Wait—is it because you have found someone interesting among the field of debutantes?"

Whit gave his friend a look that left no doubt as to the practical possibility of that particular circumstance.

The two men sat for a few minutes more, staring into the fire, each savoring the brief respite before the start of their evening activities. Whit sighed and sat forward, leaning his elbows on his knees and holding his glass in both hands. "I heard that one of the possibilities is a woman. Did you hear that?"

"No, but it doesn't completely surprise me. I've seen women take on some of the most treacherous missions—often right under the collective noses of those who think a woman can't be as dangerous or as cunning as a man. There's nothing like a smart woman to turn a man into a dumb animal. Unfortunately, once those dumb animals figure out they've been duped by a female, the consequences for her are usually more heinous than for her male counterparts. Male spies who are caught are executed on the spot or sent to prison. But if the spy is a female, she is passed around among the men and brutally used before being executed or imprisoned." Edgewood rubbed his hands together and extended them toward the fire. "And that's the work of *our* soldiers."

A sudden vision of Lady Rowden in the hands of undisciplined troops sent a shiver down the Duke of Whitley's spine.

Edgewood saw Whit's reaction. "You feel it too, don't you? No matter how close I sit to the fire, the chill remains."

More minutes ticked by, with each man lost in his

thoughts until Whit broke the silence once again. "I expect I *will* see you later tonight at Lady Evenstone's. Avery seems to have developed a *tendre* for a young lady who, rumor has it, will also be in attendance."

"Let us hope he has a more elegant manner and more success with the ladies than his older brother."

Whit raised his glass. "To Avery's success with the ladies."

Edgewood raised his glass to that of his friend's. "To Avery. And to finding the bloody traitor among us."

Whit tossed back the remaining liquid and set the glass down on the table. As he left, Edgewood was once again poking at the roaring fire.

Chapter 4

"Miss Braddock, you look exquisite this evening, if I may say so."

"You may indeed, Lord Hammond. Especially as it took me the better part of the afternoon to achieve these results. I appreciate your notice and your comment."

Lord Hammond laughed. "I thought ladies did not want gentlemen to know the amount of time they spent on making themselves beautiful—even when it produces such enchanting results."

Linney closed her fan and carelessly touched the end of it to her chin, pretending to think about his words. Finally she murmured, "Lord Hammond, it seems you are still making the error of putting me in the same category as other ladies. Did I not warn you that along that tedious path lies only confusion and disappointment?"

"You did warn me, Miss Braddock," said Avery, with a slight inclination of his head, "but I must respectfully respond that *you* are in error if you believe anything in your sphere of influence could ever bring me disappointment. In truth, it is only those things that take me *out* of your orbit which have the capacity to disappoint." He took Linney's hand and raised it to his lips. "And I would never be so foolish as to try to put you in the same category with other ladies."

"You are quite the expert at flattery, Lord

Hammond. I do wonder if I should be concerned about how you came by such skill and perhaps correlate that skill to your sincerity?"

"You wound me, Miss Braddock. I assure you that it is not practice that makes my remarks perfect, but rather the subject of those remarks."

"Lord Hammond, you make me blush." Linney gently moved her delicately painted fan in front of her face and glanced up at the earl through her eyelashes. "I am quite warm from your compliments, sir, and your words leave me quite speechless—which anyone who knows me will tell you is a feat of great enormity in and of itself."

"Then allow me to change the subject to assist in your comfort. Did you enjoy the first part of the musical entertainment? I did not see you before the performance started."

Linney leaned toward Lord Hammond and whispered so she would not be overheard. "I expect I enjoyed it more than those who sat through it. Never tell me that being prompt is a virtue."

Lord Hammond struggled to contain a shout of laughter. "Miss Braddock, I must tell you that I have not enjoyed an evening this much since I don't know when."

"Indeed, brother, I cannot recall the last occasion when I saw you with such a smile on your face."

Lord Hammond turned to see his half-brother standing behind him. "Whit! I did not expect you here tonight."

"You certainly seem to be enjoying your evening, Avery. Will you share your secret?"

"I'll do better than that. I will introduce you to my

secret. Miss Braddock, may I make known to you my brother, the Duke of Whitley? Whit, may I present Miss Linea Braddock, artist, amateur philosopher, music critic, and daughter of Lady Thea and Mr. William Braddock?"

Linea dropped her best curtsy and held out her gloved hand. Whit took her hand and bowed over it, touching her fingertips briefly to his lips. "Delighted, Miss Braddock. Your father is the senior partner with the firm of Braddock and Longmere, is he not?"

"He is, your grace."

"I am well acquainted with their excellent work. Is he by chance present at tonight's entertainment? I must be sure to pay my respects."

"He and my mother are talking with Lady Evenstone near the refreshment table. I'm afraid our arrival was a bit late, so they wanted to make their apologies to our hostess."

Whit took a sip of his punch and said just under his breath, "A brilliant strategy. I would expect nothing less from your father."

Linney slapped open her fan to hide her smile at his grace's comment on the evening's initial offerings. "I do believe that Larette—Miss Evenstone—is the only musician playing for the rest of the evening, your grace, and I know her to be quite talented. It is my understanding that her sisters' only role will be turning pages."

"I cannot tell you how happy you have made me with that extremely important information, Miss Braddock." The duke's smile enhanced his already handsome visage. "I will stay my departure based upon your recommendation then, and look forward to the rest of the evening. Please excuse me. I would like to catch up to your father before we are called back to our seats. It was a very great pleasure to meet you, Miss Braddock."

Linea curtsied again as Whit took his leave.

Avery issued a low whistle. "That was well done, I must say. Kudos to you, Miss Braddock. I almost never get to introduce Whit to any of my friends, and even when I do, he is always quite aloof. He never compliments them—much less takes their advice. In one brief interlude you managed to accomplish both. You have made a conquest, it seems."

Her fan returned to action, Linney peeked over it at Avery. "I warned you, did I not, Lord Hammond? I am not like most others."

Lord Hammond chuckled for what seemed the hundredth time that evening and offered Linney his arm as the audience slowly began to reconstitute itself for part two of the musical evening.

****

"Your grace, what a delightful surprise to see you here. I had no idea you were an enthusiast of amateur musicales."

The soft, sultry voice at his elbow could belong to no one else. Excusing himself from the conversation, Whit turned to see the Countess of Ferrington gazing up at him, her full lips in her signature pout. Her curtsy was precisely correct, but Whit's height gave him an excellent view of lovely cleavage framed by a low-cut evening gown.

Whit raised her from her curtsy and bowed over her hand. "Good evening, Lady Ferrington. Is your husband here tonight? I did not see him in the crowd."

"He is here, your grace, but I left him chatting with his fellows so I might have a word with you."

"You're looking beautiful tonight, Angelina, as usual. Is it that new gown that has drawn so many drones to your side? I thought to greet you earlier but could scarce locate you amid the admirers buzzing around such an exotic flower."

"That's certainly one explanation, your grace, although I prefer to think it's anticipation of a taste of the nectar that attracts them to the ripe fruits."

"My goodness, madam, you *are* on the prowl this evening. Take care or you'll have me blushing at your pointed…ah…remarks."

"*Au contraire*, your grace, I think it is I who will blush at such innuendo. Perhaps you would care to inspect the full effect of your words in a more private setting later this evening? My husband, alas, has a previous engagement and would not be joining us."

"I fear I must decline, my lady. I, too, have other pressing matters to attend this evening."

"Would that I were one of those matters…pressing on you, your grace." Angelina's whispered response reminded Whit of how long it had been since he had parted ways with his mistress. He was hard put to decline Lady Ferrington's offer—the operative word being *hard*. The heady gardenia scent she wore invited his surrender, especially in the close quarters of the music room, but suddenly he found himself wishing for the fresher scent of lavender with maybe just a hint of something spicier.

"I sincerely appreciate your offer, my dear, but I fear I must beg off tonight."

"I leave you to enjoy your evening, then, your

grace. Do let me know if you change your mind." This time, Angelina dipped a deep curtsy with the intention of showing Whit what he would be missing.

Whit enjoyed the view, even as he fought to maintain control of his body's reflexive response. Angelina certainly knew how to get a man's attention. Whit bowed stiffly. When Angelina turned to greet another potential admirer, he breathed a sigh of relief.

"You did not accept her offer, then, your grace?"

"I thought we had earlier determined that neither you nor I were connoisseurs of amateur musicales, Lord Edgewood."

"And you are correct as usual, your grace. My attendance here is in spite of, rather than because of, the entertainment. I would have a word with you, if you can be dragged away from that rather tempting display of treats."

"I did not know you had a sweet tooth, Edgewood. Who would have thought it?"

"I was referring to the lady, not the dessert table."

"Yes, well, it is rather difficult to ignore such a…bountiful offering. Although I seem to be in the mood for something lighter, something different."

"I thought you loathed surprises."

"In most circumstances, I do. But a little something different in certain areas of one's life might be interesting."

"I will assume you do not mean in the area of your business, and yet I am about to surprise you."

The two men had walked away from the main crowd so they would not be overheard. Edgewood's voice was barely above a whisper. "We have chanced upon a cipher. Its previous owner was reluctant to inform us of its origin, but one of the lads recognized the name from the puzzle page of the *London Mail Observer*. It's quite a clever strategy, actually. A widely distributed cipher that changes weekly and can be used by anyone who picks up the newspaper. The solution is in the next day's paper. If we can trace the creator of the puzzle, we might have a lead into our leak."

"I see." Whit barely acknowledged the words of his friend and colleague.

"You are not surprised, I can tell. Why the devil not? This could not possibly be something you expected," said Edgewood.

"It was not expected, but you are right, I am not surprised. It makes sense. If the code changes that often, it explains why we have been unable to make progress in knowing their plans. My thanks for bringing me word of this. May I interest you in some lemonade? Or perhaps *you* have an interest in dessert? I understand Lady Ferrington's husband has other plans for the evening."

"Good lord, no. I have plenty of problems already. *That* one I do not need. I am going to make my exit before the young ladies take their place at the piano again."

"I have it on good authority that the next selections will be more palatable."

"That's certainly damning with faint praise. Good evening, your grace."

Chapter 5

The book was not at all what she needed.

It was interesting, of course, but she needed something with more details about specific celestial events—not just a timetable of when they occurred. If she didn't find what she needed at Mr. Alexander's this morning, she would simply have to make do with the puzzles she already had. Even if the *Mail Observer*'s editor immediately decided he wanted to publish her new collections, she would still have a few days to finish the remaining puzzles.

Drat that man anyhow. His appearance in Mr. Alexander's bookstore and his...well, his *appearance* had so befuddled her brain that she had taken this book without even looking at it. He had befuddled her brain—and, if she were being absolutely honest—he had befuddled other areas of her person as well. Areas that she had assumed were no longer susceptible to... befuddlement.

The pleasure she normally felt about an anticipated visit to Alexander's was pierced by a shiver at the prospect of encountering Mr. Alexander's patron from the previous afternoon. He was so very overwhelming. His presence seemed to monopolize all the air in the room—at least she had found herself quite breathless after exiting the shop. His broad shoulders, crowded into the narrow spaces between the shelves of books, had given the impression of great height. And whereas Vivian usually disliked crowded spaces, her moment in the presence of this gentleman had not been unpleasant and had, in truth, made her feel things she'd not felt in a long time. They had not touched, but she had felt his heat and was aware of something else between them.

Enough! Another trip to Mr. Alexander's was required—this time with no distractions. Since it was extremely unlikely that anyone would visit the same bookstore two days in a row—even *she* didn't frequent the bookseller's shop that often—the chances of her running into the aforementioned gentleman were very small.

So why did she feel a tiny twinge of disappointment?

Vivian shook her head to clear her errant thoughts.

What was wrong with her? Why should she care one way or another whether she saw the gentleman again? She tied the ribbons of her bonnet and pulled on her gloves. A brisk walk to the bookseller's would help clear her head.

Vivian closed the front door quietly behind her with a certain pleasure. As Linney kept reminding her, one of the benefits of her status as a widow was that her every step was not dogged by a chaperone. It was early still for most of the *ton*—many of whom had gone to bed only a few short hours ago. Vivian stepped out to the sidewalk and walked briskly in the direction of her first destination. She had plenty of time to stop by Mr. Alexander's before dropping off her cipher at the offices of the *Mail Observer*. She still had not decided how to tell Mr. Davis about her idea for a series of more puzzles. More to the point, she had not decided how to tell him that she was V. I. Burningham, the puzzle maker.

Since arriving in London, Vivian's busy schedule had made creating the Tuesday puzzles and Thursday ciphers quite a challenge. So far, she had been able to honor all but one of her deadlines. She smiled, remembering the conversation from last week with Mr. Davis, the managing editor, when he assumed she was a secretary of sorts dropping off the cipher for *Mr.* V. I. Burningham.

"Please let Mr. Burningham know that I would be delighted to meet with him to discuss some additional business opportunities," said Mr. Davis. "His ciphers and puzzles have proven quite popular with our readers."

That certainly boded well for a presentation of her proposal, did it not? The wild card was whether Mr. Davis would be as enthusiastic about puzzles and ciphers coming from a *Miss* Burningham.

At this time of day, the city was in transition—like a back stage between acts. The tradesfolk who had made an early morning entrance now headed home to fish and farm and prepare for the next day, but the business of society was just beginning to stir. Vivian could hear the sounds of the city moving from morning into daytime—horses jingling their harnesses, carts rolling on the cobbled streets, even the rhythmic footsteps of clerks, assistants, and fellow early risers.

The way to Mr. Alexander's was familiar, but this time of day was not. Reviewing the route in her mind, Vivian found she had failed to remember several dark alleys she must pass in a rather neglected area of the city. She deftly stepped around the detritus and droppings that dotted her path and walked a bit faster. She did enjoy her freedom, but the company of a brawny footman would not have gone amiss this morning. Rounding the corner just as the morning bells rang the nine o'clock hour, Vivian was struck by a new concern. She had never visited Mr. Alexander's shop this early before. What would she do if the shop was not yet open?

Oh, *when* had she become such a nervous Nellie?

If the shop was not open yet, she would simply wait, of course. She was a grown woman, a widow. She knew things. She had seen things. But to wait alone in front of a store? What would people think? Oh, for pity's sake! What did she care what people might think? It was broad daylight. What possible harm could come to her in the middle of the morning?

Pausing at the edge of the sidewalk, Vivian considered the prickling of hairs on the back of her neck. Was she being watched?

She listened for the footsteps that had been behind her from the start, willing them to continue, but like her, they had paused. Was she being followed?

She turned suddenly, but the view behind her showed only a bustling street scene with everyone intent upon their own business. In truth, *she* was the only one who looked out of place. Vivian turned back, and with a small sound of relief, sighted her destination in the next block. Not until she opened the door to Alexander's and set the bell ringing did she realize she was still holding her breath.

****

The front space of the bookseller's store was empty, and the shades were still drawn.

"Mr. Alexander? Good morning." Hearing no response, Vivian stepped into the store and closed the door behind her. "Mr. Alexander? I hope you don't mind, but I need one more book to help with my current study."

This time she heard muffled shuffling from the back.

"I'll just help myself, Mr. Alexander. No need to hurry."

Vivian walked quickly to the first shelf. She should probably wait for the proprietor to show himself before she started rifling through his inventory, but she had no intention of waiting outside for a proper opening. She ducked around the second shelf and barreled straight into the gentleman from yesterday.

Catching Vivian against his chest, the gentleman let out an audible "umpf" and pivoted back a step to keep his balance. "Lady Rowden, we meet again."

"Oh, I do beg your pardon," said Vivian, horrified to find herself being held so intimately against the tall, broad-shouldered gentleman. She blushed to the roots of her auburn curls and tried to remember why she was here…in his arms. Luckily, the gentleman gathered his wits more quickly.

"Mr. Alexander is locating a book for me and should be out in a trice." He set Vivian solidly on her feet and then bowed, taking the opportunity to peer beneath the brim of her bonnet. "I say, are you quite all right? You provide quite a punch for a lady."

"Yes, thank you. I am fine. I do apologize for running into you, but…"

"Don't tell me. You assumed you were alone?"

Needled by the repetition of his admonition from

their previous encounter, Vivian straightened her spine and replied frostily, "Actually, I was going to say that you do seem to skulk about quite a bit."

The gentleman laughed outright, crinkling the area around those brilliantly blue eyes. "I do, at that. In which case, it is I who should be begging your pardon, Lady Rowden. Please accept my apology for…well, for skulking about, as you put it." He took her hand and brought it to his lips. Suddenly his head bobbed up. "Never say you have already read the book you purchased yesterday?"

Vivian smoothly withdrew her hand and placed it beside the other one, safely holding her reticule. "Actually, sir," she said, "you have me at a disadvantage, since we were not actually introduced yesterday but merely exchanged pleasantries."

"Most remiss of me, my lady." Mr. Alexander appeared from nowhere. "You and his grace are both such frequent patrons of this shop that I had not stopped to think you might not have been introduced to each other. Lady Rowden, please allow me to present His Grace, the Duke of Whitley. Your grace, the Viscountess Rowden."

"The pleasure is mine, Lady Rowden." The duke recaptured her hand and bowed more precisely, just brushing his lips to her fingertips. But this time he maintained his hold. Sparked by his touch, a shiver of excitement raced down her spine. She looked up to see those eyes staring intently—curiously—into her own. For several complete seconds, her mind, usually full to bursting with tidbits, tasks, and trivia, was utterly and totally blank.

"I admit I did not think after seeing you here

yesterday that I would be so fortunate as to encounter you again today, Lady Rowden. Have you in fact finished reading the book you purchased? It was a book of astronomy, if I recall. Do you have a particular interest in astronomy?"

Vivian found her tongue at last. "As a matter of fact, I do, your grace. And in botany and early religions. You look askance. Is it that you do not approve of educated women? Or is it that you think females incapable of comprehending such lofty topics?"

"On the contrary, Lady Rowden. I believe women are capable of anything they desire to be capable of doing. It's simply that, in my experience, the interests of most women tend toward more…ah…domestic topics."

"Yes, well, I am not most women, your grace. And it has been *my* experience that most women's interests tend to be determined by their husbands, not themselves."

"And did your husband choose that book of astronomy for you, Lady Rowden?"

"I am quite capable of choosing a book for myself, your grace. Besides which, I am a widow."

"My condolences, then."

"There is no need to offer your sympathy, your grace, and you needn't bother pretending you haven't heard the scandal. It's common knowledge that my husband died in the bed of his mistress."

"I do beg your pardon, madam. I had heard that yours was a love match destined to withstand the test of time and tumult."

"Yes, well. As it turns out, it was not. Things change."

"Then may I offer my condolences on the stupidity of your late husband?"

Vivian smiled. "Thank you, your grace. Those I will accept."

The blue eyes were amused at her response. Vivian snatched her hand away and took a step backwards. "And to answer your previous question, your grace, once I started reading the book I purchased yesterday, I realized that I needed additional information. So I came this morning to purchase...*this* book."

Vivian grabbed a book at random from the shelf beside her. A discreet throat clearing from Mr. Alexander registered in the back of her mind.

"I have a passion for astronomy, Lady Rowden. May I?" asked the duke holding out his hand for the book she had plucked from the stacks.

The throat clearing turned into a cough.

"Certainly, your grace, although I must point out that I have not yet had a chance to determine whether this book will suffice. I may need one with more detail for my purposes."

The coughing had progressed into a rather loud episode.

Vivian looked over at the bookseller with concern. "Mr. Alexander, are you quite all right?"

"Yes, my lady, but I don't believe that was the book you were looking for."

"Ah, yes," said the duke, and he read from the title page, "*A Young Man's Guide to the Erotic Art of the Roman Empire* by Brutus Gigantus. I'm afraid I'm not familiar with this author, but I must say that, were I fortunate enough to have a wife, as her husband I would definitely encourage her interest in this book." He handed the book back to Vivian, his cornflower-blue eyes holding hers, one eyebrow raised.

Wordlessly, Vivian transferred the offending book to Mr. Alexander's outstretched hand, wherein it promptly vanished. She ducked her eyes to escape the penetrating blue gaze and took another step back. "That was not the book I thought it was," she mumbled. "Thank you, Mr. Alexander, but I didn't see the title I was looking for today. Good day. Good day, your grace."

She nodded to the duke, who inclined his head and murmured, "Your servant, madam." As she walked out the door, she felt rather than heard the chuckles from the two men. She was halfway down the street before her embarrassment turned to fury.

How *dare* he?

The bookstore was *hers*—well, obviously it belonged to Mr. Alexander, but Mr. Alexander had always welcomed *her* patronage. What right had that pompous duke to haunt her haven? What kind of person goes to a bookstore two days in a row? Didn't he have laws to pass or mistresses to drive in the park or friends to meet at his club? And why did she never seem to be able to put two words together in his presence? After yesterday's disturbing encounter, she had assumed the bookstore was the one place where she would be safe from seeing him today. Unbidden, the duke's words from their first meeting came back to her. "I never assume," he'd said.

Damn it, maybe he had a point.

Chapter 6

"What is she about? This *cannot* be another coincidence."

The front door bell jingled, and Whit withdrew into the shadows, waiting impatiently while Mr. Alexander attended to the new customer.

Alexander continued to insist she was harmless, but every instinct Whit possessed screamed otherwise. She had clearly been surprised to see him—and not in the pleasantly surprised way most women of marriageable age expressed acknowledgement of his presence. Any other woman would have been simpering and flirting the moment after being introduced to a duke. She was right, he admitted to himself. She was not like other women. He grinned. In that, at least, he was in complete agreement with the mysterious Lady Rowden.

But there had been something between them. He'd seen the—what, alarm?—on her face when she first saw him. She licked her lips nervously—full, kissable lips, as his body's inconvenient response confirmed. Lips that he wanted to nibble and could almost taste even now.

She was pale—too pale, really. The shock of finding him there, perhaps? Or perhaps she didn't get enough sleep? Maybe it was because of her recent loss—although the rest of her didn't look like what he thought a widow would look like. She looked more like a siren—especially her eyes. Their eyes had locked, and she stared at him as if she knew him. It had given him time to see that her eyes were not black, as was his original impression, but rather the dark, rich brown of molten chocolate, with a darker black outline that made them look absolutely huge. Enticing eyes. Sensual. Secretive.

Vulnerable.

When she was around him, she made him feel things he wasn't expecting to feel, and he wasn't sure he liked it. He was a duke, for God's sake. He was *never* out of control, but this was twice now that he'd felt like a besotted suitor—his body reacting like a green boy with his first woman. Even now he hardened at the thought of learning more about this quixotic female.

Perhaps Edgewood was right. He just needed to scratch the itch and be done with it. That was the most logical solution, and he certainly prided himself on his ability to be logical. Not to mention that it would definitely help with the waiting. But the idea of initiating a liaison with someone like Lady Ferrington lacked appeal. Maybe it was her marital status that was off-putting. As a rule, he did not dally with other men's wives, no matter how tempting...or how willing. And certainly an unmarried woman was not acceptable. Which left...a widow, perhaps? Maybe someone with extremely kissable lips, whose sharp wit made him smile? Perhaps someone who left a whiff of lavender in her wake?

Whit groaned. He definitely needed to find a new mistress—the sooner the better. He really could not afford to be distracted right now—not while the fate of *Masquerade* and the lives of hundreds of British soldiers hung in the balance.

Another jingling signaled the departure of Mr. Alexander's customer, and the bookseller quickly sought out Whit. "Your grace, I assure you, Lady Rowden is simply a customer. As I told you yesterday, she is absorbed by her puzzles and by her family."

"Tell me more about the puzzles."

"She likes to solve all types of puzzles—enigmas, word graphs, conundrums, math challenges, that sort of thing. She is working on creating her own series of puzzles, all with a common theme. I believe she hopes to sell them to a publisher. *That* is the reason she is here all the time. For her research. But, your grace, she told me all this in strictest confidence, and I would not want her thinking I take her privacy lightly."

"For God's sake, man. I'm not going to expose her little pastime, but you must admit it is damned odd. I must insist you keep careful watch, Alexander. It is always possible that someone else is using Lady Rowden without her being aware of it. I intend to look into her history further—especially her marriage and the sudden death of the viscount. Where is she staying in London?"

"With her maternal aunt and uncle on Sudbury Street in Mayfair—she is here for her cousin's debut. You might know of her uncle, Mr. William Braddock? She has had me deliver books to her at that address on several occasions."

Lady Rowden was related to the Miss Braddock he was introduced to last evening? The one who was occupying so much of Avery's time? Another coincidence? The duke was not convinced, and he was definitely not amused.

"I'll start there, then. If you notice anything—*anything*—unusual, send word through Robbie. *Masquerade* is nearly upon us, and we cannot take any chances. In the meantime, I will see what else I can find out about the viscountess."

"Very well, your grace." Alexander bowed as Whit made for the door. "Ah, your grace?"

"Yes, what is it?" snapped Whit.

"The reply?"

Whit sighed. This damned leak was making him churlish. He reached into an inner pocket of his coat and retrieved a folded piece of paper, which he placed inside the volume of poetry on the counter. He quickly closed the book and handed it to the proprietor. "My apologies, Alexander. And my thanks."

Whit never assumed anything, and he did not believe in coincidences. At the corner, he stopped to get a signal from the street sweeper as to the direction of his prey. It appeared she was headed farther into town. Very well. He would take it upon himself to ensure that the lady arrived safely at her destination.

The information he had managed to gather so far about Lady Rowden and her late husband confirmed that Viscount Rowden had been a philanderer of the worst sort. As Alexander said, the viscount and viscountess had started out as the *ton's* most adored couple of the year, but after their wedding, the bride and groom had essentially dropped out of society. Even allowing for a passionate honeymoon period, their total absence from public life was odd. They reportedly lived the entire time at the country home of the viscount, less than a day's ride from London. For the most part, Lord Rowden ignored his responsibilities in Parliament but was often seen betting deeply at the gaming hells and taking full advantage of the female companionship in the back rooms. According to his sources, the viscountess never came to town. Perhaps there had been an illness. Perhaps she had been in the family way and had lost the pregnancy. Either could explain her solitude and could even explain the bevy of mistresses. It did not, however, explain the sudden death of the viscount or the rumors of a French connection.

That the gentleman's scandalous demise had driven his widow from polite society was titillating, but it was the man's death itself that interested Whit. An inquisition had ruled it a natural death, but it was rather a superficial investigation. Poison could imitate natural causes—he knew that from first-hand experience. Maybe the viscountess resented the string of mistresses and hastened her husband's death. Maybe the mistress was a black widow spy—a female who, once having procured the information she sought, killed her unfortunate mate. But what information would the viscount be privy to? If half of the rumors were even partially true, there was a long line of suspects who would not mourn the viscount's death. Maybe Alexander was right. Maybe the lady's appearance in the bookstore at the same time he was receiving and then sending his missive was simply a coincidence. Maybe the viscount's death was a simple matter of having too many enemies.

Or maybe the explanations were more sinister.

The only thing Whit knew for sure was that there were too many unanswered questions, and the subject of almost all of them had just entered the offices of the *London Mail Observer*.

****

Vivian stopped momentarily outside the offices of the *Mail Observer*. Taking a deep breath, she entered the building and walked briskly up to the reception desk. "Good morning," she said to the clerk. "I should like to speak with Mr. Davis, please."

"Advertisements and announcements are to your right, madam," said the clerk.

"I should like to speak with Mr. Davis if he is in."

The clerk looked up at her and smiled. "Oh, it's you again, is it? You're in early today, miss, and looking quite fine, if I may say so. I can take the puzzle from you if you like."

"Thank you, but I would like to speak with Mr. Davis if I might."

"Very well, miss. I can see if he is in. What would this be regarding?"

Vivian smiled. "Puzzles, of course."

The clerk returned her smile. "Certainly, miss. Please wait here, and I will see if Mr. Davis is available."

Less than a minute later, the clerk returned and motioned to Vivian. "Come with me. I'll show you to Mr. Davis's office."

Vivian followed the clerk down a long hall and into a huge room that had all the comforts of a well-appointed library. The small, rather wiry man sitting behind a huge carved desk jumped to his feet as she entered the room. The juxtaposition of the small man and the big desk made Vivian smile as Mr. Davis greeted her. "Please come in, Miss...ah, I beg your pardon, ma'am. My clerk did not tell me your name."

"Miss Burningham," said Vivian.

"Yes, well, please come in, Miss Burningham." Mr. Davis motioned to a chair in front of the gigantic desk. "I assume you are some relation to Mr. Burningham? We at the *Mail Observer* are very proud to be able to publish his work. Our readers are quite mad for them, and our circulation always increases on the days we run his puzzles and ciphers. Might I offer you some refreshment?"

"Thank you, no, Mr. Davis. I wanted to drop off this latest cipher, but I also have a question for you, if you would be so kind."

Mr. Davis took the folded paper Vivian held out and handed it to his clerk, waving the man toward the door. "Splendid! This will run in tomorrow's edition as usual. I wonder if you would be able to deliver a message to Mr. Burningham for me. I assume he is here in London? I would very much like to meet with him about additional business opportunities. At his earliest convenience, of course. Our readers are asking for more—more puzzles, more ciphers, more varieties of puzzles—more of everything. Our advertisers also want to see more puzzles. If Mr. Burningham would contact me, I can definitely make it worth his while. We like to please our readership whenever possible."

"I work very closely with Mr. Burningham," said Vivian, "so perhaps you could tell me more about what you have in mind."

"You're a very attractive young lady, Miss Burningham, and no doubt a great asset to Mr. Burningham, but I need to speak with the gentleman directly—man to man, as it were. I'm sure you are very helpful to him, but this is business, and I don't discuss business with women. I'll have my clerk write out a note for Mr. Burningham so you don't have to worry about remembering what I said."

"It's not a very complicated message, Mr. Davis," said Vivian icily, "and, as I said, I work closely with him on all of his puzzles. He is currently—"

"Miss Burningham," sighed Mr. Davis, "I'm a very busy man. It's not that difficult to understand. Mr. Burningham makes puzzles, we publish them, and we want to publish more. I need to talk with the man who created the puzzles—not to his sister or his niece or whoever you might be. As I said, I'll have my clerk write a note. Do you think you can remember to deliver the note to Mr. Burningham?"

"Actually, Mr. Davis," said Vivian rising from her chair, "Mr. Burningham is traveling and won't be back in London for quite some time. I am in charge of his correspondence in the meantime, and I am perfectly capable of representing his interests. If you are not interested in dealing with me, then I will suggest to Mr. Burningham that he discuss the publication of future puzzles with one or more of the other daily papers in London. The *Mail Observer* does not have a monopoly on readers who enjoy solving puzzles. Good day, Mr. Davis."

Outside the offices of the *Mail Observer*, Vivian turned toward her uncle's house and then stopped. What had she just done? Had she really just severed her relationship with the most popular paper in the city?

Vivian closed her eyes and shook her head. What would have been wrong with just listening to Mr. Davis and then sending him a letter from V. I. Burningham?

Why couldn't she have figured out some way to get her ideas and new samples to the paper now that she knew Mr. Davis would react poorly to the knowledge that she was the creator of the popular puzzles?

Now, instead of having more work and more opportunities, she had nothing. And all because she'd lost her temper…again.

It was unclear whether Vivian was angrier with Mr. Davis or with herself. She rather thought it was the latter.

Chapter 7

Mr. Davis stood automatically when Miss Burningham took her leave, but, after she left, he sat down heavily in his chair.

Something was not as it seemed. The lady... puzzled him—no pun intended. Was she trying to effect some swindle? Maybe it was Burningham she was swindling. One thing was sure—he damned well wasn't going to let the *Sun*, or the *Globe*, or the *Star*, or any other London paper publish Burningham's puzzles. Not on his watch! Blast it all, the man was *his* creation. *His* paper had made the man famous. He knew everything there was to know about him—at least everything that needed to be known—and no slip of a girl was going to take that away from him.

Davis spoke the truth when he'd told the lady that circulation rose dramatically on the days when the newspaper carried Burningham's puzzles. All of their advertisers wanted their ads to appear in puzzle editions. As a result, the paper could charge significantly more for advertising space on those days. He could not afford to lose Burningham's puzzles and would dearly like to see more from the man.

Davis sat back in his chair for a few minutes more and then called to his clerk. "Gregson, come in here. I need to send a letter."

"Very good, sir. To whom are you writing?"

"V. I. Burningham."

"What does V. I. stand for, sir?"

"What? I don't know. V. I. will suffice. Send it by personal messenger to be handed to the man himself."

"Certainly, sir."

"Say that the young lady who delivers his puzzles, who also claims to be in charge of his affairs, may have mistakenly thought we were not interested in continuing to publish his puzzles, which is certainly not at all the case. Say that if he would care to send information about his new idea for more puzzles, along with samples of the same, I would be happy to make him a very lucrative offer."

"Yes, sir. Do you have his direction, sir?"

"Send it to where we always send his correspondence. And see that it goes out immediately."

"Yes, sir. Is there anything else?"

"No. Close the door behind you."

The *Sun* and the *Globe* could go to the devil, thought Davis, as he resettled himself in his chair. Burningham was a *Mail Observer* man and would continue to be. And that young lady should limit her interests to more feminine pursuits. Who was she to threaten him?

"Mr. Davis, sir?"

"What is it now, Gregson? Can't you see I'm busy? I have an evening edition to get out."

"Sir, there is a gentleman to see you."

Was he running a tea house? "Can you not deal with the man yourself?"

"He insists on speaking with you personally, sir." Gregson handed Davis the card of the Duke of Whitley.

Mr. Davis sighed. "Very well. Show him in."

Mr. Davis stood up and inclined his head as Mr. Gregson showed the Duke of Whitley into his office.

"Your grace, it's an honor. Please have a seat. May I offer you some refreshment?"

"No, thank you, Mr. Davis," said the duke, taking the chair in front of the very large desk. Mr. Davis was not a large man, and the thought came to Whit from nowhere that the man's feet might actually dangle when he sat down across from him.

Setting the thought aside, the duke continued, "My time is short, Mr. Davis, and I'm sure you're a busy man as well, but I do have a few questions I need to ask, if you would be so kind."

"Certainly, your grace."

"I understand your newspaper publishes puzzles on some days."

"We wish we could publish them every day, your grace, but you are correct. On Tuesdays, the afternoon edition of the *Mail* carries several riddles and a word puzzle or some other type of conundrum. The solution is published on Wednesday. And then on Thursdays, in the morning edition of the *Observer*, we publish a cipher and a coded message. The solution for the cipher runs on Fridays. Are you a fan of our puzzle pages, your grace?"

"I regret to say I am not—thus the need for my visit today. Who creates the puzzles that you publish? Is it one or more persons on your staff?"

"My staff is responsible for some of the content. The riddles, for example, are usually from generally known sources that we simply compile."

"I am specifically interested in the ciphers."

"Yes, well, that is something we're quite proud of.

The ciphers—actually all of the other puzzles—are created by a Mr. V. I. Burningham from Somerset. Each week he provides us with a puzzle, a cipher, and their solutions. Both puzzles usually arrive on the Monday before they are to be published."

"How long have you been publishing puzzles by this Burningham fellow?"

"It's been about a year now. We started out with just the ciphers and then added a second puzzle because the ciphers were so popular with our readers."

"Do you have Mr. Burningham's direction?"

"I do, although it may not be the best way to reach him at the moment. Until about a month ago, the puzzles were always delivered by post from Somerset, arriving, as I said, on Mondays. The return direction merely said Burnham-by-Sea. But last month, the puzzles started being delivered by a messenger the day before each was to be published. I had the impression that Mr. Burningham was actually in London."

"Is he still in London?"

"I'm not certain he ever was. However, as of this morning I have it on good authority that he is traveling."

"On whose authority? And where is he traveling?"

"I do not know where he is traveling, but the lady who has been delivering the puzzles mentioned that Mr. Burningham would not be back in London for quite some time. She did not give his itinerary, but said she was handling his affairs in his absence."

"Does this lady have a name?"

"Actually, she calls herself Miss Burningham. She evidently shares some sort of kinship with Mr. V. I. Burningham. To be frank, your grace, it struck me as suspicious that a woman would be handling the affairs of such a brilliant man, so I have had my clerk send a letter to Mr. Burningham at his previous address."

"Is that where you send payment for the work?"

"No, your grace. From the beginning of our relationship with Mr. Burningham, we have been instructed to send payment to an account at Barclays, and we have continued to do so—even when the puzzles were delivered by messenger."

Whit was disappointed. He needed to find V. I. Burningham, and he needed to find him now. Following the money would eventually lead him to Burningham, but if the man were traveling, it would take some time to find him. He could send someone to Burnham-by-Sea and have them poke around, but if Burningham were not in residence, it would come to naught.

"So all the puzzles are now being delivered to your offices?"

"That's correct, your grace. That's the way we've been receiving them for about a month now."

"And they are always delivered by this Miss Burningham?"

"The puzzle today was delivered by Miss Burningham, but I do not know about the other ones. They are not delivered to me personally but simply dropped off at the front desk."

"Would the clerks at your front desk be able to tell us if the same person has delivered all the puzzles?"

"I can certainly ask, your grace. I'd be happy to inquire and send you my findings."

"Mr. Davis, as I mentioned at the outset, my time is short. Is it possible for us to question the clerks now? I would consider it a great personal favor."

"Certainly, your grace. Excuse me for just a few moments, and let me see who was on duty when the puzzles were delivered."

Mr. Davis disappeared into the rabbit warren of hallways and desks outside his office while Whit calmly reviewed what he had learned. Lady Rowden arrived in London for her cousin's debut about a month ago. Until a month ago, the puzzles had been delivered by post for weekly publication from somewhere in Somerset, but they were now being dropped off by messenger. Today that messenger was a woman, a Miss Burningham. Lady Rowden had entered the offices of the *Mail Observer* with a package and had left—some three quarters of an hour later—without the package. If it was Lady Rowden who was delivering the puzzles, what was her connection with V. I. Burningham and why was she using an alias?

Whit's instincts were on high alert. He had every reason to believe this was an important piece of the puzzle—he apologized to no one for the all-too-apt play on words. The difference was that *his* puzzle involved human lives. If successful, *Masquerade* would expose a string of traitors who continued to smuggle British arms to Napoleon's army—arms that were then used to kill British citizens. It was one of the largest operations of the war, and the stakes were enormous. If the plan failed, it would most likely be because of the leak in *his* organization.

"Your grace?" Mr. Davis stood in the doorway with another clerk. "Edwards here says that the same lady has delivered all of the puzzles. Twice a week, for the past four weeks, she's left a puzzle or cipher at the front desk."

Whit stood and inclined his head to Mr. Davis and the young man. "Thank you for your time, Davis, and for your help in this matter. I am in your debt. Good day, gentlemen."

****

What was Henri's widow up to?

This was twice in two days she'd been at the booksellers and then, when she went to the newspaper offices, she stayed inside for more than three quarters of an hour. She had never spent more than a few minutes inside before.

When he'd given the order to terminate Henri, he'd factored in the regrettable realization that they would also be losing his wife's brilliant ciphers in the local gazette. Henri's death was unfortunate, of course, but necessary, and he'd counted on the ensuing scandal to keep the mourning widow isolated and away from polite society.

After Henri's death, he toyed with the idea of tracking down the widow and perhaps blackmailing her to continue creating ciphers under his direction. But before he could decide how to approach Lady Rowden, similar ciphers under the name V. I. Burningham started appearing in a London paper. He soon realized Henri's widow was selling her puzzles to the *Mail Observer*, which made them readily available to his entire network. It was a happy coincidence and one he immediately used to his advantage. Later it might be necessary to take a more "hands-on" approach with the widow, but as long as she stayed isolated in Somerset, there was no need.

And then she showed up in London, right in the middle of things.

From the minute he was alerted to Lady Rowden's presence in the city, he kept her under observation. As far as he could tell, she was still unaware that her ciphers were being used to encode missives to Napoleon's army. The only reason he could unearth for her trip to London was her cousin's debut. Was it all as innocent as it seemed, or was there a more interesting explanation? And why was she so long in the newspaper offices today?

Too many things were coming to a head at the same time. His best intelligence confirmed that the British were planning "something big," but he needed to know more—much more—and quickly. The time for his operation was growing shorter. Would they be able to count on Lady Rowden to continue publishing her ciphers, or was it time for him to take her under his control? His sources said she was being paid a pretty penny for the puzzles, and she *had* been consistent, missing the weekly publication of a new cipher only once in the past year. They had been forced to use the same cipher two weeks in a row—risky even in the best of times, and these were not the best of times. The Emperor had been furious

No, he could not afford a missing cipher now. And, in addition to making sure she delivered a new cipher each week, he also needed to know how much that idiot husband of hers had let slip about his involvement with Napoleon's army of spies.

Having Estelle work from the inside would be of great value, although he would miss her in his bed—the woman had amazing stamina and enough of a repertoire to satisfy even his demands. As one of Henri's mistresses, she had been surprisingly competent about eliciting secrets from the viscount. Having her infiltrate Lady Rowden's new London residence would get him the information he needed. Soon he would know what Lady Rowden was up to and whether she, like her late husband, needed to be silenced.

He watched Vivian climb the steps to the Braddock house and breathed a sigh of relief. He had plenty of time to finish his errands before stopping by his club for a brandy.

Chapter 8

Linney was right, and, in hindsight, Vivian was glad to have been badgered into taking a walk. It *was* a beautiful afternoon—one of London's infrequent perfect days. The few clouds in the sky were too fluffy to threaten rain and the late afternoon sun was warm on her shoulders.

And who knew? Maybe a walk in the park was just the thing to help her straighten out her convoluted thoughts—starting with the fiasco she had created with Mr. Davis and moving on to her inexplicable reactions to His Grace, the Duke of Whitley.

"Did you say we are supposed to be meeting someone, Linney?" Her cousin was trying very hard to seem as if she was not looking for someone. "Linney?"

"I'm sorry, Vivian, what did you say? Are we meeting anyone? Oh, I don't know. I was just looking to see if there was someone else strolling that I knew, but I don't see anyone."

"Well, I do. There is Lady Yeardon with her sister, and we just passed Miss Pruett. Perhaps you are looking for someone in particular?"

"No. No one in particular."

"A gentleman, perhaps?"

"I don't know what you're talking about. I'm simply enjoying the fresh air."

Linney was obviously too distracted to chat, so

Vivian's thoughts turned back to the morning and her visit to Mr. Alexander's. Was she the only one who had found it difficult to concentrate in the bookstore today, or had *he* felt it too? When she collided with the duke, her whole body had felt the shock and sent an involuntary shiver down her spine. It was probably just nerves—he *was* a duke, after all, and not known for his genial countenance. He was quite formidable, and his manner was invariably cold, which was probably why they called him the Ice Duke.

Vivian took a deep breath and exhaled slowly. There was absolutely no reason why the Duke of Whitley should have any interest in her and absolutely no reason why she should be distracted by him.

That was that, then. The man had taken up quite enough of her time and had definitely overstayed his welcome in her head. She would use the fresh air and a brisk walk to figure out what to do about the rather chauvinistic Mr. Davis.

She *had* been a bit hasty, Vivian acknowledged to herself. By telling Mr. Davis that she—or rather, Mr. V. I. Burningham—would not be providing any more puzzles to the *Mail Observer* until and unless he changed his mind about doing business with her—or rather, with Miss Burningham—she had totally eliminated her best option for having her collections published.

Would it not have been a better strategy to continue sending the puzzles—and thereby continue receiving the payments—while she discussed—or rather, while Mr. Burningham discussed—the merits of such an arrangement and the possibility of more work? Clearly Mr. Davis was eager to have more puzzles. And surely he had worked with women before in his line of business. There were any number of established female writers and essayists. While doing business with a woman was not the usual thing, it was certainly not unheard of. He ought to be amenable to it if it resulted in him getting more puzzles from V. I. Burningham.

But instead, she had seriously overreacted and by doing so had done damage, not just to her own future but possibly to the future of all women who wanted to do business in a man's world.

Talk about cutting off one's nose to spite one's face.

Even a gorgeous afternoon wasn't going to change the facts. She had made a mistake, and now she needed to own up to it. She should write a note and apologize to Mr. Davis and see if she could convince him of the benefits of working with her—or rather, with Miss Burningham. That was the only thing to be done. The only question that remained was whether that note should come from Miss Burningham or from V. I. Burningham?

Vivian took a deep breath. Her multiple identities were giving her a headache.

She looked over at Linney to see how she was enjoying the stroll and smiled. The beautiful day was completely wasted on her cousin. It could have been snowing for all she noticed. Her head bobbed as her eyes darted from figure to figure, searching for a particular gentleman. Ah, young love.

"For goodness' sakes, Linney. Stop fussing with your bonnet strings. You'll wear them out. Why are you so nervous?"

"Oh, Vivian, what if he does not come? What if his

sisters don't like me? What if they *do* like me and I disappoint them at some point in the future?"

"So we *are* meeting someone?"

"I told you there was a chance that Lord Hammond would be strolling in the park this afternoon with his sisters."

"I don't recall your saying that."

"Well, I did. You were somewhere solving puzzles in your head. Anyway, that's what he said last evening when we spoke at the musicale. But since he is nowhere to be found, he has obviously changed his mind and never wants to see me again. Oh, I should have worn my other dress—he said he likes seeing me in blue—although this one looks nicer with this parasol."

"The green looks lovely on you, Linney. I'm so glad you had it made into a walking costume. The only reason Lord Hammond said he liked seeing you in blue is because he has never seen you in green. I'm sure he will have eyes only for you."

"But where is he? What if I got the date wrong and it is tomorrow that I am to meet him and his sisters?"

"Then we'll have a lovely walk today and come back for another tomorrow."

"But what if we do come across him and he and I have nothing to talk about?"

"It would be perfectly understandable that he would be tongue-tied at your beauty, my dear, so you must simply be kind and allow him to slowly come to his senses."

"But what if he decides he doesn't like me after he spends more time with me?"

"Then we will send him straightaway to the physician, for there will indeed be something dreadfully wrong with him."

Linney finally giggled at the absurdity of their conversation. "Oh, Viv, what would I do without you?"

"You would do very well, of course. Lord Hammond is a gentleman, and he would not have arranged to meet you for a stroll if he had other plans or if he did not want to spend time with you. And everyone loves you, so I'm sure his sisters will be charmed by your gaiety. But you must calm down. Just take a breath and then let it out. Shall we sit down on this bench?"

"No, I'm much too nervous to sit. Let's stroll along this path until—wait, is that him?" Linney squinted. Her vanity did not allow her to wear her spectacles in public. "I don't see his sisters, but someone is with him—a gentleman. I think it is Lord Hammond's half-brother, the Duke of Whitley. Oh, Vivian, I do so want Avery to like me. I think I may faint!"

"You are not going to faint," hissed Vivian, not feeling at all steady herself. "Take deep breaths. Why didn't you tell me that Lord Hammond's brother was the Duke of Whitley?"

"Half-brother. I didn't *not* tell you. I just didn't think *to* tell you. I met him last night at Larette's recital. Avery told me they had the same mother who had twice married dukes. Avery's father is still alive, but he is somewhat of a recluse and mostly stays in the country since Avery's mother died. His sisters are in London, staying with their aunt, Lady Charlotte Asbury."

"And you could not have mentioned before now this family history with which you seem so familiar?"

"Why would I? Do you know the family?"

"Actually, I met the duke just this morning in Mr.

Alexander's bookstore."

Vivian could not believe her luck as she watched the two gentlemen approach. They were both tall and quite ruggedly handsome. But only one of them had piercing, cornflower-blue eyes determinedly fixed on her.

****

After introductions—including an explanation from Lord Hammond as to why his sisters had failed to accompany him and his good luck in running into his older brother, and an explanation from the duke of how he and Lady Rowden had met just that morning and his good luck in running into his younger brother—Lord Hammond offered his arm to Linney, and the duke did the same to Vivian. Soon both couples were strolling along the footpath that paralleled Hyde Park's Rotten Row.

"Perhaps another time we might go driving," offered the duke. "I have just recently acquired a matched pair of grays that are giving my groom a run for his money. He would be grateful for any extra workouts for them."

"Whit, we would not want to endanger the ladies with a pair that's too high spirited," said Lord Hammond with a frown.

"I think it sounds delightful, your grace," said Linney, and then to Lord Hammond, "I'm sure his grace would never put us in harm's way, my lord. Oh, Avery, look, the swans!"

And with that, Vivian watched as the younger couple went closer to the Serpentine for a better look at the elegant birds.

"Are you usually this quiet on your strolls with

gentlemen, Lady Rowden?" The duke had walked her past the trail that forked off to the water, and they now continued down a less traveled path. "I had not pegged you for the taciturn type."

"You are correct," said Vivian. "While I will never be thought of as a chatterbox, I do pride myself on my ability to have an interesting conversation with just about anyone. However, this afternoon, I am trying to work out a mystery."

"Tell it to me and perhaps I can be of service. In some circles, I am seen as mystery personified."

Vivian came to a full stop and turned to the duke. "Your grace, have you been following me?"

A full moment of silence passed before the duke drew her hand under his arm and continued to stroll down the empty path. "What an unusual question, Lady Rowden. Why would you ask that?"

Vivian cocked her head and looked up at him, waiting until those blue eyes met hers, and then she looked away.

"Honestly, at first I was just making conversation, but now, with your taking so long to answer the question, I think I should ask it again in earnest. You have to admit, it *is* rather odd that I have seen you on every outing I have been on over the past two days. I was only formally introduced to you this morning, so I am inclined to assume that it is more than a coincidence, but," she added, peering up innocently at her escort, "I have it on the best authority that one should never assume."

The duke smiled. "That sounds like good advice from a wise man," he said.

"How do you not know that it was from a wise

woman, your grace?"

The duke laughed out loud. "*Touché*, Lady Rowden. Either way, it sounds like good advice."

"So then you *were* following me. May I ask why?"

"If I *were* following you—and mind you, I'm not saying I have been—but if I were following you, I daresay it would simply be to occupy the same space as such grace and beauty personified in such a single, glorious example of womanhood."

Vivian snorted.

"I beg your pardon, Lady Rowden?"

"I am sorry, your grace, but your explanation is...let me see if I can put this delicately...no, I cannot. Let me be blunt, then. You will have to come up with a better story than that or risk insulting my intelligence—if, of course, you were in fact following me."

The duke acted offended. "Was something I said amiss, Lady Rowden? Or in error?"

"Your grace, I am well aware of my attributes. I know that I am tolerably pretty and have an inquisitive and agile mind. But if I am the glorious personification of womanhood, then England is in dire straits." She did not look up into his face, but Vivian could feel the duke smiling.

"Very well," he continued, "let us say—hypothetically—that I wanted to gain the attention of a lady but belatedly realized that following her would not be the most effective approach. How would I let her know that I am attracted to her and would like to get to know her better?"

"Well—hypothetically—there would be the normal avenues of introduction at an event or gathering."

"In our hypothetical example, let us say that she

and I have already been introduced by a mutual acquaintance."

"Very well, then perhaps you might arrange another public meeting with her—perhaps a stroll in Hyde Park during the fashionable hour."

"That sounds like a splendid idea. Perhaps on a gorgeous day with a blue sky and fluffy clouds? And then, after that?"

"Perhaps during your hypothetical stroll, you might inquire as to what mutual activities you and the lady might be pursuing in the future, and then ascertain if there were any that you might have in common."

"Such as trips to bookstores that feature pleasurable, but, alas, fleeting embraces in certain sections? I must confess that I have never enjoyed browsing among the stacks quite as much as I did this morning."

Vivian blushed but replied, "I am not at all sure that would count as a mutual activity in and of itself, your grace. I would classify that as more of an errand."

The Duke leaned closer to Vivian's ear and said softly, "I know when you blush even without seeing your face. I can feel your heat through my sleeve."

"It was very ungentlemanly of you to refer to that incident," Vivian whispered back, darting her eyes up at him.

He stopped and turned to face her, still holding her hand. "Perhaps you are right. I do beg your forgiveness, Lady Rowden." He held her gaze as he raised her hand with both of his and touched his lips to her fingertips. "I would very much like to make amends for my less than gentlemanly behavior. Are you perhaps attending the Calloway ball tonight?"

The very sight of a duke—*this* duke—kissing her hand had Vivian's thoughts on the run. "Ah...yes, I...I believe...actually, Linney...uh...that is, Miss Braddock and I will be attending with my aunt and uncle."

"Splendid. Avery and I are taking our sisters to the theatre tonight, but I'm sure I can convince him to accompany me to Lady Calloway's afterwards—especially with the knowledge that Miss Braddock will be in attendance." The duke nodded slightly toward the aforementioned couple walking slowly up the path behind them, their heads together. "Might I be permitted to hope that you would save a dance for me later in the evening?"

"Are we still speaking hypothetically, your grace?"

"We never were, Lady Rowden," whispered the duke in her ear just as Lord Hammond escorted Linney to meet them.

"Whit, I'm afraid we must be off," said his brother. "The Furies will be chomping at the bit."

Vivian and Linea traded looks and then burst into laughter.

"The Furies?" asked Linney. "Who—or what—are the Furies?"

"That's what Whit calls our three younger sisters," said Lord Hammond with a broad smile. "The Furies, goddesses of vengeance. Whit is convinced that Rose, Lily, and Marguerite live only to seek vengeance on him. They *can* be a little much sometimes."

"And what was the duke's crime that inspired this thirst for retribution? Did he embarrass them? Follow them up and down public streets? Dog their every step?" Vivian looked pointedly at the duke and raised her eyebrows.

"Well," said Lord Hammond, "this morning, I believe his grace told them they could not accompany us to the theatre tonight unless they had completed their lessons. And just yesterday, he insisted they apologize for hiding from their governess. As you can see, he's nothing but an ogre." Lord Hammond smiled, and then leaned in with a stage whisper to the ladies, "And they adore him."

"They do nothing of the sort," said the duke, drawing himself up to full ducal pompousness. "They appropriately respect that I maintain a strict and very proper household in every regard."

"Yes, well, perhaps you could tell Lady Rowden and Miss Braddock why it is that you are wearing your second-best hat today, your grace, and what it was that happened to your best hat?"

"I'm sure the ladies have better things to do with their time than to listen to the destructive tendencies of your younger siblings toward my outerwear, Lord Hammond."

"They are your siblings as well, your grace."

"Half-siblings, if you please. I believe you said we were going to be late?" The duke bowed to Linney and touched the brim of his second-best beaver hat. "It was a pleasure to see you again, Miss Braddock. I do apologize that you had to spend so much of the afternoon in the company of my rather dull brother." He flashed that brother a grin and then moved to take Vivian's hand.

"And I hope you'll give consideration to my request, Lady Rowden. I look forward to your answer this evening."

He once again raised her fingertips to his lips,

never taking his eyes from hers, and murmured, "*Au revoir, cherie.*"

****

A duke's presence in the park at the fashionable hour never goes unnoticed, and today was no exception.

On their walk home, Linney and Vivian were stopped no fewer than seven times by friends and acquaintances. People whom Vivian had known before her marriage—including those who seemed to forget her name when scandal rocked her world—were all of a sudden plying her with greetings, invitations, and compliments on her new walking dress, which did, in fact, look stunning.

Once free of the throngs of well-wishers and hangers-on, it was Linney's turn.

"Exactly *when* did you say you met the duke, cousin? This morning? He certainly seems smitten with you. The two of you looked quite cozy. I felt that Avery and I were the ones chaperoning."

"Don't be ridiculous, Linney. As I told you, Mr. Alexander introduced his grace to me at his bookstore this morning. We discussed books. That is the end of it."

"Is it, *cherie*?" mocked Linney. "And to what question does he await your answer this evening?"

"It is nothing. He simply mentioned that he and Lord Hammond would be attending the Calloway ball later tonight and asked if I might save a dance for him."

"A dance? Everyone knows that the Duke of Whitley never dances at the balls he attends. You have made a conquest, Vivian! And will you? Save a dance for him?"

"If I remember to, I don't see why I shouldn't. But

really, it is nothing of significance."

Tell that to her traitorous heart, which only now had settled down to a normal beat.

Chapter 9

"It's my amethyst gown for this evening, please, Margie, and have you any experience with terribly uncooperative hair? I'm at sixes and sevens without Annie. I cannot even manage a French twist."

"I'm not one for fancy hair doings," said the first upstairs maid, "but Mrs. Jacobs said you were to have the new maid help you once she knew her way about. Maybe she knows something about fixing up hair."

"Any help at all would be very much appreciated. I have a velvet ribbon to weave in there somewhere, but I have no idea how to start it. Will you help me out of this dress and unlace my stays? I can manage the rest by myself."

"Yes, my lady. The water for your bath is ready. I put the oils in like you asked. Oh, and Mr. Thomson said this letter came for you while you were out."

"Please put it on the table, Margie. I'll look at it later. Oh, and do take my walking dress to clean and press when you go down."

"Yes, Lady Rowden. I'll be back with your gown within the hour, and I'll bring Estelle up to do your hair."

The hot bath relaxed her, allowing her mind to wander back to the variations of her day. The pinnacle was undoubtedly her stroll in the park with the duke. That whole episode required further thought and much

80

more reflection. But more immediately there was her decision to send a note of apology to Mr. Davis. In her note, she needed to figure out a way to convince him to change his mind about working with a woman. It was either that or accept that she would be forever going back and forth between identities. If he refused, perhaps she *could* find another publisher—one who would not object to working with a woman. It was probably worth a few letters of inquiry.

The lavender scent relaxed her, but the spicy scent of carnation gave her energy. After washing and rinsing her hair, she rubbed it dry with a soft towel and donned her dressing gown. The letter Thomson had sent up was still on the table. Putting the towel aside, she opened the heavy folded paper. The words were written quite clearly, but after an initial scan of the contents, everything blurred in front of her eyes.

She sat down in the nearest chair. It couldn't be. It simply wasn't possible. She read the letter again, but the words were the same:

Dear Lady Rowden,

I regret to inform you that your monthly stipend from the estate of the late Viscount Rowden has been suspended, effectively immediately. A number of outstanding personal debts which were sanctioned by the viscount before his death have come to light, the amounts of which are quite substantial. These claims have severely depleted the monies from which your stipend was paid.

In addition, we have it on good authority that more claims will be forthcoming. To that end we must stop payment of your monthly allowance and, in fact, may need to seek repayment of monies you have already received. We will keep you apprised as the situation develops.

Yours, etc.
Msers Finial and Harp, Solicitors

A scratch on the door signaled Margie's return.

"Come in," said Vivian automatically.

Margie entered, reverently carrying the amethyst gown and matching silk slip. Behind her a younger maid stood quietly.

"Your gown is lovely, my lady. I'll hang it here. I've never seen such shimmer and so many shades of purple. Lady Rowden, this is Estelle. I've brought her up to do your hair."

Estelle dropped a curtsy but said nothing while Margie continued. "Will you be wearing your pearls tonight, my lady?"

"My pearls?" Vivian's mind was still trying to absorb the contents of the letter from Henry's solicitors.

"Yes, my lady, the ones you said your husband gave you as a wedding gift. They will be perfect with your gown. Shall I—?"

"No! I mean, no, thank you, Margie. I'll wear my cameo or the amethyst beads. Anything except the pearls."

"Certainly, my lady. The amethyst beads will look lovely. Now come and sit here so Estelle can get started on your hair while I collect the rest. You'd best hurry, Estelle. Lady Thea and Miss Linney are already dressing."

Vivian sat down in front of the looking glass as if in a dream. She couldn't believe it. Was she a pauper?

In the end, had Henry left her destitute? The contents of that letter would have to be shared with Uncle Will and Aunt Thea, but not right now. Not tonight, when Linney so wanted to make a good impression on Lord Hammond. Tomorrow would be soon enough to deal with this devastating news.

With an outward composure that belied her inner turmoil, Vivian pasted on a smile and sat while Estelle did her best to tame and style her unruly tresses.

Chapter 10

Outside the London Theatre, the Duke of Whitley took leave of his family.

"Avery will escort you home," he said to his Aunt Charlotte and to the three young ladies trying to appear oh, so very grown up after their first evening at the theatre. "I have a business matter that I must attend to. Rose, please inform your governess that I will be in tomorrow morning before luncheon to speak with her about your studies in mathematics. I was unimpressed with your understanding of percentages as they relate to the cost of your share of a glass of lemonade."

He gave his favorite aunt a peck on her still-smooth cheek, and then turned to the young ladies in front of him and bowed. "Good night, my Furies."

"Why do you call us that, Whit?" Rose was the queen of stalling tactics.

"Why do I call you the Furies?"

"Yes. Miss Satterwhite told us that the Furies were goddesses of vin gents."

"Miss Satterwhite is quite correct."

"What kind of gentlemen are *vin gents*, Whit?" asked Lilly, who always hung on his every word.

"*Vengeance*, not *vin gents*," said Whit, struggling to keep the straight face required for the serious conversation in which he was engaged. "Vengeance means punishment. The Furies were goddesses of vengeance. They punished men who had committed crimes."

"Have you committed a crime, Whit?" inquired Marguerite. "We would not punish you even if you had—as long as you promised to take us to Vauxhall Gardens."

"Your sense of justice seems to suffer from the same malady that too many of our MPs have contracted, Marguerite. It's called bribery. I will take you to Vauxhall Gardens sometime, but only if you pay more attention to your lessons. Miss Satterwhite is quite beside herself trying to deal with your antics."

"If she is beside herself, does that mean there are two of her?" asked Lilly, who would have made a fine barrister.

"Would that that were true," muttered Whit to Avery and his aunt. "I leave this last inquiry to the two of you."

"Girls, really," said Lady Ashby, "you should show your brother more respect—especially in public. Sometimes I think you forget he is a duke."

"Oh, we could never forget that, Aunt Charlotte," said Lilly.

"Never," echoed Rose, and Marguerite's echo was only a second behind.

"Well, see that you don't," said their aunt as her second nephew handed her into the waiting carriage.

Before Whit could turn away, he was treated to three very proper curtsies and a rather giggly farewell chorus.

"Good night, your grace."
"Good night, your grace."
"Good night, your grace."

Whit shook his head at his little sisters' disrespectful mocking and met his brother's eyes.

"Shall I see you at Lady Calloway's later, your grace?" asked Avery.

"Yes, although I anticipate that my arrival will be somewhat later than yours. I hope to have a report from Edgewood to share with you by then."

"I will be on my way once I have dropped these sassy baggages at home. You do not need your carriage?"

"I prefer to walk, thank you. We can ride home together afterwards, and I will bring you up to date—unless, of course, you have other plans?"

"None at the moment, although you should know that I am hoping a particular young lady will be there, and I may ask for the privilege of seeing her home."

"By all means, if you find you have need of the coach, let me know. I'm sure I can find an alternate means." The duke started away from the coach and then turned back to speak quietly to his younger brother.

"Avery? Be careful. I do not know the lady's family well, and I would be remiss if I did not remind you that this soiree will be replete with debutantes who would love to have a title in the family, especially in the person of a handsome young earl who is heir to a dukedom. Tread carefully unless you are feeling the need for more responsibility to add to that of keeping the Furies on the straight and narrow. And keep your wits about you. Lord Calloway is overly generous with his spirits."

"Thank you for the warning, brother. Would I be out of line to suggest that you take the same care?"

"I always do."

Chapter 11

The line of carriages stretched for blocks, so by the time Vivian, Linney, and the elder Braddocks were announced at Lady Calloway's ball, guests had filled the great ballroom and were spilling out into every other possible location.

"What a complete crush," said Vivian directly into Linney's ear after they made their way through the receiving line and had been announced.

"I know," said Linney. "How will we ever see anyone or be able to find anyone? More importantly, how will they find us?"

"Anyone in particular, Lin?" teased Vivian. "I thought Lord Hammond was attending the theatre tonight. Or is there someone else who has you shredding your dance card?"

Linney looked down at the mangled card in her gloved hand and grimaced. "Lord Hammond said he would be here after the theatre, but I don't think he'll ever be able to find us in this crowd."

"All the more reason you should dance, cousin. Everyone sees the dancers."

"You're absolutely right. What a brilliant idea! Oh, but I don't have anyone for the next set. That was the one I was saving for Avery. That one and the last one."

"Surely someone else is available with whom you can take to the floor. Oh, wait, here comes Mr.

Hamilton. He is supposed to lead me out, but I'll plead fatigue and he can dance with you. I'm sure he won't mind."

"Good evening, Lady Rowden, Miss Braddock. I believe this is my set, Lady Rowden, if you would do me the honor?"

"You are right, of course, Mr. Hamilton," said Vivian, "but would you mind terribly if I sat this one out? I am all of a sudden feeling rather fatigued."

"Certainly, Lady Rowden. May I bring you some refreshment instead?"

"Actually, Mr. Hamilton, if you don't mind, I think I will just sit here, but would you mind if my cousin took my place on the dance floor with you?"

"It would be my greatest pleasure, madam—if the lady herself would not object?"

"I would be delighted, Mr. Hamilton. Thank you, Vivian."

Vivian watched while Linney and Mr. Hamilton worked their way to the center of the room where the sets were forming for a country dance. Maybe she should have danced, she thought in retrospect. Performing the intricate steps might have taken her mind off the letter she had received from Henry's solicitors.

When at last the dance was finished, Mr. Hamilton returned Linney to Vivian's side and made his bows. Linney nervously fanned her face, her eyes still searching the room. "It's past midnight and I still don't see Lord Hammond. Do you think he was leading me astray when he made me promise to save a dance for him?"

"I would think by now you would have learned to

trust his word, Linea. He was escorting his family to and from the theatre, was he not?"

"Yes, but the theatre let out over an hour ago and there's still no sign of him."

"Linney?"

"Yes, Vivian?"

"Have you misplaced your spectacles again, dear?"

"Oh, I don't need them, Vivian. I only wear them sometimes when I attend the theatre."

"Because you have difficulty distinguishing figures at a distance?"

"Yes, that's right. I don't need them for dancing or for chatting with people."

"Yes, I understand that, but you might have saved yourself some anguish had you been wearing them sometime during the last half hour. Lord Hammond has been trying to make his way over here for at least that long. Lady Waller and her daughter have him trapped. I must tell you, Linney, that in my opinion, he is much too gentlemanly. He will never be able to extricate himself from his current conversation unless someone rescues him. Perhaps we should stroll over that way and remind him of his obligation on the dance floor."

"Oh, thank you, Vivian. Lady Waller will never let him go. She may as well tie him to a chair. You're right. He really must learn how to remove himself from such situations. There's still half the season left. Whatever will he do toward the end when the mamas are more desperate?"

"Lord Hammond," called Vivian as they approached the gentleman in question. "How good it is to see you again. I *told* Linea that it was you. She almost gave away your dance to Sir James, but I told her you were on your way to escort her for the set when you were dazzled and detained by Lady Waller and her lovely daughter. Good evening, ladies. Tina, you are a vision. That is the most cunning lace—wherever did you find it? Linney, you and Lord Hammond had best be off or the set will form without you."

Vivian inserted herself between Lord Hammond and Lady Waller—there simply was no other way to describe it—and in the interim, much to Lady Waller's dismay, Lord Hammond offered his arm to Linney and they disappeared into the crowd.

Vivian slapped open her fan and continued the conversation, whispering a titillating piece of gossip that she'd just made up into Lady Waller's ear and rationalizing to herself that, in the interest of distracting and calming the savage beast—or the thwarted mama—all's fair in love and war.

When Lady Waller left Vivian a few minutes later, it was with a tasty tidbit to share—in strictest confidence, of course—with her nearest and dearest friends.

Vivian breathed a sigh of relief. *This* she had not missed. She always felt like an outsider at gatherings of this size. And even though she was perfectly capable of holding her own, something in her reacted to the crowded corridors, airless ballrooms, and pressing masses of human beings. Sometimes she felt as if she couldn't breathe, and when that happened, she felt self-conscious and vulnerable.

She strolled past a group of chattering women and smiled at their sudden silence. She did not need to hear the words to know the topic of *that* conversation. She could practically write the item for the papers herself:

"And what of the appearance in town of the wealthy widow whose late husband spent his final moments in the nest of his ladybirds instead of his wife? Has she come to town to find a cure for her broken heart?"

Perhaps the gossip rags would put it about that she had fallen for Mr. Alexander and was conducting a torrid affair in the back room of his bookstore. Vivian chuckled to herself at the terror that would be seen in Mr. Alexander's eyes were she so much as to flutter an eyelash at him.

Holding her head high, Vivian tried to find space in the pulsating tide of people. The perfumes were overpowering and did not mix well with the smell of too many bodies in one place. It was one of the odd things about being in the middle of a mass of humanity, she thought—one feels all alone even though one is quite literally surrounded by people. Tonight, she felt that isolation keenly.

The other odd thing, she mused, is how easily one can overhear conversations of people—especially men—who don't realize how their voices carry to everyone around them. Or maybe they do realize and simply don't care.

"...the Viscountess Rowden—you know, the one whose husband died while he was...attending his mistress."

"Which one? I heard he had several."

Several men guffawed.

"I heard there were five."

"At the same time?"

"Well not all five at the same time in the same location, surely, but five that he was...ah...servicing."

"Lucky man!"

Like a murder of crows or an unkindness of ravens in their black evening clothes, the gentlemen cawed loudly.

"What of the viscountess? I heard she was quite lovely before she married. Perhaps marriage didn't suit her and she let herself go."

"To the contrary. I saw her tonight, and she is striking—if anything, marriage made her more beautiful."

"Perhaps he was simply a man of huge…appetites."

"Aren't we all?"

"Yes, but somehow he was able to get away with it."

"If you call being murdered getting away with it."

The ungentlemanly laughter sounded careless, and it was. But the ladies' tittering carried an even harder edge.

"What kind of horrible wife must she be for her husband to have need of so many other women?"

"I heard he visited her bed only on their wedding night."

"I heard that too. Lucky woman."

"Do you think she killed him?"

"There was never any evidence to implicate her…"

"There never is, is there?"

"I would never be able to show my face in town again."

"Hush, there she is."

"Did she hear us?"

"She couldn't possibly hear anything in this crush. I can barely hear myself!"

It seemed that every which way she turned, she was the topic of conversation. Vivian spotted the ladies' retiring room with relief, but as she entered that room, she was met with a deafening silence and stares that ranged from pity to speculation. She smiled brilliantly and made herself breathe steadily as she walked slowly over to the looking glass. After carefully patting her hair and inspecting her reflection, she brushed at an invisible thread on her bodice before putting her shoulders back and adjusting her skirts. She turned, murmured, "Good evening," to a lady of her acquaintance, and walked back out, closing the door behind her. She paused for just a moment and soon heard the growing buzz of the ladies returning to their gossip.

Suddenly she was in need of fresh air. Now.

Rather than take the steps down to the crowded ballroom and to the terraces beyond, Vivian moved toward the open French doors on the other side of the staircase. They opened out onto a balcony that spanned the back of the enormous ballroom and overlooked the lighted patio and gardens. The balcony itself was dark and offered the solitude she so desperately needed. She walked directly to the railing and closed her eyes as she tried unsuccessfully to gulp fresh air.

What had she been thinking? How could she possibly have believed that she *wouldn't* be the topic on the tip of every tongue in the *ton*? Against her better judgment, she had allowed Linney and Aunt Thea to talk her into coming back to town. She had pretended everything would be fine, even though she knew her appearance would resurrect the scandal.

She knew it. And she did it anyway.

And now, if that letter was correct, she had no money—and might actually owe great sums.

The letter. Her interview with Mr. Davis. The fear that her scandal would ruin Linney's season. Despair washed over her like a wave, and she struggled to keep her head above it.

Everything was too much. Vivian clamped her hand over her mouth to keep a sob from escaping. She couldn't seem to catch her breath. Her corsets strained as she tried desperately to fill her lungs with cooler air. Drat these tight lacings. The edges of her vision dimmed and a silky blackness beckoned. She felt herself falling…

Chapter 12

The very last woman he expected to have faint dead away in his arms was his sparring partner from the bookstore and, more recently, from their walk in Hyde Park. Lady Rowden. Vivian. His own personal enigma.

His? Where had that had come from? He must remember to examine that later. At the moment, he was concerned with the motionless shimmering violet bundle he held in his arms. Instinctively, he moved to a shadowed area of the balcony and gently placed the lady on the chaise lounge beside the chair he had just vacated. Kneeling beside her, Whit softly spoke her name. He traced a finger down her soft cheek and rubbed the inside of her delicate wrist.

"Lady Rowden? Can you hear me? Vivian?"

This was a first, he thought dryly to himself. He had been responsible for a lady or two swooning before, but it was usually after some sort of eye contact—either the heavy-lidded, smoldering ducal gaze or the scathing ducal glare. This was the first time a lady had swooned in his arms without so much as a backward glance.

Perhaps he was losing his edge. He'd been told he was devilishly handsome, which he always took to be a sincere if somewhat backward compliment. He encouraged comparisons between himself and the Lord of the Underworld whenever possible, as it suited his overall mystique and served to further his cover—a positive thing in his line of work.

"Vivian, my dear, open your eyes. Look at me." This time when he touched her cheek, his fingers on her wrist registered a strengthening pulse and he saw her eyelashes flutter.

"Ah, the lady returns."

When her eyes opened he saw confusion in her gaze. As her huge velvet-brown eyes focused, he cupped her chin with a caress. He knew the instant she recognized him because her whole body tensed.

"What happened? Why are *you* here?" She tried to sit up.

He pushed her gently back to the cushions. "Stay right where you are. I don't intend for you to faint again and topple over into the rose garden below."

There, that got some reaction.

"I was beginning to wonder if I might have the honor of carrying you down the stairs to commandeer help and thus, of course, ensuring the complete success of Lady Calloway's soiree. Take a deep breath. That's it. No, don't try to sit up yet. Let's see some color in your cheeks before we attempt that." He held her shoulders to the cushion, surprised at the strength he felt in her pique.

"I know you don't like others telling you what you must and mustn't do. I understand perfectly because it's a characteristic that we share. In this particular case, however, I win because I am stronger and can hold you down. Now, tell me who I am and I will *think* about allowing you to sit up."

A faint smile touched those perfectly shaped lips. "You are the skulking Duke of Whitley, are you not? The one who steals books from widows?"

96

"Correct on both counts, my lady. Now let's have you sit up and see if you can find other items to add to your list of my character flaws."

"On the contrary, your grace. It seems that I should be thanking you, not insulting you. I beg your pardon, but how did I end up here on the chaise?"

"You fainted, my lady. It was all quite romantic."

"I fainted? I never faint."

"Right into my arms. It was a thing of beauty."

"I rather doubt that, your grace," she said dryly.

Her breathing was soft and measured now.

"You came out onto the balcony—I assume for some fresh air—where I was skulking about as usual. You were unable to catch your breath adequately, and you fainted. I, being the essence of gentlemanly conduct, carried you to this chaise and have been debating whether to seal our collective fate by loosening your laces. Luckily, you revived yourself, so you will not be saddled with an indecisive duke as your second husband."

Vivian giggled. He loved the sound of it.

"Well, I owe you my thanks, your grace. Perhaps my life. As you said, had I fainted and toppled forward instead of backward into your convenient arms, I would have landed on my head on the terrace and given the *ton* yet another death in my family to gossip about."

Still holding her wrist, Whit felt her pulse accelerate. "My lady, why *did* you come out onto the balcony? Has someone done or said something that is causing you distress, in which case, may I be of service? When you appeared in the doorway, you appeared to be having trouble breathing. Are you prone to attacks of this nature? Perhaps an aversion to crowds or close spaces?"

"So many questions, your grace," said Vivian with an elusive smile. "I think trouble breathing is a malady that I share with all women wearing tight laces. I am not aware of any other conditions—it's just that the crowd was so close, and everyone was talking so loudly to be heard above the din. I remember coming out onto the terrace to get some fresh air and…"

"And?"

"To escape."

"To escape? The crowd?"

"The crowd, yes. Partly. But also what the people in the crowd were saying. It was difficult not to hear them. Or, in the case of a sudden silence, as I found in the ladies' retiring room, it was difficult not to assume what they had *been* saying."

The duke started to interrupt, but Vivian continued.

"I know, your grace. I should never assume. But to be perfectly honest, I'm not assuming. I heard them talking about me—and not in a flattering way."

"Tell me who it was and I will have a word with them."

Vivian laughed. "In that case, you would need to have a word with the entire *ton*. I think that would be difficult—even for you. Now please, I think it best if I return home."

"I will escort you to your uncle so he can call for your carriage."

"That will not be necessary. I don't want to bother him. He would insist on taking me home and collecting my aunt and cousin as well. I will have Lady Calloway's footman call for a hackney cab. Do you know if there is an exit from the garden to the front?"

"I do and there is, but I will not have you taking a cab alone at this time of night. I will escort you home in my carriage and send my footman with a message to your uncle so your family will not be concerned."

"That is very kind of you, your grace, but I am—"

"It was not an offer, Lady Rowden. It was a statement of what will happen."

Vivian was silent, but only for a moment. "As I was saying before you so imperiously interrupted, your grace, I am quite well now and must insist on a cab. My uncle's home is a ways away, and I cannot take you away from your evening's entertainment."

"The quality of my evening's entertainment rose considerably when I caught you in my arms. You can consider my escort to be an extension of that and a way for you to repay me."

Vivian scowled, but the duke only chuckled and assisted her to her feet, carefully holding her elbows while she regained her equilibrium. It was as close to an embrace as one could get without actually embracing, and all his senses registered her presence. He felt her take a deep breath and heard her exhale slowly. Her eyes were closed as if readying herself for a battle—or maybe her prayers? Long, dark eyelashes kissed her cheeks, taunting him with their good fortune, and the perfect lips—the lips he all of a sudden would give his entire dukedom to taste—parted ever so slightly.

As in his other meetings with Lady Rowden, he was surrounded by the comforting scent of lavender and—something else. Something he knew, but couldn't name. What *was* it? He had been aware of the same scent during their walk in Hyde Park, and it was driving him mad not to know what it was.

When Vivian finally opened her eyes, he searched the brown velvet depths for confirmation that she could stand on her own.

"If you will not tell me who it was that drove you out onto a dark balcony, will you answer another question for me?"

"If I am able to, your grace."

"Please, call me Whit."

"Why would I do that, your grace?"

"Because I plan to call you Vivian, Lady Rowden," he whispered into her ear.

Vivian sighed in defeat. "Very well, then. I will take it under consideration. What is your question, your grace?"

"What is the scent that you wear that so complements the lavender?"

Laughing, Vivian smiled brilliantly up at him. "Carnation, dianthus. In Greek, *dianthus* means 'heavenly flower.' It is also the flower for January, my birth month. The scent can be difficult to find, so I make my own oils."

"Well, that is one mystery solved."

"Are there others that need solving, your grace?"

"Too many to name, Lady Rowden." He offered his arm.

Sighing again, she placed her hand on his sleeve and scowled up at him as he smiled and tucked her hand close under his arm.

****

The duke—Whit, as he insisted she call him—had been the perfect gentleman. From the moment he'd handed her into his carriage until the coach pulled up in front of her uncle's house, he had been solicitous, entertaining, and nothing short of charming.

She was highly suspicious.

What was his interest in her? Why did he feel the need to insert himself so into her life? And was she the only one who felt the air crackling between them? There was definitely something there—she just had no idea what it was or what it signified. Did he feel it too?

She had not expected the kiss.

When she turned back around from collecting her reticule and evening wrap from the seat beside her, he brought her hand to his lips. He then placed that same hand on his shoulder and used his free hand to tip her chin up. The light from the carriage lantern made his blue eyes glow, and the last thing she registered before closing her eyes was that his second-best hat was in grave danger of being crushed, thus precipitating the need for him to bring out his third-best hat.

He brushed his lips over hers, once, twice, and again as if searching for the perfect spot. When he found it at last, she was more than ready to return the pressure. He cupped her face and slanted his lips on hers for a better fit. His tongue first traced her top lip, then the lower one, and then the seam between, coaxing them to part.

Opening to the insistent pressure, she breathed him in, desperate to be closer. He explored her mouth, his tongue tasting and taunting as it tangled with hers.

He tapped on the roof in an obviously prearranged signal to his coachman to resume driving, and for a moment, she was annoyed, but only for a moment.

Still holding her close against his broad chest, he moved his other hand from her chin down the nape of her neck to her side, molding her form with his hands.

His kisses intensified, and her cloak fell back to show how very low cut her gown really was. He groaned at the sight of her full breasts all but overflowing her bodice and whispered her name. When he moved her to his lap, she felt the hard ridge of his arousal under her thigh. He kissed the tops of first one breast and then the other, and, with his thumb, softly caressed below the neckline of her gown to find the hardened tips that attested to her desire.

She arched her back at the sensation and pressed against him, trying wordlessly to communicate her need. She kissed his neck, inhaling his masculine scent as she used her tongue to trace the contours of his ear. Her hands found their way through his cravat to unbutton his waistcoat and his shirt underneath and then—finally—to touch his warm smooth skin. She wanted to kiss his hard muscled shoulder and nuzzle her way through the soft dark hair on his chest.

He caught his breath and moved her so that her knees were on the edge of the seat as she straddled his lap. He ran his hands up her sides, cupping and freeing a breast to expose the dusky areola. He lowered his mouth and gently laved the tip with his tongue while his thumb found and circled the other taut peak.

Moaning, Vivian put her arms around his neck, pressing closer as she offered herself to him. He moved between her thighs and she circled her hips, caressing his hardness more fully. He groaned, and suddenly his mouth was everywhere—kissing her lips, suckling the escaped nipple, and whispering in her ear.

"Vivian, my love, what are you doing to me? I need to see all of you. I—"

The horses stopped with a forward jolt.

Whit swore under his breath. His hands stilled on Vivian's back, holding her close and stroking her as he regained his senses. When his breathing had calmed, he put his hands on her waist and tilted her back to see her face. Her wide eyes were black with passion—he was not the only one frustrated by the too-short carriage ride. He kissed her lips and slowly eased her off his lap and onto the seat beside him, groaning at the movement. Silently, he helped her adjust her bodice.

She spoke first. "Well, that certainly was..." Her voice quavered just a bit as she searched for the right word.

"Unexpected? Presumptuous? Inappropriate?"

"I was going to say 'lovely,' but your adjectives are also correct."

The change in the air was almost visible, and he didn't like it. "I apologize, Lady Rowden...Vivian. This is not what I had planned when I offered to see you home."

Wasn't it? What *had* been his intentions? He could have easily called a hack to transport her, as she'd first suggested. He could have even sent her home in his carriage, alone. His footman would have seen her safely inside. What *were* his intentions when he'd insisted on accompanying this beautiful woman home in his carriage? She had every right to be furious.

Her actual response was a complete surprise.

"I quite understand, your grace. It also was not my intention, and yet...it seemed to be quite the right thing at the time." She avoided his eyes, but he saw a hint of a smile touch her lips.

He smiled at that smile. Unable to resist, he caressed her soft cheek with the back of his fingers and tilted her chin up. "Lovely? Really?"

Her eyes finally met his. "It was uncomfortable, cramped, awkward, and all in all, quite lovely."

He kissed her lips softly. "If I am to protect your reputation from aspersions, I should assist in putting you back together."

"I think if you can help me pin up these curls and untangle my skirts, my cloak will cover the rest. However, it is probably best if you allow your footman to see me to the door, as your cravat is quite undone and other parts of you are…" She gestured vaguely in the direction of his still-hard erection.

Whit pulled the offending scarf from around his neck. There was nothing to be done about the other at the moment. "My lady, you are not the only one with a cloak that camouflages. I refuse to relinquish the privilege of seeing you to your door or to forfeit even one second of time in your presence."

He gathered his cloak and stepped around her to open the carriage door and then held her hand as she descended the three steps to the ground. In the light from the street lamps, he could see a smile still on her face.

"You are quite the accomplished flatterer, your grace."

"There is no skill needed to speak the truth, my lady…Vivian." He pressed her fingertips to his lips as Thomson opened the door at the top of the stairs.

"Good night, Whit," whispered Vivian. Then she dipped a small curtsy. "Your grace."

"Lady Rowden." One chaste peck on the cheek and she was inside. He walked the few steps back to the carriage, not at all sure what had just happened.

Chapter 13

For a man tasked with coordinating and implementing the activities of a vast network of individuals who were involved in complex operations requiring the procurement and analysis of thousands of details and bits of information, and for a man in charge of the lives that provided that information, as well as the thousands more who were dependent upon that information, he had certainly made some serious miscalculations this evening.

Putting aside for the moment the immediate discomfort of his physical state, which he assumed would pass eventually, he was more concerned with the sea change that seemed to be taking place with his emotions.

He was the Duke of Whitley—the Ice Duke they called him, mostly because of the icy glares he parceled out without respect to rank or relation. The Ice Duke was as likely to thwart the actions of a peer as those of a lowly bootblack. Even the Prince Regent kept his distance. But the coldness of the Ice Duke went further than that. Although only two men had felt the chill of staring across loaded pistols at the steady hand of the Ice Duke, many more had experienced his icy blue stare of disdain—a glare that caused grown men to cower and grown women to weep.

His few friends knew him better, but even they

were not always immune to the cold, haughty demeanor that had them reassessing their positions and priorities.

The duke was not a sociable peer even though he was seen at society events as often as he was seen in the halls of government. As one hostess put it, his attendance was really more of a *presence* than that of an actual participant at gatherings. He seldom danced—the last recorded sighting being when he was prowling for a new mistress—and he usually arrived late and left early.

The duke was quite aware of what was said about him and, for the most part, he encouraged the generally accepted opinions. Those who needed to know differently, did. They knew how committed he was to every last one of the men—and women—who engaged in the difficult, dangerous, and mostly unacknowledged work he oversaw. They also knew the extent to which he would go to protect and defend them all.

So what the hell had just happened with the suspect he had under surveillance—the suspect also known as Lady Rowden?

As might be expected of a man with such weighty responsibilities, the duke was also a man of strong sexual desires, needs that were met quite satisfactorily with a professional mistress paid handsomely to ensure that very thing. Granted, it had been several months since he had released Claire, but that would only explain his physical response to Lady Rowden…Vivian—surely once one had undressed and tried one's best to mate with a woman in one's carriage, a more familiar address was acceptable.

But it was not his physical response that bothered Whit. Letting her go inside her house a few moments ago was one of the most difficult things he'd ever done. It was as if a great storm had ravaged through his whole being. He'd had to fight the urge to wrap his arms around Vivian and carry her away to his lair. He had never experienced such a longing to be with a woman, to hold her, and to have her in that most intimate act of joining. He had never felt such a fierce desire to protect and cherish anyone. And he'd never felt such emptiness as he experienced watching the door close behind her.

He shifted uncomfortably in his seat. Not to mention that he had never been this hard for so long. Even now, more than several blocks away from Lady Rowden's residence, with the windows of the coach wide open and the cool evening air running over his person, even now, he was trying to find a position that did not cause him significant discomfort—and was, thus far, failing miserably.

His instincts were screaming at him, but he was damned if he knew what they were trying to say.

The only thing he *did* know was that this could not happen. He simply could not afford to be distracted like this. He could not afford to see the lady again—at least in the social sense. It simply was not safe for him or for anyone else. Especially if, as it seemed, the lady was somehow involved in transporting the puzzles that the enemy was using for their ciphers.

He frowned as the coach pulled up in front of his townhouse. A light shone in the library window, and he could see the shadow of a figure on the closed draperies. He had no meetings scheduled. Something must have happened.

Whit opened the door to his library and was not really surprised to see Edgewood standing by the fireplace, where the flames had been built up to a small inferno.

"May I offer you a nightcap?" said Whit, noting the snifter already in Edgewood's hand.

"I'm fine, thanks. But feel free to help yourself."

"That is good of you." Whit poured a generous portion of Scotch whiskey into a glass and inhaled deeply before taking a long drink.

"To what do I owe this...honor? Or have you just run out of places to spend your evenings?"

Edgewood laughed. "A little of both, I guess. There's news."

"I thought as much. What is it?"

"That French operative we captured—now on his way to the Tower, by the way—told Reggie that his contact is a woman. He was to meet her next week at a house party given by Lord and Lady Haversham. The prisoner confirmed that their operation has been scheduled, but he did not know exactly when or where it would happen. Reg says he thinks that information was to come from this next meeting. He figures that the specifics will be sent out using this week's cipher."

"So this female contact would also have a connection to the maker of the puzzles that run in the *Mail Observer*?"

"Most likely, yes."

"I talked with the editor-in-chief at the *Mail Observer* today," said Whit, moving to behind his desk. "Davis is his name. He told me that the V. I. Burningham who creates the ciphers is from Somerset. I've already sent Withers there to see what he can find out about the man. Davis told me the ciphers were originally sent to the paper by post, but for the past four weeks, a messenger has dropped them off at their London office. We talked to the clerk who's been receiving the puzzles, and the clerk confirmed that the messenger has been the same woman each time. I think the messenger is Lady Rowden, the wife of the late viscount. I followed her to the *Mail Observer* this morning."

For some reason, Whit failed to mention to Edgewood that he had also just had a rather intense romantic interlude with that same lady in his carriage.

"The plot thickens," said Edgewood. "We need to get an operative into the Haversham house party. I was told that the festivities begin on—"

"Monday. Yes, I know. Avery and I both are invited. I sent my regrets, but I'm sure I can appeal to Lady Haversham to find room for me."

"You? You're going to be the operative at the house party?"

"Why not?"

"Well, apart from the fact that you have several other matters that need your attention, you are not the most inconspicuous person in the world."

"That can work both ways. No one would dare question the actions of a duke—especially not the Ice Duke—and I can manage the other matters from there just as well as I can from anywhere else."

"Do we know whether Lady Rowden will be attending?"

"I can find out, and then I can keep an eye on her."

Edgewood was silent for a moment and then took a sip from his glass. "Word has it that you're already doing that." He looked up at Whit, who stared back at him coldly.

"What are you saying, Edgewood?"

Edgewood put his snifter down on the table beside him. "You've always said the *ton* is the very best spy network in the history of espionage and, as you might imagine, they have not been silent on this particular subject. All I'm saying is to make sure your motives are clear and make sure you're thinking with your brain and not your cock. The lady is said to be very beautiful, and she is extremely available. But she is also a suspect."

"If you were anyone else, I'd call you out for that," Whit said mildly. "As it is you, I'll simply ask if you have a better plan. Is there someone else we can get in there on such short notice?"

"No, you're right. As usual. No one else would have such access or as much freedom to move about. I'll establish a command post nearby, and we can send you information as soon as we get it. You can use Cooper or Avery to send any information you can't get out personally."

I'll use Avery. Lady Haversham's house parties always have a theme and a costume ball, and if I recall correctly, the theme for this event is the Olympics of ancient Greece. Cooper will be too busy assembling a costume for me that won't show my bare arse."

Edgewood snorted. "Perhaps I should apply as a footman to help out for the evening. I would really hate to miss seeing you in a short toga."

"Knowing you as I do, I posit that what you don't want to miss are the ladies in their costumes—or lack thereof."

Edgewood laughed. "You know me too well." He raised his glass. "Let the games begin."

Chapter 14

"Are you feeling better, Vivian? I've brought up tea."

"That was very nice of you, Linney, but as I have told you six or seven times already, I am quite well. So to what do I owe this honor?"

"Do I need to have a reason to spend time with my favorite cousin? We're family—no, we're more than family, we're family *and* we are friends. We do things for each other. That's just the way things are between us."

Vivian wrinkled her brow at Linney's effusive soliloquy and raised an eyebrow as it continued.

"I'm so sorry I wasn't there to help you last evening, although I do think it is terribly romantic that the duke was there to rescue you—especially after the two of you shared such a lovely stroll in the park. Avery said his brother was rather pensive on the way home from the park. I get the impression they are quite close—but then, they are family and really there is nothing more important than that, don't you think? We should take every opportunity to show the members of our family how much we value them, don't you agree?"

"I would agree that you have just about worn out that sentiment. Would it be too rude of me to ask that you just tell me what favor it is you require of me?"

"Very well," said Linney, flopping down on the

floor in a most unladylike position. "Although I did have several more very flattering lines."

"For goodness' sake, Linney, what is it?"

Linney sat back up. "Mother is not feeling well and has decided she is not going to go to Lady Haversham's house party next week. She told me to send our regrets."

"So...is it paper you lack? Ink? I'll ring and have both brought immediately. I'll even provide sealing wax and a flame. And once you finish, we can have your missive delivered to Lady Haversham personally. Now may I get back to my work?"

"Vivian, you *know* how much I've been looking forward to this house party. Mother has said I may go if you go with me. So I'm begging you..." At this point Linney knelt in front of her cousin. "I am literally on my knees, Vivian, begging you to change your mind and say you will go with me to Lady Haversham's house party."

"Linney, you are the one who keeps telling me that a widow need not do anything she doesn't want to do. That a widow doesn't have to go anywhere she doesn't want to go. And I will tell you that a house party is at the very tippy-top of the list of things I don't want to do and places I don't want to go. In fact, I can think of very few things I want to do less, but only a few—and they involve boiling oil and stepping on snakes while wearing no shoes. I do *not* want to go."

Linney stood up and started pacing around the room. "I understand, Viv, honestly, I do. And I wouldn't ask under normal circumstances, but these are not normal circumstances. If mother sends her regrets, I'm unlikely to be invited ever again in my whole entire life. Lady Haversham has a very strict policy."

"Since when have you become such a devotee of Lady Haversham? I would think such a tame time would not be to your liking. From what I've heard, her entertainments are all rather quaint. Not at all the type of amusements your set seems to favor. Why the change of heart?"

"It's not a change of heart, exactly. I love charades and picnics, and of course there's always the fancy dress ball..." Linney picked up the feather quill from Vivian's desk and trailed it thoughtfully across her cheek. "Perhaps...well, perhaps I am getting a little tired of my friends—at least I thought they were my friends. I'm not so certain anymore."

Vivian narrowed her eyes at her younger cousin in an expression that clearly said, *Explain, please.*

"It's nothing really. Just..."

"Just *what*? Tell me, Linney. Have you had some kind of falling out with your friends?"

Linney resumed her pacing. "It's just that sometimes they can be so juvenile. The way Nadine gossips and makes fun of everyone—even when she doesn't know them."

"My dear, you have just described the whole of the *haute ton*. It's what they do. What about Annabeth? You and she have always gotten on. Weren't you chums at school?"

"Annabeth won't take a breath unless Nadine tells her to, and Gordon and his friends are always foxed—even at luncheon."

"Most likely left over from the previous night's festivities," observed Vivian dryly.

"Yes, well, Nadine thinks her brother can do no

wrong, so we're forever waiting for Gordon to take us walking or for Gordon to escort us to the shops or for Gordon to take us driving in his new carriage. When he's in his cups—which seems to be all the time—he acts like he is God's gift to women."

"Linney!"

"Well, it's true." Linney paused, glancing around as if waiting for lightning to strike her dead for invoking the Lord's name in vain, but then she continued. "Gordon is... I mean, sometimes he... Well, just the other day, Avery had to remind him that there were ladies present, and Gordon looked right at me and said, 'I don't see any ladies.' It was terribly insulting, and for a horrible minute I thought Avery was going to call him out. Gordon just laughed. I didn't know what to do, so I just turned my back on him and walked out into the garden."

"Turned your back on Gordon or Avery?"

"On Gordon. Do pay attention, Vivian! Avery escorted me as we walked ahead of the group and out to the garden. He told me that if Gordon insults me again there will be hell to pay. And then, of course, he begged my pardon for using such language in front of a lady. He must have said something to Gordon, though, because later that day, Gordon found me standing alone and asked my pardon. He said he'd been thinking about a certain actress he'd seen crossing the street when he said what he said, and that it was all a misunderstanding. He asked for my forgiveness and I gave it. But then when I tried to rejoin our group, he stood in my way and refused to move. I used my coldest tone and asked him to please let me by, but he wouldn't budge. He just laughed and said he wanted to explain to me all the ways the actress wasn't a lady."

"Linea! Why didn't you say something sooner? You didn't tell Lord Hammond, did you?"

"I didn't, but I was so embarrassed. I told Gordon to stop, but he said that I was being too prudish. I finally pushed past him and found Avery and the others, but I'm sure he has made up stories about me and is telling them to his friends and to Nadine and Annabeth. And honestly, I don't care. I just don't want to spend so much time with them anymore."

"So these friends of yours have not been invited to Lady Haversham's house party?"

"No, thank goodness."

"Has Lord Hammond per chance been invited?"

"I…uh…I'm not certain…"

Vivian's eyebrows flew upward.

"Oh, very well. You needn't look at me like that. Yes, it is altogether possible that Lord Hammond might have mentioned something about attending the house party, now that I think about it. In fact, yes, he did say he planned to attend. Vivian, I do wish you would reconsider. I would—"

"You might have saved us both a great deal of trouble if you had just put it all out there for me at the start."

"You mean you'll go?"

"Of course. Just because *I* have no interest in finding a husband doesn't mean that everyone should stop looking. I'm perfectly willing to accompany you to Lady Haversham's house party—oof!" She was interrupted by a huge hug from her cousin.

"Oh, thank you, Vivian! How can I ever repay you? You are such a good friend to me."

"I promise I will even find my own amusements so that you and Lord Hammond can become better acquainted. When are we expected at Haversham House?"

"We can travel down on Monday. The ball is Friday. Everyone is supposed to dress like the ancient Greeks." Linney giggled. "I wonder if the men will wear short tunics?"

"What of you, cousin? Will you go about wrapped in a toga with no stays underneath and a laurel wreath in your hair?"

"I will if you will."

Vivian laughed. A house party would be just the thing to take her mind off debts, dead husbands, diabolical editors, and a certain duke with cornflower-blue eyes—who, by the way would look devastating in a toga. Vivian shook her head to erase the picture before her brain had a chance to fill in all the details, and she pulled her thoughts back to her cousin.

"A pact, then," said Vivian, raising her teacup in salute. "Authenticity is king—or in this case, queen. When in Greece, we will dress as the Greeks dressed, down to the very last detail."

"God save the queen," said Linney, raising her cup in response. "Oh, Vivian, thank you. You can't imagine how much this means to me."

"Perhaps a change of venue would be distracting, at that. I, too, might benefit from a change in scenery and inhabitants. I do seem to keep seeing the same people over and over again."

"I'll send our acceptances to Lady Haversham right now." Linney danced toward the door.

"Linney, wait! I just realized... I can't go without a

maid. Annie won't be back for at least another week." Vivian sighed. "Maybe it's not meant to be after all."

"Nonsense. Besides, you promised. We have a pact. Mama said you could have Estelle help you here, so I'll just go and ask if Estelle can go with us to Lady Haversham's. I'm sure Mama will be happy to oblige—especially since you are doing all of this for me. You know—anything for family and all that."

Linney grinned at Vivian before shutting the door behind her.

Chapter 15

The Earl of Haversham had been married to his countess for more than thirty years. Theirs was an anomaly in *ton* marriages, having the characteristics of both love and fidelity.

Many things had contributed to their long and happy relationship, but as Lady Haversham told anyone and everyone who would listen, the most important thing was that they were *friends* before they were ever *lovers*. And, once they did become lovers, she explained with a demure smile and a twinkle in her eye, both of them took responsibility for making sure their relationship was an ongoing adventure and something neither took for granted.

The other thing the earl and his countess would tell you about their marriage was that they trusted each other completely. Even after four children and frequent separations, and even though they had very different interests, they were always united in their love and respect for each other. For example, the Haversham house parties—legend within the *ton's* upper echelon—happened in spite of, not because of, Lord Haversham. The earl was usually in residence when the house parties were in progress, but his participation was limited to leading out his countess for the obligatory first dance at the fancy dress ball that always marked the midpoint of a successful event. He never dressed in costume, he never joined in any of the games or activities, and he seldom joined Lady Haversham's guests for dinner, preferring to dine alone in his study.

On the other hand, Lady Haversham adored bringing together disparate guests to create house parties with a unique flair. While many of her guests were members at every level of the *ton*, many were not, occupying instead roles in politics, in the arts, and even in trade. Gossip surrounding a Haversham house party often lasted months after the event, and it was not unheard of for an engagement to be announced after a couple attended one of the gatherings at Lady Haversham's country home.

"A true Haversham house party always has a theme," Linney explained to Vivian as they rode through the countryside on their way to the hallowed Haversham home. "The theme for this particular party is 'Greek to Me' and the activities—actually the invitation refers to them as 'Olympics'—run the gamut from archery contests to wildflower gathering. Tuesday will see the opening ceremonies that mark the beginning of eight days of festivities, with the costume ball on Friday evening. Lady Haversham eschews the tradition of having a ball at the *end* of a house party because she enjoys reliving the evening with her guests over the days that follow the event. The last full day of the party is Tuesday week. It features the closing ceremonies when laurel wreaths are to be given to the champions of each event. Lady Haversham has been quite hush-hush about any other details, but there is a rumor of fireworks. It is said that Lady Haversham adores fireworks, so I am quite hopeful."

"That certainly sounds like a very full schedule. I

was hoping for some time to read and stroll around her gardens. I hear they are quite beautiful."

"Oh, I'm sure there will be time for that, too. Not everyone participates in every activity. I think that's one reason she always puts a fancy dress ball in the middle of the party. It's really a brilliant hostessing strategy—the ball draws everyone together, and then gives them a common experience to talk about for the next few days. Nadine said it's because Lady Haversham wants to make sure everyone has time to get their stories in order before they travel back to London to spread all the gossip they learned."

"That's not a very nice thing to say, Linney."

"*I* didn't say it. Nadine said it. But you're right, it wasn't very nice. I think she said it because she's never been invited to a house party at Haversham House."

"So how do guests know what to wear to the ball?"

"It's right here on the invitation." Linney read from the elegant card:

"You are invited to a Fancy Dress Ball.
Friday Evening at Nine o'clock.
When in Rome, do as the Romans do,
but when in Greece, in both custom and in dress,
all things are Greek to Me.
Let the games begin!"

Linney handed the card to Vivian for her perusal. "I do hope we brought enough material for the togas."

"Well, if anyone knows how much material it takes to make two togas, Madame Augustine does. I trust her judgment implicitly."

"Perhaps Lady Haversham will have additional

materials available."

"I say we just use what we have and stop wrapping it around us when we run out. I'm sure it will be fine," said Vivian absentmindedly.

"I hear that this party is one of the largest Lady H. has ever given. In addition to Lord Hammond, I know several people who will be in attendance."

"That's nice." Vivian's reply was noncommittal, but Linney persevered.

"Avery should already be there when we arrive."

"Is that right?"

"Yes, and he said that the duke might be coming later in the week."

"Mmm-hmm."

"Yes, in fact he said that the only reason the duke was coming was to see you."

"That is a shame."

"And to ask you to marry him."

"That's lovely, dear...I'm sorry, what?"

"Oh, good. I have your attention at last. Whatever are you thinking about so deeply?"

Vivian sighed. "I'm sorry, Linney. You're right, I wasn't paying attention. I just keep thinking about the letter from the Rowden solicitors and about my conversation with Mr. Davis, at the *Mail Observer*. I handled it poorly and have decided to send an apology letter, but I just don't understand why he is so set against working with a woman. I would so love to confide in him that I am V. I. Burningham and that I am the one who created all those puzzles that were responsible for the paper's increase in circulation. I could do so much more for him, if he would only let me, but I don't dare even tell him who I am."

Vivian had shared the letter from her late husband's solicitors with her cousin and with her aunt and uncle. Aunt Thea had gone on and on about the unfairness of it all and how despicable a person Henry was—which Vivian did not dispute. Uncle Will seemed quite confident that it was all an act of caution on the part of the estate's solicitors. He was convinced that the eventual dispensation of Henry's assets would see Vivian's monthly stipend reinstated. Vivian felt no such optimism, but, as she anticipated, Aunt Thea and Uncle Will insisted on providing her with a monthly income while it was all being sorted out.

"It's wonderful to have family to help me muddle through these difficult times," said Vivian, "but I must find a way to repay your mother and father. I'm convinced that if I could have my puzzle collections published, they would be a success and would provide enough income for me to keep my house in Somerset. Before Mr. Davis voiced his opinions about doing business with women, he implied that a very lucrative deal could be worked out if Mr. Burningham were interested. Why should that change just because I'm a woman?"

"Are you sure that it is Mr. Davis who has the problem working with women?" asked Linney.

"What do you mean?"

"I mean, maybe his prejudice is coming from someone else."

"Such as whom?"

"I don't know. Perhaps the owner of the paper has made such a rule and Mr. Davis is just carrying out the policy. Or..."

"Or what?"

"Maybe it is someone's wife who has set the policy that says they will not do business with women. Have you thought of that?"

"No, actually, I had not," said Vivian. "That's an interesting idea. So what you're saying is that perhaps it is not Mr. Davis who is opposed to doing business with a woman—maybe it's his wife or his boss. That's a very good point, Linney. Thank you. I can see that I need to find out more."

"You needn't sound so surprised," sniffed Linney. "I have been known to have an inspired thought or two. What I want to know is why don't you just get married again?"

"Why would I do that? I don't want to get married again. I've been married before and, if you recall, it didn't work out well. Plus, if I am unmarried, I have great amounts of freedom. Married, I am literally the property of my husband."

"You've said that before like it's a bad thing, but I think it would be lovely to belong to someone you love who also loves you."

"Yes, well, I thought so too, but I found out differently."

"You can't judge every man by your first husband, Vivian. If you found someone you loved and who loved you very much, would you get married again?"

"Honestly? I try not to give it much thought."

"Why ever not? Wouldn't you like to have children and a family of your own?"

"It sounds nice when you say it like that, but I'm not sure it's even possible anymore. I think you have to be looking for a love like that in order to find it. Besides, what if we each have only one chance for true love, and what if I wasted mine on Henry? Besides, most *ton* marriages are based on property settlements rather than love anyway."

"I know that, but they aren't always. I know there are some husbands and wives who are very much in love. Look at Mama and Papa, or Lord and Lady Haversham. Both are very successful marriages, and both couples seem committed to making each other happy."

"Again, when you say it like that, it sounds lovely. And yes, if I could be sure I had found a man who was as interested in making me happy as I was in making him happy, then I might marry again. But I'm not holding my breath, and I'm not going to spend all my time looking for such a Prince Charming."

"How about a charming duke?"

Vivian suddenly had a vision of sitting in the Duke of Whitley's lap in his carriage, kissing him. She blushed and turned away so Linney wouldn't see her flushed face. "I'm sure the duke has many other things that need his attention, as do I. Plus, I doubt we will see him at an event so far from London. And even if we did, the duke is much too proper to attend to a lady with a past as scandalous as mine."

"Through no fault of your own."

"Even so. I have a feeling the duke is quite the dutiful peer and will find a most obedient and suitable lady to marry when he is ready to fill his nursery."

"Well, when I see Avery, I will ask if he knows his brother's plans. Oh, look, Vivian! We're turning into a lane. I think we have arrived!"

Chapter 16

"Good evening, Lady Rowden. I had not heard you were back in polite society."

"Lady Smythson. It *is* you. I had so hoped..." Vivian chose not to complete the thought aloud.

Of all the luck.

Upon their arrival at Haversham House, Vivian and Linney had been ushered to their respective rooms. Vivian's corner room overlooked the side and front of the house, offering stunning views of the Haversham hills beyond the well-kept park. Linney's room overlooked a vast courtyard which occupied the southern vista and included the entrance to the formal gardens. After their arrival, a sumptuous tea had been sent up for them to share in Vivian's more spacious rooms. There was time for a luxurious bath before Vivian rang for Estelle to help her dress and do her hair for dinner. She went to gather Linney, and the two went down together to the drawing room where guests were gathering for an aperitif. Everything had been lovely— until now, when Vivian was cornered by Lady Smythson, one of the *ton's* most prolific gossips.

Vivian smiled at the lady known for her perpetually turned-up nose and soldiered on. "Doesn't Lady Haversham have a lovely home?"

Lady Smythson made a great show of looking around at her surroundings. "It's a little too quaint and too democratic for my tastes. My husband insisted we accept the invitation even though we could at this very moment be sitting at table with a second cousin of the Prince Regent himself, with only those of the bluest blood on our left and right." She lowered her voice to a whisper. "I understand Lady Haversham has invited an *actor*—and not just to perform, but to dine and associate with the guests."

"How very intriguing," said Vivian. "I wonder if he is a Shakespearian actor. I understand Lady H. adores anything to do with Shakespeare. Perhaps he will dress in his toga and entertain us with Marc Antony's speech from *Julius Caesar*?"

"Well, I, for one, have no intentions of flaunting myself about in society with only a bed sheet draped about my person, and I assume all ladies of quality will comport themselves with similar restraint."

Vivian could not help it. "I was recently informed by a duke that one should never assume anything, Lady Smythson, and I must say that I think it to be very good advice. If you will excuse me, I—"

Lady Smythson stepped in front of Vivian, effectively blocking her path. "Oh, yes," she said, smiling slyly at Vivian. "And would that be the Duke of Whitley? The same duke you were walking with in Hyde Park the other day? Perhaps you are not aware, since you've only recently come to town, but his name was recently paired with a dear friend of mine, Lady Monroe. She is a great beauty, and she caught the duke's eye when she returned to society after a period of mourning for her husband. *He* was killed in a tragic carriage accident about which there was only sorrow—no scandal. Well, after my friend returned to town, she and the duke were seen together *constantly*. She thought—well, really, *everyone* thought—they would make it a permanent connection, seeing as the duke has yet to produce an heir."

Lady Smythson lowered her voice. "My friend did confide to me that marriage was the *only* thing stopping the duke from producing a legitimate heir, if you understand my meaning. He certainly had all the other…requirements. He had recently broken off with his mistress, so he was always suggesting that they…well, *you* can imagine, I'm sure. My friend said she had to keep reminding the duke that there was a time and place for such activities and that the time was *after* they were married and the place was in the ducal bedchamber—not in a carriage or wherever the mood struck him."

"Yes, I can see how—"

"Well," continued Lady Smythson, as if Vivian had not said a word, "my friend told me that when she assured the duke she would look quite favorably upon an offer to be his duchess, he smiled that icy smile of his and told her that now was neither the time nor the place. He took his leave and never returned. As you can imagine, my friend was furious. Not only had she wasted *days* catering to the duke's every whim, but she had told all of her friends it was only a matter of time before she landed the biggest prize of the season— although, I dare say she overstepped just a bit with that. Don't you agree?"

"It certainly—"

"My friend did confide in me that perhaps it was just as well because his grace was a very difficult man to abide and quite the cold fish." The lady sighed. "Of course, with the duke's reputation for always having a beautiful woman on his arm, I wasn't surprised to hear that he and Lady Ferrington were having a rather public tête-à-tête at the Evenstone musicale. Now, *she* is quite the beauty—just like her mother. My friend was at the musicale, and she said the two of them looked quite cozy. They both left the gathering early—not together, mind you—that would have been terribly indiscreet— but no one saw either of them afterwards. And word has it that Lord Ferrington was out until all hours with his own gaming and other...ah...diversions."

"Yes, well—"

"So you can imagine how shocked I was when I heard the duke was walking with *you* in Hyde Park. I wondered if he had already tired of Lady Ferrington and was looking elsewhere for a diversion. Although I do think he would prefer a connection with someone less notorious than yourself. And of course marriage with you is out of the question."

"And just for curiosity's sake, why is that, Lady Smythson?"

"My dear, the duke has his reputation to think of, and his duchess must be above reproach. Given your...history...well, let's just say it's rather obvious you wouldn't suit. Don't you agree?" Lady Smythson smiled a very condescending smile and cocked her head to one side. Then, as another thought popped into her mind, she lowered her voice and stepped closer to Vivian.

"I hope you don't mind my asking, Lady Rowden, and mind you, I would never speak ill of the dead, but is it true that when they collected your husband's body, he was still...ah, *engaged* with the woman?"

"Actually, Lady Smythson, I *do* mind your asking. And I would not regale you with the lurid details of my husband's death even if I knew them. If you are so desirous of knowing what went on between the viscount and his mistresses, then I suggest you ask them. And now, if you will excuse me, my cousin is in want of my company. Good day, Lady Smythson."

Vivian schooled herself not to run, but she took her leave as fast as humanly possible, walking quickly in the direction opposite the wretched gossip. Part of her had a grudging admiration for the lady who was only *saying* what everyone else was *thinking*, but nothing, absolutely nothing, could make her say a word about Henry and the circumstances of his humiliating demise.

And what did she care that the Duke of Whitley had dismissed his mistress and was searching for a new liaison? Although that did perhaps shed some light on his actions in the carriage. The man had been deprived of his regular sexual encounters, and she had simply been the closest available female. Not to mention, she reminded herself, that she had quite literally fallen into his arms up on Lady Calloway's balcony. Any man would be excused for taking advantage of the situation that had presented itself.

The *real* question was, what was *her* excuse?

Hearing Lady Smythson's voice in the hall behind her, Vivian looked around frantically for an escape route. The door to her right was almost but not completely closed, so she slipped inside and found herself in what appeared to be…heaven. Or perhaps just a well-appointed library. The room was huge—on the scale of London's best reading rooms—with shelves of books that drew her in before she noticed the man sitting at a big desk at the far end.

"Oh, I do beg your pardon," she said when the gentleman stood and gestured her in. "I did not mean to intrude."

"Come in, come in. You are most welcome, madam. I am Lord Haversham. Welcome to my home and to my haven."

"Thank you. Your home is lovely, and this library is... Oh, I beg your pardon again, sir. I am Lady Rowden, a guest at your wife's party. I saw the door was ajar, and as I was looking for a...a less crowded venue, I thought—"

Lord Haversham smiled. "Won't you have a seat? I know that look. You were trying to escape someone, weren't you? Let me guess. Lady Smythson?"

Vivian laughed. "How did you know? Am I that transparent?"

"You do have a bit of a hunted look about you, but mainly because I know Lady Smythson. She is a distant cousin of mine, and every time my wife has a house party, she feels obligated to invite the woman. It doesn't matter much to me because I spend most of the time holed up here in my library. But I can always identify the parties where Lady Smythson is in attendance by the number of guests seeking refuge."

"Thank you for letting me take temporary shelter. I will not bother you further."

"You are more than welcome to stay or to come back at any time and avail yourself of the books or the seclusion. I am very proud of my library, especially my collections in horticulture and astronomy. I leave tomorrow on business and will be away until the day of the Grecian Ball, but I will leave the door unlocked if you would like to return."

"That would be wonderful, Lord Haversham. I have several letters to write, and I did want to work on a puzzle that I was creating for the *London Mail Observer*, so having access to your library would be extremely helpful. Thank you."

"You're not by any chance related to that V. I. Burningham who does the ciphers on the pages of the *Mail Observer*, are you?"

"Can you keep a confidence? Actually, I *am* V. I. Burningham. The puzzles, ciphers, and enigmas are my own creations."

"What a wonderful happenstance! I am a great fan of your work, Lady Rowden. Wherever do you get your ideas?"

Vivian smiled. "My ideas come from everywhere—from my daily walk, from *ton* events—anywhere. I am also working on collecting a library of my own to assist in the development of my puzzles. Thank you for your very kind offer, Lord Haversham. I will most assuredly take you up on it, but for now I will leave you to yourself. Good day."

Vivian looked both ways before she scampered across the entryway to the terrace to find Linney.

****

"Where have you been?" asked Linney as Vivian walked up behind her.

"Talking with Lord Haversham in his library and escaping Lady Smythson. In the opposite order."

"Well, I certainly hope you didn't bring her with you. She is the most exhausting gossip—in every sense of the word. I am quite in awe of her ability to gather and disperse information with such efficiency. Oh, here's Avery with our punch."

"Good day, Lady Rowden. Would you care for some refreshment? The punch is flavored with pineapple and is quite a refreshing change from lemonade, don't you agree, Linea? I would be delighted to fetch you a glass. In fact, do take mine, and I will procure another for myself."

"Thank you, Lord Hammond. I am indeed in need of some refreshment."

"Excellent. I'll return in a trice."

As Lord Hammond made his way back to the refreshment table, Vivian took a sip, trying to appear blasé. "My, this *is* delicious. Have you tried yours, Linney?"

Linney smiled at Vivian with a maternal look. "You are so adorable when you pretend you don't care about something. I haven't asked yet and Avery hasn't volunteered anything, so I don't know anything about the duke's plans. Shall I ask Avery when he returns? Or shall we talk more about the punch? Or maybe the weather? Or perhaps the lavish decorations that Lady Haversham has created to provide such ambiance? Or maybe we should—"

"Hush, you horrible creature! Why would I want to know about the duke's plans? According to Lady Smythson, he hardly has time to stand upright because he's constantly holding auditions for a new mistress, having thrown over all the old ones as well as a number of ladies in the *ton*—including Lady Ferrington and Lady Smythson's bosom friend, Lady Monroe."

"From what I hear, he has trespassed on several others as well," murmured Linney from behind her punch cup.

"Linney! It is terribly inappropriate for you to say something like that."

"I was just repeating what I heard others saying," answered Linney with a recalcitrant look on her face.

"Who was talking like that in front of you, an innocent young lady in her very first season?"

"I'm young, Vivian, but I'm certainly able to put two and two together to get four. And besides, no one said anything in *front* of me. I have found that the conversations held behind my back are much more interesting, so it is quite possible that the persons speaking were unaware I could hear them."

"Why were they unaware?"

"There might have been a potted plant between us." Linney took another sip. "You're right, this *is* delicious."

"Oh, Linney, you are a terror, and I have been such an absent chaperone. I do apologize. You deserve better."

"I think you're doing an admirable job as chaperone." Linney blushed as she said, "Avery thinks so too."

Vivian groaned. "Please, just tell me that the two of you are being discreet. Aunt Thea and Uncle Will are trusting you with me."

Linney smiled. "Don't worry, Vivian. I'm not as innocent as some girls my age. I understand more than I should. And as far as Mama and Papa are concerned, the last thing Mama said to me before we left was to watch out for *you*. They still blame themselves for your marriage to Henry. So you see, you're off the hook." After another sip, she said, "By the way, don't look now, but that gentleman over there has not been able to take his eyes off you since you joined me."

"I can't see—the sun is in my eyes. Who is it?"

"I don't know him, but he is tall and quite attractive. Or maybe it's just that his blondness makes him so." Linney sighed and continued. "I have always thought that those with blond hair have a distinct superiority over all the rest of the world."

Vivian rolled her eyes.

"Whoever he is," continued Linney, "it seems you have yet another admirer. And this one seems to laugh and smile a great deal. He is not as…severe as the Duke of Whitley, who tends to look as though he is well aware of my every misdeed and is deeply disappointed. Oh, the blond gentleman looks as though he might be heading our way. No, don't look! He's coming over here—Oh, no!"

"What? What happened?"

"Lady Smythson accosted him. What a shame. Now we will never know his intentions."

"Oh, Linney, you make me laugh."

"Well, there really is no other word for it, is there? She is horrible. I wonder what the Duke of Whitley would do if Lady Smythson accosted *him*? Now *that's* something I would like to see. I expect she would be frozen solid by the coldness of his stare."

"Linney, hush. Here comes Lord Hammond. Not a word about the duke, do you promise?"

"Oh, very well. If you insist."

"Ladies, I come bearing sustenance." Lord Hammond offered a plate of golden-brown shortbread biscuits with Grecian designs stamped into them, along with a small bunch of grapes and a very flaky layered pastry with walnuts. "The maid called this baklava. I tried one and it was delicious! Very sweet."

"Thank you, Lord Hammond," said Linney taking a tiny square of the baklava and popping it into her mouth. As Linney's eyes grew wide, Vivian laughed.

"Oh, my!" said Linney. "Vivian, you must try it. It is so good. I've never tasted anything like it. Tell me, Lord Hammond, how were the Furies when you left?"

Lord Hammond smiled as he offered the plate's contents to Vivian. "When last I saw them, the Furies were explaining to their governess exactly why they should not have to do lessons in my absence. I declare there is not enough gold in the world to compensate Miss Satterwhite for what she does. I've recently thought to leave my entire estate to her as a token of my esteem. I know Whit is thinking similar thoughts."

Lord Hammond shook his head while he took a bite of the shortbread. "And mind you, the girls were not demurely putting forth random pleadings or petulant demands. They were triple-timing Miss Satterwhite with well-organized rationalizations worthy of the most respected barristers. Their arguments would sway any jury and make any opposing decision seem ignorant at best and criminal at worst."

Lord Hammond took a sip of his punch and then added, "I left as soon as I could decently make an escape. I am sorry to say, however, that Whit had business to complete before he was able to leave, and…"

Lord Hammond heaved an exaggerated sigh and shook his head sadly. "I think we may have lost him. Such a pity. He was so young, and I know he was looking forward to the Grecian Ball on Friday." Lord Hammond's dancing eyes belied his serious face.

Linney and Vivian dissolved into giggles that caught the attention of other guests, who smiled at the three and whispered behind their fans.

"Lord Hammond, you are terrible," said Vivian wiping her eyes. "If the Furies are anything like their brothers, then I agree. There is no amount of compensation enough for Miss Satterwhite. And now that you have made a spectacle of us all, which will, in all likelihood, result in our being the very first guests ever to be expelled from one of Lady Haversham's house parties, I will take my leave."

"I can guarantee you, Lady Rowden, that we three by no means represent the worst behavior seen at a Haversham house party, most of which is unfit for the ears of well-bred ladies and certainly inappropriate for an innocent like Miss Braddock."

Linney rolled her eyes as Lord Hammond continued.

"In short, Lady Rowden, let me assure you. I have been to several of these house parties—Lady Haversham is a cousin on my mother's side—and we have not even gained the first tier of outrageous behavior."

Vivian smiled. "I leave you in good hands, then, cousin." She opened her parasol and started down the path toward the garden. When she looked back, Linney was whispering in Lord Hammond's ear and Lady Smythson was nowhere to be seen.

Chapter 17

The next morning after breakfast, Vivian disappeared into Lord Haversham's library. The night before she had decided upon a plan of attack, and today was all about putting that plan into action.

The first thing on her list was to finish the sample puzzle collection she had been working on. It really is a good idea, she thought to herself—even if I am biased.

The idea was to expand on the number and types of puzzles the paper offered on its twice-weekly puzzle pages. Vivian knew the types of puzzles were limited only by her imagination, so she could constantly offer new challenges to the *Mail Observer* readers or to whomever she ultimately convinced to publish her collections.

A collection would contain a riddle, a letter or number cipher, one of a variety of word puzzles—some new and some familiar—along with one or two mathematical challenges. All puzzles in a collection would have the same theme, and there would also be an overarching puzzle that incorporated solutions from each of the other puzzles. Readers would know the week's theme for certain only when they solved all the puzzles—although they could certainly guess the theme at any point. The paper could even sponsor a contest and randomly choose a winner from all correct entries submitted before the given deadline. Businesses that advertised on the puzzle pages might offer prizes to the winners. The winner's name could be published in the paper along with the next collection.

Vivian had been experimenting with a type of puzzle based on an acrostic poem. Late last night, she had figured out a different way to align the clues so that the second letter of each correct word solution spelled out the theme for the collection. She painstakingly inked the puzzle—both with and without its solution—and then put it aside with the three other puzzles that shared the same theme.

Of course, providing all of these puzzles and their answers was a lot of work—especially, she thought wryly, for a mere woman—but by having control over all of them, she was certain she could keep up with the weekly demand. As with many things, the trick was to get ahead of the deadlines and work on puzzles *now* that wouldn't be published for months. Vivian had already completed three puzzle collections—each showcasing a different set of puzzles and each with a different theme. Now all she had to do was to get the *Mail Observer*—specifically, Mr. Davis—to accept this new idea. More to the point, all she had to do was to get Mr. Davis to accept this new idea after telling him that she, not the fictitious V. I. Burningham, was the creator.

Might it be better to offer the puzzles first and then let Mr. Davis know the truth after he had made a commitment? Perhaps she *never* need tell him—many females used male pseudonyms to disguise their gender. But did they keep their identities secret from their publishers as well? Vivian sighed and worried the pen wipe on the ink stand in front of her. Lord Haversham had not balked upon learning that she was V. I.

Burningham. Why would other puzzle aficionados be less understanding?

On the other hand, Mr. Davis had made it perfectly clear that he was not interested in working with a woman. But might he change his mind if he saw something new and different that he liked, and only *later* found out that it was from a woman? Once he had a chance to think it over, maybe he *would* be interested. But what if Mr. Davis, like the Duke of Whitley, was not fond of surprises?

Continuing to chase thoughts round and round in her head was getting her nowhere. She had to make a decision.

Maybe there was a third option. Who was it that said, "Compromise, while not always the clearest or even the most direct path, is often the best way—and sometimes the only way—forward?" She could certainly try to pique Mr. Davis' interest with samples of her collections and then—before they signed a deal—tell him that she was the true face behind the puzzles. That was a compromise she could embrace. Decision made.

Which brought her to her next task—composing a letter to Mr. Davis from V. I. Burningham.

Channeling her best interpretation of a male persona, she dipped her quill into the inkwell and began.

Dear Mr. Davis,

My niece has recounted her conversation with you of Wednesday last and has pointed out several problems that result from your refusal to work with her as my surrogate.

As my current plans and certain physical issues prevent me from traveling to London to attend these matters in person, I would consider it a great favor if you would allow me to speak through her on issues regarding the dispensation of both my current work and any new assignments we might agree upon.

While I do not at this time intend to seek out other establishments to publish my puzzles, I must insist that my niece be allowed to represent me in all business dealings. If you find that you are unable to accommodate me and cannot work with her, then I will be forced to make other arrangements.

Please inform me of your decision at your earliest convenience.

Yrs Truly,

V. I. Burningham, Somerset, 21 May 1815

Vivian added another flourish to the signature and then sat back to assess. Luckily her handwriting was not overly feminine. Anyone who saw the letter might well believe it was written by a gentleman, or at least his secretary. Vivian added her new puzzle samples and a brief description of the three themed collections she had created. As she folded the papers and wrote Mr. Davis's direction on the outside page, she felt a huge weight lifted from her shoulders. All she could do now was wait for Mr. Davis to respond.

Vivian carefully dripped sealing wax onto the folded paper and was just pressing a seal into the soft blob when the library door opened. The blond gentleman who had been staring at her the night before stood in the doorway. He looked around and finally caught sight of her at Lord Haversham's desk, and then he smiled. When she returned the smile, he walked toward her.

"Lady Rowden?" he said, "I was told I might find you here. I do hope I'm not intruding."

"Not at all. Please come in. I beg your pardon, sir, but I do not know your name."

"Baron Blount at your service, madam. I have been wanting to speak to you since I saw you yesterday afternoon with—I believe it was your cousin?"

"Yes, Miss Braddock. She is making her bow this season."

"Yes, well, I was foiled in my attempt to speak to you last night by the effervescent Lady Smythson, so I set out on my quest again this morning."

Vivian laughed. "Lady Smythson is a force to be reckoned with, is she not?"

"She is, madam, and one does not cross her without significant fortification." He lowered his voice and confided, "I had breakfast sent up to my room this morning just so I could avoid an early encounter with the lady."

He grinned and his entire face brightened. Linney had been correct. He was a very handsome man.

"My cousin and I noticed you yesterday afternoon because of your hair. She was remarking on how few of Lady Haversham's guests had blond hair. My cousin is quite blonde as well, but you and she were the only guests we saw with such coloring—although there was a young lady with strawberry blonde hair who was quite lovely."

"My family traces its roots back to the Vikings, which explains things a bit—although it doesn't explain my distaste for ocean voyages. Seasickness, I'm afraid.

I would have made a rather poor pillager."

Vivian laughed again. "I was on my way to give Lady Haversham's butler a package to post. Would you care to accompany me on a stroll through her famous rose garden afterwards?"

"I would be honored, my lady."

Vivian bent to tidy the desk and then looked up at Lord Blount with her forehead wrinkled. "I keep thinking you look terribly familiar, Lord Blount. Have we been introduced before and you are simply being too polite to bring attention to my lapse?"

"Actually, Lady Rowden, we have met. Once. Very briefly. But, at the time, you were quite preoccupied."

"Do put me out of my suspense, my lord. I will try not to be too embarrassed if you promise to be quick."

"I'm afraid it was at your husband's funeral," said the baron. "You were so beautiful even in your grief that I could barely express my condolences. When I saw you were a guest of Lady Haversham's, I decided to try and renew our acquaintance."

"You flatter me, sir. Please accept my apologies for not recalling our first meeting." She held out her hand.

Lord Blount took Vivian's hand and pressed her fingertips to his lips. Continuing to clasp her hand, he said, "You would be forgiven for not remembering our encounter since you were somewhat preoccupied, but I remember it as if it were yesterday. You see, I was one of your husband's oldest and dearest friends. In fact, I was with him when he died."

Vivian remembered the man now. She snatched back her hand as if she had touched a hot coal and took a step back. He was correct. She had met him only that one time, but she had seen him often in Henry's company. From the rumors she'd heard, this man was Henry's constant companion in—she blushed—in *everything*. She took another step back, putting the big desk between herself and Lord Blount.

"I…I beg your pardon, sir, but I have remembered some important business I must attend to. I will not be able to take a stroll after all. Please excuse me."

"Surely you can spare a moment to regale the memory of your departed husband and allow me to express my condolences on your loss."

"It has been almost two years since my 'loss,' " said Vivian coolly, "and I am in no need of your condolences. In truth, I had counted the absence of Henry's friends as one of the good things that came from his death."

"You wound me, Vivian."

"I have not given you leave to call me by my Christian name, sir, and that permission will not be forthcoming. We have nothing to talk about and I see no reason for further conversation. Good day."

But instead of leaving, Blount stepped closer. "Henry talked about you constantly, Vivian—especially when he was with other women. He was always comparing them to you and, of course, always finding them lacking. He was obsessed with you, but your beauty intimidated him. He used his mistresses to enact fantasies about you."

The baron smiled at Vivian's shocked expression, but then held up both hands, feigning innocence. "I am just telling you what I have read in his journal—although, now that I think on it, I believe the book actually belongs to you. A green leather book with gilt edges?"

"My journal? Why would Henry give it to you? He hated that I kept a journal, and he was always threatening to burn it. When it disappeared, I assumed he had done just that."

"But you do admit that the volume I describe is yours, my lady? I wanted to be sure, you see, because the musings that it contains are of a rather…ah…intimate nature."

Vivian looked at him disdainfully. "Don't be absurd. The only things I kept in that journal were ideas for my puzzles."

"I beg to differ, my lady. The journal is quite explicit and chronicles activities you shared with your husband…and others. Perhaps you'd like it returned?"

"Lord Blount, the journal I kept contained ideas for my puzzles and had not even sentimental value. I was not overly concerned with its disappearance, and I have no need for its return."

"Perhaps you should reconsider, my lady, because it also happens to be the only record of an exceedingly large gambling debt that your husband failed to repay to me before his death. You see, he wrote his vowels on the last page. After his untimely death, I used the entry to appeal to his estate to repay the debt. It was only then that I realized Henry never signed the note. Unfortunately, without Henry's mark, the debt will not be honored by his estate."

"Lord Blount, as far as I am concerned, that journal is not a record of anything, and I do not feel the least bit obligated to repay some debt you imagine Henry owed you. Now, if you will excuse me—"

"That is disappointing, my lady, because it is that debt I wanted to discuss with you. You see, the only name in the journal is yours and, as its owner, it seems it is you who owe me the money."

Vivian sat down at Lord Haversham's huge desk, staring daggers at Blount. When she spoke, her voice was calm and pleasant.

"Lord Blount, if it is your plan to extort money from me to avert a scandal, you must understand that I have already been through a rather racy one regarding my late husband. I am not afraid of your threats. Also, even if I were inclined to pay back any supposed debts—which I am not—I have no money. Henry's excesses have also affected me. Now, if you won't leave, sir, I will."

She rose and started to walk toward the door, but like a snake, Lord Blount's hand shot out to stop her escape. She could smell the spirits on his breath even at this early hour. She shook off his hand and tried to move away from him, but the baron stepped closer.

"Perhaps *you* have no reason to fear a scandal, my lady, but it would be a shame if your lovely cousin's season were ruined by her close association with you. Tell me, Lady Rowden, do your aunt and uncle know that you shared your marriage bed with Henry's mistresses? Does your innocent cousin?"

"That is not true, and you know it!" cried Vivian. Her voice was louder than she realized. Her heart stopped for a beat as she thought about the damage Blount's lies could do—embarrassment, scandal, ruined reputations—not just for Linney, but for Uncle Will and Aunt Thea too. Surely no proper gentlemen would offer for Linney if she was associated with such a sordid story. Vivian could not—would not—jeopardize her cousin's season and her future happiness.

"As I understand it, Lady Rowden," continued Blount, "your uncle is quite well off. Perhaps you could appeal to him for assistance in making good on your late husband's debts."

The library door opened and Vivian looked up to see the Duke of Whitley standing in the doorway with a scowl on his face. "Lady Rowden? Your cousin said I might find you in here." He turned to Lord Blount and said, "I don't believe I've had the pleasure, sir."

The baron took a step back from Vivian and turned toward the Duke with a slight bow. "Baron Blount, your grace. Lady Rowden and I are old friends."

Whit's nod was barely noticeable as he acknowledged the man with an icy blue stare and a raised eyebrow. "If you don't mind, sir, I have urgent business with Lady Rowden. Private business."

"Certainly, your grace. Lady Rowden, I will be in touch, shall I? Good day." He inclined his head again before leaving the room.

Offering no further acknowledgement, Whit watched him leave and then closed the door after him. He turned to look at Vivian and in two strides was at her side. Grabbing her shoulders, he pushed her down to sit in the chair behind the desk. "For God's sake, Vivian, sit! You're pale as a ghost. No, don't talk, just breathe."

Barely registering Whit's presence, Vivian's mind was racing. She couldn't allow scandal to touch Linney. She should simply plead exhaustion and return immediately to her seaside home. If Lord Blount followed her there, she would tell him again that there was no money, but at least she would be away from Linney.

"What did he say to you, Vivian?"

"It's nothing."

"It's not nothing. What did he say?"

"It is a private matter and not your concern."

"The man obviously upset you, and that *is* my concern. Would you please just tell me what's wrong?"

"Is that a request or a command, your grace?" snapped Vivian.

Whit exhaled. "I have no right to either," he said quietly, "but it pains me to see you unhappy. In the three times I have seen you in these last few days, each time I was drawn to your smile. And now there is no smile, and there are tears in your eyes. Perhaps if you will tell me the source of your dismay, I could somehow be of service."

"Thank you, but as I said, it is nothing."

"And, as I said, it is clear that is not true."

"So you are calling me a liar?"

"That was not what I meant."

In spite of her words, Vivian wanted nothing more than to confide in this man and seek his help. She was scared to death of the damage Lord Blount could do to Linney's season. And she was drawn to Whit—not just physically, although there *was* certainly that, but also on another level, one that tugged at her heart. It scared her. She needed to stay away from him. She took a deep calming breath and then stood up, gathering her papers and quill.

"*Why* are you here, your grace? I was under the impression you had pressing business that kept you in London until later in the week, so why exactly are you here?"

Vivian suddenly remembered what Lady Smythson

had said about his looking for a new mistress and added snidely, "I believe the *on dit* is you are searching for a new mistress? It must be extremely tiring, interviewing so many applicants. Or perhaps you have already exhausted all the candidates in London and have expanded your search to include Lady Haversham's guests?"

Her sudden attack triggered a like response from the Ice Duke. "Did you intend to apply for the position, my lady? I could give you an excellent reference. You do seem to be rather skilled at providing entertainment for men in closed carriages and other secluded areas. Maybe being a gentleman's mistress has been your goal all along?"

"If it were, I would not be considering you as my protector, your grace," snapped Vivian, mortified at his reference to her behavior in his carriage. "It is said you are overly critical and quite demanding. I'm sure we would never suit."

She looked at him across Lord Haversham's desk. "Now, then, you said there was some urgent, private business that you wished to see me about? Or are you also lying to get me alone so you can take advantage of me?"

Whit narrowed his eyes and spoke his reply in a dangerously soft voice that belied his fury. "My lady, I assure you, if it were my desire to take advantage of you, we would not be standing here having this conversation, nor would your bountiful assets still be hidden by your gown." He ignored Vivian's gasp at his crude remarks and continued.

"As you well know, my lady, my words were a ruse to remove the gentleman, who was obviously bothering you. I neglected to bring along my dueling pistols, so it seemed the preferable solution."

As if vaguely aware of his boorish behavior, he added, "I regret any inconvenience I may have caused you and would like to again offer my—"

Vivian put her chin up. "Thank you for your concern, your grace, and for your offer of assistance with Lord Blount, but I assure you, I am fine."

"Vivian..."

"I do not need your help!" Vivian slammed down the lid of her writing box. Mounting fears about Blount's threat and Linney's reputation made her lash out.

"I don't know why you keep putting your great ducal nose in where it doesn't belong, but I assure you I am perfectly capable of taking care of myself. This does not concern you. I will handle it. I have no need of interference from the Ice Duke!"

With a stiff bow, the duke turned and left the library.

Chapter 18

Thunderclouds towering up from the horizon broke up the blue sky, and wind gusts whipped at Vivian's skirts as she sought refuge away from the confines of Haversham House.

Most of the guests had taken themselves into town for a shopping trip, so she was free to roam the grounds without fear of running into anyone who might wonder at her hasty exit without bonnet and shawl or at the suspicious brightness in her eyes. Her mind raced with panicked visions of Linney's ruined debut and bleak future—all because of her association with Vivian. Images of a smiling Lord Blount peppered the scenes running through her head, and at every curve stood the Duke of Whitley, blocking her way forward.

What was it about the man that made her so volatile? Apart from his epic arrogance and his patronizing condescension, what was it that made her lose all semblance of control whenever she was in his presence? Those icy blue eyes looked through her as if he could see straight into her soul and ascertain her greatest fears. Or, more likely, she scoffed, exploit her greatest weaknesses. And the nerve of him referring to that carriage ride. He certainly was no gentleman. He was pompous to an extreme, and she never wanted to see him again!

Her pace kept up with her thoughts. She *had* to get

him out of her head…or her heart…or wherever else he was. She *must* concentrate on how to protect Linney.

It was clear that she had to leave her aunt and uncle's home as soon as possible. Lord Blount's disgusting insinuations—as false as they were—could devastate Linney's chances for a successful season. No one would be interested in whether the sensational rumors were true or not. The simple fact of their existence would be enough to destroy her cousin's reputation.

Vivian finally slowed her steps. She had to think. She could hardly abandon Linney at Lady Haversham's party without a chaperone—especially with Lord Blount still as a guest. Perhaps she could convince Linney to return to London? But that thought was quickly replaced with a picture of Linney strolling with Lord Hammond, their heads close together as they laughed and talked. She could claim a sudden malady and insist that they leave early, but it would break Linney's heart.

Perhaps if she talked to Lord Blount. Met with him. Pretended to be amenable to paying him the blackmail. She shuddered involuntarily at the idea.

Perhaps she could tell the baron she needed to talk with Uncle Will in person and wouldn't be able to do so until they returned from the house party. Maybe that would stall him for a while. Maybe that would give Lord Hammond time to declare himself. With as much time as he was spending with Linney, surely he had honorable intentions. But what if Lord Blount demanded payment now?

Round and round, her thoughts chased her down the path that edged Haversham Lake and led to the forest beyond. Paying no attention to the rumblings of thunder that grew louder and louder, Vivian had already walked halfway around the lake when the skies opened up and sheets of rain began to fall. The summerhouse at the far side was her closest shelter, and she ran the final distance to the covered verandah.

Panting, Vivian leaned against one of the Ionic columns to catch her breath. Her light muslin day dress was soaked through, but the coolness felt good on her flushed skin. She stood as close to the edge of the porch as she dared, watching the streaks of lightning flash across the dark sky and letting the fury of the storm draw out her own anger. As the first fierceness passed, the storm settled into a steady rain, and with it, Vivian felt some calm returning. Shaking the drops from her hair and face and fanning her skirts to help them dry, she looked around for a chair from which to watch the storm pass.

"I feel obliged to let you know that you have once again caught me skulking about."

The familiar voice sent shivers up her spine. Shivers that had nothing to do with the inclement weather.

"Your grace?" Vivian turned to see the duke standing in front of a settee that boasted plump cushions and an unobstructed view of the summer rain on the lake. The sky crackled as a streak of lightning blazed through the clouds. The answering thunder came only seconds later.

"Like you, I am a refugee seeking shelter from the storm," he said. "Please join me. I promise not to pry into your business unless asked."

"Your grace, I do apologize for my behavior

earlier. I have such a temper, and it sometimes gets the best of me, no matter how I try. Please accept my apologies."

"I will accept yours if you will accept mine. You were right. I have no business interfering in your affairs. I was simply reacting to your distress without thinking."

She smiled up at him, her attention held once again by cornflower-blue eyes that made her feel so... wanted. "A truce, then?" She extended her hand.

He raised his eyebrows.

"At least until the storm is over?"

The blue eyes twinkled. "Agreed."

He took her hand, marveling at how perfectly it fit in his own. And then he noticed her gown.

"Uh...may I offer you my coat? Your dress seems to be rather...ah...damp."

In fact, what her dress seemed to be was the most erotic piece of clothing he had ever seen, and on a woman who already dangerously intrigued him. The damp muslin clung to her every curve, outlining her shapely legs and derriere. And whether because of a chill or because of his presence, her nipples stood proudly erect under the almost transparent fabric covering her breasts. His whole body hardened in response to the Venus in front of him.

"Thank you, yes. I am a bit chilled."

Whit draped his coat around her shoulders and, for his own sanity, pulled it closed so she could hold it in front. "Won't you sit down? The view is quite peaceful—except for the thunderstorm. And, of course, all the rain."

She accepted his hand again and stepped around

the ottoman in front of the chaise. She leaned over to adjust the cushions and when she rose, she took a step back—onto his foot.

"Oh, I beg your pardon!" Trying not to do him further injury by putting her full weight down, she teetered wildly, letting go of the covering coat in an effort to regain her balance.

In the same moment, Whit grabbed her to keep her from falling and pulled her up against his chest. Holding her close for a few moments longer than necessary, he reveled in the feel of her full, soft breasts against him and was aware of his own growing arousal.

Vivian blushed and pushed away quickly, turning her back to him. "I have a window in my house near Burnham-on-Sea that has a view of the ocean," she said, taking an unusually long time to arrange a spot on the small settee. "It's a rocky shore, and when it storms, the waves pound against the rocks and throw out great sprays of water. I think I could sit there all day and watch the waves and the sea. It's never the same."

Whit lowered himself to sit beside her. "I've been to Bath, of course, but never as far west as Burnham-on-Sea. Is the whole shore rocky, or is there also some beach so you can bathe and stroll?"

"There is some beach—it's mostly beach, actually. The rocky part is just a short stretch near my house. I often go for a stroll on the cliffs above, but I have never been bathing. I don't know how to swim."

"You live beside the ocean but you don't know how to swim?"

Vivian laughed at his astonished tone. "Is it as bad as all that?" she asked, glancing up at him. "I grew up inland and only went to the shore for the first time after my husband's death. I keep thinking I will learn to swim someday, but it's never the right time. And besides, I have no one to teach me."

"It's not so difficult to learn, Lady Rowden... Vivian. Anyone could teach you, really."

"I don't think I would trust just anyone. I mean, the person would need to know what they were about, obviously."

"Obviously."

"But they must also be willing to take the time necessary to allay my fears."

"Going slowly is often a requirement when one is doing something one has never done before."

"So you see, it must be the right person. And, of course, it must be the right time."

"A critical factor, always."

"No, I mean the water must not be too cold—I suppose the ocean never gets too hot, does it?"

"Not that I have ever experienced, no."

"And I don't think I would enjoy it if the waves were too rough."

"Gentle waves would be best for learning, I agree."

"If I were to find someone who was in agreement with me on all these things, then I rather think I would enjoy it."

"I could teach you," Whit said huskily. "I have quite a bit of experience in the area. I promise to go slowly, and I guarantee you will enjoy it." When she looked up at him, he saw his own passion reflected in her dark brown eyes and decided it was time for her lesson to begin.

In one movement, he pulled her onto his lap and into his arms, capturing her mouth with his own. With one arm he held her close as he ravaged her mouth, his tongue insisting that her full lips part to give him access. His other hand traced her shape in the now-transparent muslin, up and then down, slowly caressing her back, her waist, and her arms.

Moving his hand back up her side, he cupped her breast and then teased the sensitive tip between his thumb and forefinger. She gasped, her response fueling his own desire. He gently freed one breast from her bodice and touched his tongue to the pointed peak. Vivian arched her back as he traced around and around with the tip of his tongue, nipping and pulling and then, finally, suckling hard as she moaned beneath him.

Laying her down on the pillowed chaise, Whit knelt beside Vivian, kissing her full lips while he worked impatiently to loosen her gown. He tugged the soft fabric out of the way and caught his breath as he beheld the sight of her reclining on the chaise, her full breasts free of the high-waisted gown that still pushed them up to a prominent position. One of her hands still rested on his shoulder while with the other she cupped the side of his face, stroking his cheek with her fingertip.

"I have never seen a woman as beautiful as you, Lady Rowden." He watched with pleasure as the pink of her blush moved from her cheeks down her throat to her breasts.

She looked up at him with a coy glance. "Lady Rowden, is it? Well, I return the compliment, your grace. You are a most pleasing man to behold." She pulled his head down so he would continue kissing her, moaning when he plunged his tongue inside her mouth to meet hers.

Changing positions, he broke the kiss and captured both her wrists, holding them over her head, immobilizing her. He smiled at the feast before him and then dipped his head to take his fill, his mouth laving and teasing, nipping and sucking as she writhed rhythmically in response. He lay down beside her then, moving her hand down his body so she would feel the full extent of his arousal.

She responded gingerly at first, hesitantly stroking his hard length and fumbling with the buttons that restrained him. He groaned as she freed him at last and shuddered when, with her forefinger, she stroked the velvety tip of him and felt the first drops of his essence.

He moved his hand beneath her skirts, pushing them up over her hips as he caressed her belly and then moved lower. Cupping her mound, he sent one slow, stroking finger to find the tender bud in her soft nest. She arched her back, but he continued stroking around the same sensitive place, steady, soft, and over and over. When she moaned again, he suckled her ear lobe and whispered, "Yes, that's it. Let go, Vivian. That's right."

He stroked deeper and found her opening. His finger penetrated her and, when he felt her wet heat, he used her moisture to stroke more firmly. Taking one rose nipple in his mouth, he suckled hard as he continued stroking. And when he felt the contractions, he whispered, "Vivian, my love, come for me. Come, darling." He plunged two fingers into her wetness and felt her clench around him as she moaned and rode wave after wave after wave to her climax.

He held her close as her shuddering slowly ceased, kissing her forehead and looking down at the long dark eyelashes now fluttering on her pink cheeks. He touched her once again, stroking and stroking until he could feel her tighten. "Vivian," he whispered, "you are ready for me, darling. Tell me I can have you now. I need to be inside of you. I need to feel you all around me."

Eyes wide with desire and trust looked into his. "Yes," she whispered, "yes, please, Whit. Now."

In one movement, he straddled her and, holding himself in one hand, found the slick, wet opening between her legs. He touched his tip to her wetness and pushed slowly but steadily into her. She was so tight that he worried he would hurt her. "Vivian, relax so I can be inside you. You have made me so hard and so big and you are so tight. It feels wonderful, but I don't want to hurt you."

He spread her legs wider and put his hand down between them to again stroke her sensitive bud. He moved deeper, and she pushed up to meet him. No virgin was tighter than she, so once he was in, he held motionless, letting her grow used to the feel of him deep inside. He bent his head to kiss her lips and then suckled her nipples—first one and then the other, over and over. As he felt her relax, he pushed in deeper, all the way to the hilt. Then, watching her face, he slowly pulled almost all the way out until only the tip of him still touched her wetness. Her forehead creased with a scowl.

"Open your eyes, Vivian. Look at me."

When she did, when he could see her eyes dark with passion, he thrust into her again, going deeper than before. He pulled back out and thrust in again, harder and deeper, and all the time watching her watching him.

As his own passion grew, he saw the flush that heralded her climax creep over her breasts. He felt her contract around him and heard her call his name. He felt his own body tighten, and, thrusting twice more, he groaned into his own astonishingly powerful release as he shouted her name into the storm.

Chapter 19

Like an autumn leaf drifting to the ground, Vivian slowly regained her sense of time and place. She wrinkled her forehead and frowned up at Whit.

"Does that always happen?"

Whit stirred himself, surprised to find that he too had drifted off into that rarest of states, the sleep of one who is completely and totally satisfied. Not quite as surprising but also quite satisfying was the fact of Vivian curled up against his bare chest, completely encircled in his embrace.

"If you are referring to the rather intense finish, I must apologize. I had thought to withdraw, but I...ah...well, leaving was more difficult than I'd anticipated. I trust—"

"No, not you. Me. Do your bed mates always have that reaction...that splendid feeling of rising, almost unbearable pleasure, and then that final wave of sheer ecstasy?"

"If you're asking if I usually take the time to see to the pleasure of my sexual partners, the answer is yes. Usually more than once."

Vivian's eyes widened.

Whit returned to his previous conversation. "Again, I apologize. I—"

"That's never happened to me before. The pleasure."

"What do you mean?"

"I mean that when my husband and I had relations, I never experienced that aspect of it."

"Are you saying that in the course of your marriage, your husband never concerned himself with your pleasure?"

"I did not know such things were even possible for women."

"Your husband was a very selfish man, my lady." And a fool, he thought to himself. "Indeed, one of the great joys of making love is giving pleasure to your partner."

"So you always…ah…pleasure your partners, your grace?"

"Unless they or the situation require otherwise," Whit replied. He kissed her hair and moved to whisper in her ear, "Would you like me to help you do it again?"

Vivian's eyes flew open. "You can do that? Already?"

Whit chuckled. "*I* may need a little more time to recover myself, but there's nothing stopping me from giving *you* more pleasure." He repositioned his hand so it was free to find her again. "All I have to do is touch you here…"

Vivian gasped.

"And here…and here…and then here, like this. Is this what you want?"

Vivian moaned. "Yes…" Then she grasped his hand, holding it still. "No. When you do that I cannot think. You must stop."

"Must I?"

"No. I mean, yes. I mean…I need to think, Whit.

Please stop."

"Very well, my love. For now. What is it you need to think about?"

"Everything...nothing. I..."

"You are a woman of many contradictions, Vivian."

"It's you," she said crossly. "You do this to me. I am normally a very calm and a very rational person with a very methodical mind, who has very straightforward conversations with people. But for some reason, when I am anywhere near you, all of that goes right out the window."

He kissed her hair and said in a low sort of growling voice, "It might interest you to know that you have a similar effect on me, my lady. It's a new experience, and I'm not at all sure it is appropriate for the Ice Duke. It must be the air here at Lady Haversham's. I cannot remember a time when I was so caught up with a woman that I failed to take the necessary precautions. I do apologize again."

Whit was finding this part of the conversation not just unusual but uncomfortable. He really did not want to examine his inability to take precautions—no, that wasn't quite right. He had been able enough—it was more of an unwillingness, but not really even that. It was more that he had a desire to have the ultimate experience with Vivian. It was the same unexplainable desire he'd had for her in his carriage. It was new and it was different. And it was totally unacceptable.

And above all things, he did not want to talk about it. So he did what men do—he moved to another topic to avoid talking about it altogether.

"Vivian, I trust that if you find there are any

unforeseen consequences from my carelessness, you will let me know."

Vivian shivered. The coldness of his words robbed her of the previous warmth, and she sat up to escape his embrace. "I assume you mean if I were to become pregnant? I do not think that is possible, your grace. My late husband tried…repeatedly…but I was never able to conceive."

She flushed at the shame of her own words and quickly stood up. Turning her back to him, she started searching for the pieces of her wardrobe that had gone missing in the throes of their passion.

"The rain has stopped," Whit remarked absently, watching Vivian's bare backside as she searched for her clothes. "Shall we avail ourselves of the lake for washing up?"

"I see no basin or bucket. Did you notice one?"

"I was thinking more of a bath. In the lake."

"You mean *swimming*? In the lake?"

"I know no other place suitable for swimming, do you?"

"I have told you that I do not swim," said Vivian haughtily. "I do not know how."

"Come on," said Whit.

"What?"

"Come with me. I am going to teach you to swim."

"I don't want to go into the lake. I don't have a bathing costume, and—"

"You're already wearing the perfect bathing costume."

"I am totally naked!"

"Exactly. The best way to swim is with no clothes to encumber you."

"I am not going to walk down to the lake with no clothes on," she said, pulling on her chemise and casting about for an escape path. "I will put my feet in the water and wash off a bit, but I don't want to learn to swim."

"You're in luck, then. I can't teach you how to swim in one afternoon, but I can help you feel the freedom of being in the water and teach you how to float." He caught up two thick towels, left conveniently on a nearby shelf for guests who might avail themselves of the refreshing lake on a summer day, and held out his hand to her. "Come on."

Vivian stood there shaking her head, clutching her wrinkled gown in front of her.

"Lady Rowden, you have two choices. You can walk to the lake or I will carry you down and dump you in the water."

Vivian narrowed her eyes at him, but reluctantly draped her gown over the settee, caught his hand, and let him pull her down the path to the lake. He dropped the towels on a stump far enough away from the water to stay dry and led her toward the small sandy beach.

A little way from the water, a stubborn look crossed her face and she dug in her heels like a mule. "I've changed my mind. It looks very cold. I'll learn how to swim another day."

"Don't say I didn't warn you." With barely any effort at all, Whit whisked her up in his arms and waded into the cool water.

She clutched at his neck, holding on for dear life. "Don't you dare! Whit…your grace… I cannot swim!"

When the water reached his waist, he relented a bit. "Do you want to put your legs down and try to stand on your own? You can touch the bottom here." He laughed as Vivian, like a cat, tried to climb onto his shoulders, clutching at him, and getting as far away as she could from the water.

"This is your last chance," he warned. "Okay, hold your breath." Without further ado, he dropped her into the sparkling water with a very satisfying splash. Almost instantly she bobbed back up to the surface, kicking, splashing, cursing, and…laughing.

"I warned you," he said, grinning. He reached for the sputtering, splashing water nymph in front of him and held her afloat by her arms. He tried not to notice that her now-soaked chemise was plastered to her body and doing nothing to cover her perfect breasts. His own body reacted to the vision before him like a youth seeing his first nude woman. He moved them both to deeper, cooler water with the vague idea of stemming his arousal.

"Now relax, Vivian. Take a deep breath and put your head back on the water like a pillow."

"No!" said Vivian, tensing every muscle. "I'll go under!"

"No, you won't. I've got you. Just relax. I promise I won't let anything happen to you. Just trust me."

Against her every instinct, Vivian tried to relax—tried to trust. She felt Whit's arms supporting her, and she closed her eyes. She took a deep breath and did as he had instructed, laying her head back onto the water and willing her body to let go of the tension and relax. Her body's natural buoyancy took over, so she did not notice when Whit slowly lowered his arms. What she *did* notice was the lovely feeling of lying down on clouds.

"Don't look now, my love," whispered Whit in her ear, "but you're floating."

Vivian tensed, and immediately began to sink. Whit caught her by the shoulders to keep her head above the water.

"Vivian, put your feet down. You can touch the bottom, try it. Just put your feet down. Vivian! Put your feet down!"

Whit's words finally penetrated her panicked flailing. She put her feet down and immediately stood up. The water reached just below her breasts. Above the water her wet chemise covered her like a second skin while the rest of the material floated in the water around her. The fine lawn of the chemise was totally transparent, letting Whit clearly see rosy nipples and darker areolas and clearly imagine the rest of her body immersed in the cool water.

Vivian grinned delightedly at Whit. "I can touch the bottom. Oh, this feels wonderful." The grin vanished a second later and she narrowed her eyes at him. "You dropped me in the water! I cannot believe you did that. What if I had drowned?"

"I told you I was going to do it. And I wouldn't have let you drown. You should learn to trust me."

"And why would I be doing that?" she scoffed. But then she smiled. "It *is* a rather lovely feeling."

"Let me help you float again."

"No. I like just standing here. I can twirl and bounce…"

"Yes, I can see that," said Whit, trying very hard to concentrate on something other than the twirling and bouncing.

"And pretend that I'm a mermaid—what?"

"It's just that all the twirling and bouncing is rather…ah…pleasant to watch."

Vivian looked at him looking at her chest. She looked down and saw her nipples proudly erect. She quickly covered herself with her hands.

"Don't do that," he said in a husky voice. "I like to look at you. You are very beautiful, Vivian."

Speechless for a small moment, Vivian eventually found her voice. "So show me how to float again."

"I'm afraid that's not a good idea right now."

"Why? Did you forget how? I promise to do what you say and relax."

"I know how," he said dryly. "It's just not a good idea for me to do it right now. All of that twirling and bouncing in your wet chemise has had an…an effect on me."

Vivian's eyes opened suddenly. "Oh…I see. I mean, I *don't* see, but I understand."

A sly look came across her face. "So just looking at me in my wet chemise has…affected you?" She smiled with the knowledge of a beautiful woman who has just realized her power over a man. She made her way over to him and reached up on tiptoe to put both of her hands on his shoulders. She pulled herself up against him and whispered, "So what would happen if I were to kiss you…like this?" She pressed her lips to his and sighed when he opened his mouth for her to taste and explore with her tongue. After a moment, she moved her mouth to his ear and whispered, "Would that affect you as well, your grace?"

In answer, Whit picked her up under her thighs and spread her legs to straddle his waist. She clasped her arms around his neck and her breasts rubbed against his chest. His erection was cradled between her open legs and it only took seconds for him to guide himself to her opening. "I'll let *you* judge how much it affects me," he growled. "Now, try your bouncing again, mermaid."

The water buoyed her so that she could ride him easily, moving up and down on his hard shaft as the delicious feeling inside her continued to build. He took her higher and higher until her release came at last. She called out his name, clenching him inside her and holding on with her arms wrapped tightly around his neck. After several final thrusts, Whit pulled out—reaching his own release only moments later and holding her tightly against him as he slowly regained his breath and his equilibrium.

His mouth was at her ear. "So how do you like floating?" He felt her smile into his chest and wrapped his arms more tightly around her.

Chapter 20

"What was it that you were doing in Lord Haversham's library?"

The two had dozed for a few minutes on the towels in the sun—enough so that her chemise was almost dry. Now, as they walked hand in hand back to the summer house, Vivian remembered what had driven her from Haversham House and into the storm. With a sigh, she allowed the real world to return as she pulled on her gown, her stockings, and her shoes.

"If you must know, I was working on an acrostic poem. Are you familiar with the form?"

"The first or last letter of each line spells out a message, correct?"

"That's right. During the night, I came up with an idea for a slightly different approach to it and I wanted to write it down before I forgot."

"Do you enjoy writing poetry?"

"Actually, I wrote the poem because I am going to make a cipher out of it." Vivian laughed at the look on Whit's face. "Don't worry, your grace. It's for a puzzle that I hope to have published. There is no need to call the Home Office and have me sent to the Tower as a spy."

"I should hope not. Isn't that a rather unusual pastime for a lady?"

"Perhaps. I have always loved solving word

puzzles and riddles and other enigmas. When I went to school, I started creating some of my own for the other girls to solve. It's always been something I enjoy. I think I like the feeling of getting so totally absorbed in creating the puzzles—it helps me forget where I am."

"Like when you were married to the viscount?"

Vivian said nothing for a moment, but then replied lightly, "Yes, that's a good example. I needed something to…distract me from what my life had become."

Vivian paused, remembering, and then took a deep breath. "So I spent my time at Henry's country estate either in the gardens or solving the puzzles printed in the papers and creating new ones of my own. Henry always hated my puzzles." She laughed. "I think that might have been one of the reasons I kept doing them so religiously. But then one day he suggested—actually he *told* me—that I should have my ciphers published in the local paper. I hesitated, but he insisted, and soon I was providing the editor of the local gazette with a new weekly puzzle—all ciphers—with a solution key published the following day.

"I loved it, and Henry seemed to have come to terms with it. In fact, once, when I was ill, I had not been able to create a cipher for that week. I wrote a note explaining the situation and asked Henry to take it to the editor. He returned home with the missive undelivered and demanded that I create the cipher right then and there. I told him I was too ill, and he became enraged. He gripped my arms and shook me. He told me if I didn't create the cipher immediately there would be dire consequences. He terrified me, so I tried as best I could to pull something together. The cipher was short, and it had several errors in it. I was quite embarrassed about it later, but evidently it was sufficient. Henry never spoke of the incident or mentioned it again, but I had bruises on my arms for weeks."

Whit had listened to her story with growing fury. "Did he ever hurt you again?"

"No...in fact, he never touched me again. Two weeks later he was dead."

At the moment, Whit wanted nothing so much as to kill her already deceased husband. Instead, he said softly, "I am sorry things were so difficult for you then. Was your family aware of the state of your marriage?"

"My parents died when I was quite young. Uncle Will and Aunt Thea raised me with Linney. They were so happy when Henry and I became engaged. I didn't have the heart to tell them how awful it had become until after he died. I don't know that I would have told them even then if there had not been the scandal about where and how he died."

Whit pulled Vivian to her feet and into his arms. He stroked her back and whispered into her hair, "I wish I had been there to protect you."

Vivian's heart squeezed at his words. This...this feeling was what she had always wanted but never seemed to have. Since her marriage, she had almost come to terms with the fact that it was something she would never have in her life. Was it possible there was still a chance for her? A chance to be the love of someone's life? To feel safe and loved? To belong to someone who belonged to her?

She quickly tamped down that spark of hope and pushed back from Whit's embrace. "Of course, after

Henry died, the scandal made it impossible for me to return to London, so I retired to Somerset. I still subscribed to the London papers, though, and I always solved the challenges on their puzzle pages. One day I found an error in one of their ciphers and wrote to the editor, pointing it out. He wrote back asking if I would be interested in creating puzzles for them to publish in his paper and offered to pay me for them. I said yes."

"So the acrostic cipher you were working on in the library was for the *Mail Observer* to publish?"

"Well, that depends on whether Mr. Davis, the editor there, is willing to publish puzzles created by a woman."

"I don't understand."

"I've been publishing puzzles in the *Mail Observer* under the name of V. I. Burningham. You can tell they're mine because I always put a tiny V in the lower right-hand corner at the end of the last clue—like the end marks that newspapers sometimes use at the conclusion of a story or article. It's my signature and it's always the last thing I do on a puzzle. Mr. Davis is under the impression that V. I. Burningham is a man— an assumption that I never bothered to correct. My acrostic cipher is part of a collection of new puzzles that I'm hoping he will—wait…"

She cocked her head and furrowed her brow. "I didn't say that the *Mail Observer* was the London paper that published my work. How did you know?"

"The *Mail Observer* is one of several papers in London that publish puzzles."

"Yes, exactly. But it is not the only paper to publish puzzles. Why did you assume my puzzles were published by the *Mail Observer*?"

She waited, but Whit said nothing.

"You never assume anything, your grace—that's what you told me. How did you know my puzzles were being published by the *Mail Observer*?"

The duke said nothing as he continued dressing.

"Whit?"

Finally he turned to face her. "Because I followed you there. I saw you enter their offices with a package and come out with none."

"So," said Vivian slowly, "when we were walking in the park and I asked if you were following me, the correct answer was 'Yes'?"

"Yes."

"I see. May I ask *why* you were following me?" The silence again was deafening. "Whit? Why were you following me?"

"There has been some concern that you were supplying ciphers to the enemy through your puzzles."

Vivian started to laugh, but she stopped abruptly when she saw the seriousness of Whit's face. "I? A spy? Working for the French? I don't even *speak* French very well. Why would you think I was a spy?"

"We had intelligence that a woman was supplying the ciphers the French are using to code their messages."

"We?"

Whit took a deep breath. "I do clandestine work for the Home Office. I needed to find out if you were the person providing codes to the French."

"So you followed me? To Alexander's bookstore, to Hyde Park, and here to Lady Haversham's party—so you could spy on me?"

She stopped suddenly and gestured around her.

"Was all of this because you wanted to see if I was a spy? Did you think I had codes hidden in my bodice, so you decided you needed to see me without my clothes, just to be sure? Surely you could have made such an assessment without expending all of that passion and...and pleasuring. Or is that just part of the service—the complete seduction experience? How dare you? How *dare* you?"

Vivian flung the still damp towel at the duke and stormed out of the summerhouse.

Whit stared after her and, for the second time in less than a week, realized he was not at all sure what had just happened.

What was it about this woman that attracted him like a moth to a flame? She intrigued him as no woman ever had before, and she irritated him beyond words. He had never really understood the expression about someone getting under your skin, but now he did. She was not just under his skin but in his head as well. Her scent was in his blood and even his arms craved the feel of her in his embrace.

And if he wasn't careful, she would capture his heart and end his career—and perhaps his life.

Chapter 21

Vivian didn't remember the way back to the house as being quite so long. Of course, it had been the middle of the day when she'd first fled the duke's meddling presence in Lord Haversham's library. Now, with twilight approaching, she was fleeing the man again.

The irony of the situation did not amuse her.

A spy? They thought she was a *spy* for the enemy. It certainly was not a very good recommendation for those in charge of the Home Office. Was *this* how they ran the operation? Spying on widows who created puzzles for the papers? No wonder Napoleon had managed to escape from Elba.

Vivian stopped suddenly on the path. *The Duke of Whitley was a spy.* How many people knew that? Surely it was not something that he confessed to very many people—especially if he thought those people to be enemy spies.

Behind her, Vivian heard Whit calling her name. She quickly resumed her walk, increasing the pace.

When he caught up with her, he grabbed her arm, bringing her to an abrupt stop. "Didn't you hear me calling you?"

"I heard you." She jerked her elbow from his hand. "Leave me alone."

Whit exhaled and let his arms drop to his side.

"Why didn't you stop? We have to talk."

"A request, your grace? Or a command?"

"Which one will compel your obedience?"

"Neither," she said angrily, crossing her arms over her chest. "Aren't you concerned that I'm going to tell all my French friends that the Ice Duke is a spy?"

"*Are* you?"

She looked him in the eye and sneered. "Perhaps you should have thought about that before you told me your secret, your grace."

"Vivian, this is not a game. I should not have told you what I told you. I have put people in grave danger. I have put *you* in grave danger. People would kill to know the information you now know—they have killed for much less. I must have your word that you will not breathe a word of this to anyone."

"And you would trust the word of a traitor such as myself? You're not a very *good* spy, are you?"

"Vivian, I have told you too much. I admit that. If you say I can trust you, then I will trust you, but I cannot let you go until you promise me that you will not say a word to anyone about this and until I know what you are planning to do."

"You can go to hell. I won't tell your precious secret. Not for your sake, but because I do believe other people might be harmed if I do."

"That's all I ask."

Vivian started again on the path toward the house, but turned abruptly. "Was it all a ruse? In the carriage? In the summerhouse? Was it all so you could figure out if I was working for the French?"

Whit was silent for a moment. "Vivian, I…"

"Never mind. You don't have to say it." She turned

back and continued up the path, pretending not to notice when he caught up with her again.

"It was not a ruse. The feelings that I had…that I *have* for you are unrelated to my work. I did not make love to you to find out if you were a spy."

"Then why did you?"

Whit was silent. What could he say? That he was overcome with a desire like none he had ever experienced in his entire life? That he, the Ice Duke, had been sabotaged by his own traitorous heart— among other organs. He did not understand it himself. How was he supposed to explain it to her? Luckily she was more able to express herself than he was.

"How could you possibly think I was a spy?" Her brown eyes were huge and bright with unshed tears. "That is the part I absolutely do not understand. I have never done the first thing that was the least bit suspicious. Please explain to me how and why you came to believe I was a spy for the French and willing to betray the country of my birth."

"I should not have told you that I am a spy. You could be arrested for conspiracy and I could be hung for treason if those above me learn what I did, but I wanted you to know I had a legitimate reason for following you. We received word that ciphers published in the *Mail Observer* by V. I. Burningham were being used by the French to code their messages. I followed you when you left Mr. Alexander's bookstore simply because I was headed in the same direction. I was on my way to set up a watch at the offices of the *Mail Observer*. I soon realized that the *Mail Observer* was your destination as well. I had already asked Mr. Alexander what he knew about you, other than the *ton* gossip, and he called you a puzzle maker. He said you created all sorts of brilliant ciphers and enigmas. He said you were hoping to publish your puzzles in the newspapers. It seemed just too much of a coincidence, so I decided to get to know you socially so I could determine if you were, in fact, working as a spy for the French. And then this morning you were meeting with Baron Blount in Lord Haversham's library. We have had *him* under surveillance for a while now, Vivian, and you seem to have a connection with him that you cannot or will not explain."

Whit stood quietly, waiting for some sort of reaction from Vivian.

She folded her arms over her chest again and looked up at him. "Is that all?"

"Vivian, *someone* is using your puzzles to kill British soldiers. The most obvious person was you. I had to find out the truth. Everything else was coincidence. *You* fainted at the Calloway ball. How could I have planned that? I was intrigued and overwhelmingly attracted to you when I took you home that evening and again when we met—purely by accident—in the park. And this afternoon was…"

Whit's voice turned husky. "You are a beautiful woman, Vivian, and I find myself dangerously attracted to you—not just physically, although that is a huge distraction—but I am drawn to you in a way that I've never experienced before. I don't understand it, but it has nothing to do with my work for the Crown."

"Have I convinced you that I am innocent?"

"If you say I can believe you, then I do."

"Well, then I will tell you this. If someone *is* using my ciphers, they are going to be disappointed tomorrow morning because my last cipher was published this past Thursday. There will be no Thursday cipher tomorrow. They will have to get their codes from somewhere else."

"I don't understand."

"When I met with Mr. Davis last week, I lost my temper." She glared at Whit's feigned look of surprise. "I told him that V. I. Burningham would not be sending any more puzzles to the *Mail Observer* unless he agreed to work through *Miss* Burningham—me—which Mr. Davis adamantly declined to do. As a result, V. I. Burningham is no longer providing puzzles to the *Mail Observer*. So you can report *that* to your spymaster. Perhaps then he will have you follow more promising suspects."

Whit furrowed his forehead. "If they don't have a new puzzle cipher tomorrow, then they will most likely use the one that just ran. This may be the opportunity we've been waiting for."

"I don't want them using *any* of my puzzles at all!"

"No, it's good. We already have last week's puzzle, so we will know in advance what cipher they will be using. We can use it to set them up. You're absolutely sure that Davis has no other puzzles of yours to publish?"

"Yes. I have sent him a note apologizing for my outburst—that's part of what I was doing in the library this morning. I did include some examples of my acrostic puzzles, but no ciphers. Tomorrow's *Mail Observer* will not have a new cipher from V. I. Burningham."

"What about Lord Blount?"

"Not that it is any of your business, but he

is…was…a friend of my husband's. He had appealed to Henry's estate to collect on a gambling debt but was turned down, so now he thinks to collect the debt from me."

Whit narrowed his eyes. "I will speak to him. I can—"

"No. Please. I thank you, but I don't need your help. I can take care of it myself."

Vivian noticed that Whit's jaw twitched as he finally said, "Very well. I will honor your wishes…for now."

"That is very kind of you, your grace. I appreciate your granting me the ability to handle my own affairs. You and Mr. Davis would get along well together." Oh, she did love sarcasm.

"Vivian, my love, as much as I would enjoy a resounding argument with you right now, I need to get this information out straightaway. And you must hurry back so you have time to dress for dinner. I'll make my excuses and go directly to the stables. Don't tell anyone that you've seen me this afternoon. Hopefully no one will see us returning. I will be back as soon as I can."

"Will you let me know when you've returned?"

He looked at her. "Have you decided to believe that my attraction to you had nothing to do with my work?"

"If you say I can believe you, then I do."

He pulled her to him and gave her a quick kiss. "I will come to your room when I get back, but don't wait up for me. It may be early morning before I return."

Chapter 22

Fate was not on their side.

Guests were already gathering for pre-dinner conversation and aperitifs as Vivian and Whit scaled the path to the house and emerged from the woods. Before Whit could change course and head to the stables, Vivian saw Lady Smythson drawing the attention of several other ladies on the terrace to look their way.

"Damn," he said, quickly tugging Vivian behind a tree. "Maybe they didn't recognize us?"

"I think that is very unlikely," Vivian said, peeking out toward the terrace. "Don't worry. What can she do? I'm a widow, and my reputation is already spoiled." She smiled up at Whit.

"She is not a nice woman," he said, stroking her cheek with the backs of his fingers. "She can make your evening miserable if she decides to do so."

"I'm not afraid of—" began Vivian as he covered her mouth with his. She kissed him back and for just a few seconds again felt the bliss of being held in his arms. She broke the kiss before she lost herself entirely.

"Lady Smythson is just jealous," she whispered as he rested his forehead gently on hers.

"I will see you later." He kissed her once again before disappearing down the path toward the stables.

Of all the luck, thought Vivian as she made her

way up the back stairs to her room. It had to be Lady Smythson.

In her room, she struggled with her stays and quickly washed. As she rang for Estelle, she noticed a slight sunburn on parts of her body that had never been directly exposed to sun before today. She hoped Estelle would focus on bringing order to her hopelessly tangled hair and wouldn't notice the parts of her that now sported a tan. She laid out a new dinner gown of silver silk with tiny seed pearls sewn in a design along the neckline and hem. As she dressed, her summons was finally answered by Lydia, a maid sent by Lady Haversham's housekeeper.

"Is Estelle unwell?" she asked as Lydia started brushing out her hair.

"I don't know, Lady Rowden. None of us have seen her all day. Mrs. Daniels told me to come up and help you dress."

"That's odd. I wonder where she can be."

"If you need any help while she's away, I can do hair and press gowns and help you dress. My mum has been Lady Haversham's maid since before I was born."

Happily, Lydia was even more adept at hair styling than Estelle, and in no time at all, she untangled Vivian's long tresses—making no comment about the occasional twig or leaf—and then artfully piled it all high upon Vivian's head. As Vivian sat patiently, Lydia arranged curls along the nape of her neck and covered her upswept hair with a silver net. Vivian pulled on the long white gloves that reached above her elbows and covered most of the tan on her arms. She stepped into the silver slippers encrusted with seed pearls that Lydia held for her, and then turned to glance at her reflection.

The bodice of her gown was shockingly low, and it showed much more of her bosom than she was used to showing. She thought about finding a bit of lace to provide more coverage, but then remembered how she had spent much of the afternoon and blushed. The plunging *décolletage* was definitely not her most grievous disregard of propriety for the day. Oh, how she hoped that Lady Smythson had not recognized her returning with Whit.

The hunt for the lace abandoned, Vivian grabbed her evening shawl, smiled her thanks at Lydia, and ran out the door just as the dinner gong sounded.

****

The numbers were uneven at dinner that evening, and although Lady Haversham elegantly dismissed Whit's absence, it was obvious to all that the duke's departure had been unplanned.

As they went in to dinner, Vivian had a moment of panic until she saw Lord Blount was seated at the far end of the table from her. But her panic returned when she saw his place was set beside Linney and he was already using his charm to establish a rapport with her as a fellow fair-haired guest.

The current fashion for ladies was a high-waisted style that elevated the bosom and gathered the gown beneath. Like Vivian, Linney had more bosom than most to elevate, and Lord Blount was taking every opportunity to view the assets displayed by her gown of pomona green silk. Had Linney been a more experienced matron, the trope might have been comical, but Vivian was disgusted at the picture of the baron leering at her innocent cousin.

Two things prevented Vivian from switching

places with Linney. First, Linney was holding her own and replying quite icily to Lord Blount's attempts at innuendo. Probably, thought Vivian, because Linney saw him as one of Vivian's suitors and would never usurp her cousin's beau. And secondly, because Lord Hammond had also registered the baron's untoward glances. If she was reading the situation correctly, it would take only a little more provocation for Lord Hammond to issue a challenge and call Lord Blount out for his ungentlemanly behavior. Not wanting to add fuel to that fire, Vivian could only watch and fume.

After dinner, the ladies left the gentlemen to their port and cigars and adjourned to the parlor for sherry and gossip. It was not long before the gentlemen rejoined the ladies for charades—a venerable Haversham party tradition. Vivian, however, found herself playing an entirely different game with Lord Blount. As he stalked her, she roamed the room with the agility of a doe, never stopping for long in one place. Only in the company of Linney and Lord Hammond did she feel remotely at ease. Not wanting to intrude on their growing romance, however, she kept moving to stay ahead of the blond baron as he moved stealthily among the guests.

At long last, Lady Haversham called for everyone's attention and ordered two teams—half of the guests on the right side of the room and half on the left. Luckily for Vivian, she and Linney were on the same team and *not* on the side of Lord Blount. Unluckily for Lord Blount, Lord Hammond was his teammate. Before the game began, the earl invited the baron out on the terrace and was seen in a rather serious, one-sided conversation with the baron. Seeing the blond giant properly cowed did Vivian's heart good and improved the evening considerably—at least for a while.

The game was a variation on traditional charades. The rules required one team member to stand apart while the rest of the team read the name of a famous person—each player having already put the name of a famous person and a single word describing their choice into a gentleman's tall hat. The object of the game was to help the single team member guess the name of the famous person by calling out one-word clues that described the person physically, by their accomplishments, or in any other way, but without saying any form of either the famous person's name or the single word description. Members of the team could say as many words as they could think of within a one-minute time span—Lady Haversham's special "one-minute hour glass" was the official word on times. If the team member did not correctly guess the name of the famous person within one minute, then the other team had one minute to offer their guesses. The team that ended up with the most names guessed correctly was the victor.

Vivian's team, which included Lady Smythson as well as the two friends Vivian had seen with her on the terrace, was the second team to go, and Vivian was the team member selected to guess. Lady Smythson drew a name from the hat, but then quickly put it back and picked another. Vivian raised an eyebrow. Surely that wasn't allowed.

Lady Smythson kept the second name from the hat and showed it to everyone on the team. Several snickers were heard from the gentlemen and from Lady

Smythson's friends. When the timer was turned, Vivian smiled at her team, but her smile turned to surprise and then embarrassment as the ladies began to offer their clues and nudged certain gentlemen on the team to shout clues as well.

"Courtesan!"

"Paramour!"

"Hetaera!"

"Demimonde!"

"Ladybird!"

"Harlot!"

"Concubine," called Linney, blissfully unaware of the *double entendres* being flung like rotten tomatoes by Lady Smythson and her friends.

Stunned that Lady Haversham's guests would call her such names, Vivian blushed beet red and stood silently as her teammates continued to hurl insults at her. The truth—and the solution—finally dawned on her with Linney's clue of "Craven." Vivian quickly called out the name of the Earl of Craven's infamous mistress.

"Harriette Wilson!"

While several ladies blushed and feigned innocence about the nature of Miss Wilson's occupation, Lord Hammond caught Vivian's eye and raised his eyebrows at her in a mute question. Vivian looked down and joined the other ladies in their communal blush—but for a very different reason. When she chanced another glance at Lord Hammond, he was smiling broadly.

Chapter 23

Whit made good time to the meeting place and immediately sent a message to Edgewood in London. He then began the long wait until morning.

He took his horse to the nearby stream for water and then back to the clearing to graze. He ate the cold bread and meat he had scrounged from Lady Haversham's kitchen.

And he waited.

He tried to review the pieces of the puzzle he had lately acquired to see if they still fit. Too often, however, the game board in his head was interrupted by visions of his afternoon with Vivian—recalling her wonder at what was evidently her first orgasm and her delight in the freedom of swimming in the almost nude. He laughed out loud at her crack shot about his not being a very good spy.

And he waited.

As late evening turned into early morning, he climbed a nearby tree and settled into the surprisingly comfortable saddle created by the big branches. He drifted off for a few minutes as he waited.

Finally he heard the sound of another horse and saw Edgewood in the clearing. Jumping down from his perch, he handed his friend a bundle of cheese and bread. "It's about time you arrived."

"I got here as soon as I could."

"I thought my note conveyed some urgency," persisted Whit. "If I'd known you were going to wait on me at your leisure, I would have met you in London. It would have been faster."

Edgewood narrowed his eyes at Whit. "If I were in a better mood, I'd go a round with you—just for the chance to pound your pretty face. But I'm not, and once I tell you the news, you won't be either."

"What's happened? You did get my message about there being no puzzle in today's paper, did you not?"

"I did, and I waited until the early edition came out so I could bring you confirmation. That's what took me so long."

"Were you able to alert the encryption chaps to use the old cipher?"

"No."

"Why the devil not, man?" Whit rarely showed anger, but this time he turned on his friend. "This is the break we've been waiting for, damn it! It's our chance to know their plans before they can even send them out to their own. What the hell happened?"

"Take a look for yourself," said Edgewood, handing Whit a folded news sheet—the early edition of the *Mail Observer*. It was rumpled and had been turned to show the back page where the puzzles ran.

Whit felt a feeling of dread creep over him. "This is this morning's paper?"

"From the boy right out in front of their offices. The cipher ran, just as it always does. There's V. I. Burningham's name, right there. Somebody played you, Whit. Who was it? Where did you get your information? What else do they know?"

Whit looked at the paper in front of him, still trying

to absorb all the implications of what he held in his hands. "Damn it to hell!"

Edgewood continued, "I waited to get the paper before I sent out your orders. If we had used the old cipher as you suggested, our lads would have been sitting ducks. Who told you the cipher would not run?"

Whit was silent for a moment. He was still grappling with the fact that, had his friend not taken the time and initiative to confirm the information from Vivian, dozens of men would have been delivered up to the French for capture or—more likely—slaughter.

"She did."

"She? You mean Lady Rowden?"

"Yes."

"Does she know who you are?"

"Only partly. I told her I worked for the Home Office, but I didn't tell her that I was in charge of the whole bloody network."

Edgewood said nothing. There was nothing to say.

More than anyone else, Whit knew the implications of what they were now facing. Luckily, his orders had been countermanded because of Edgewood's obsessive attention to detail.

Chances were good that Lady Rowden had already disappeared into thin air—probably to meet her French counterparts. If she hadn't, then she would be arrested and tried for treason. And, if found guilty, she would hang for her crimes. And he…well, only because of his friend's caution were good men still alive this morning.

Whit's mind raced to remember what he'd told Vivian. Was there anything else he'd let slip? Any other information he'd given away? Damn it! He should have listened harder and paid more attention. With his brain instead of his cock, as Edgewood said. If he had, then surely he would have picked up the signs that she was one of Napoleon's agents. He should have trusted his instincts to tell him that she was simply using him.

He deserved to be shot.

But there was time enough for blame and self-recrimination later. Right now he had a score to settle.

The Ice Duke spoke deliberately as he always did. "Have Edwards send two men to Burnham-on-Sea to search her house. I don't know if they will find anything there, but we need to be sure. If I can get to her before she disappears, we might be able to extract information about her contact." He put the morning's newspaper in his saddle bag and pulled himself up on his horse.

"Whit, wait. There's one other thing. One of Edwards' men was following a known operative—a small-time rough that mostly does local jobs. They followed him to an abandoned mill just east of Reading where they found a woman being held captive. When they rescued her, she told them she was Lady Rowden's maid. Her name was Anne...Annie. She said she was returning to Lady Rowden from a family visit in the North when she was abducted. She was unhurt, but scared. We didn't get anything else from her, and we sent her back to her family for the time being. Does any of that mean anything to you?"

Whit shook his head. "No. This is the first I've heard that the woman with Vivian is not her regular maid. Just one more thing I'll be interrogating the viscountess about if she is foolhardy enough to still be there when I return."

He started his horse toward Haversham House but

then turned the beast around to face his friend. "Thank you for having my back, Edgewood."

"You've had mine too many times to count, your grace. Part of the job."

Whit nodded. "Please tie up one other loose end for me. Send word to the *Mail Observer* and ask them when today's puzzle was delivered and by whom. I want all of our evidence in good order when we make the case against Lady Rowden."

"I'll go myself. Keep your head with her, Whit."

Whit nodded his understanding and disappeared into the shadows.

Lord Edgewood looked thoughtfully after his friend. Whit never said "thank you" and he never said "please." Edgewood had just been the recipient of both.

Chapter 24

Vivian awoke slowly, aware of a chill in the air—a draft in her room. Her heart beat faster. It must mean that Whit was back. She had waited up for him as long as she could, but finally fell asleep on the sofa before the fire.

Someone was in her room, and they were quietly opening and closing doors and drawers. No light shone from the window—even the moon had set—so she could only just make out a figure in the darkness. She made herself continue breathing. Slowly. Steadily. For some reason, she was not afraid. It was as if, at some subconscious level, she knew who was there and she knew she was in no danger.

The intruder moved to her dressing table, closer to the faint light from the fireplace. She moved her head slightly so she could see over the blanket's edge. It *was* the Duke of Whitley, but instead of preparing to join her in bed, he was methodically rifling through her possessions like a thief. She watched him a few minutes more as he carried out his persistent search.

At last she could stand it no longer. Speaking in a low, sultry voice that belied her anger, she asked, "Did you find what you were looking for?"

To his credit, the duke showed no reaction to being discovered in such a compromising situation. "Not yet, but I am not finished."

The nerve! Oh, how he aggravated her!

"Perhaps if you told me what it is you are looking for," she drawled, her voice dripping with sarcasm, "I could point you to it and save us all a great deal of trouble. Estelle will not thank you for creating such disorder."

"That would be extremely helpful, madam, but I'm not exactly sure what I seek. Additional ciphers, maybe? More puzzles that can be used to help the French take more British lives? Information about your contact, perhaps? Or maybe just something that tells me more about your role in all of this."

Confused, Vivian sat up to see what What was doing. "Whatever are you talking about?"

"Why don't *you* tell me, Vivian? And why don't you tell me the truth this time?"

"I have already told you what I know about the puzzles I sent to the paper. I told you there wouldn't be any more until Mr. Davis and I make a new agreement. Why are you asking me about more puzzles?"

"You seem genuinely perplexed, Vivian. The consummate liar. How skilled you are. When your husband 'often' performed his husbandly duties, did the two of you laugh about the soldiers you planned to kill? Who is your contact, Vivian? Now that your adoring husband is gone, who gives you your orders?"

"You despicable man!" Vivian's eyes sparked as she threw back the blanket and stood up. Her long-sleeved, high-necked nightgown was pristine white and of the finest cotton, and it billowed about her bare feet as she stalked toward him.

"How dare you accuse me of such a thing? So my word is good enough when you want to bed me but not good enough to trust me once you have taken what you want?"

"I don't have time for theatrics, Vivian. This has nothing to do with yesterday or with us. I—"

"It has *everything* to do with yesterday and with us. Maybe *you* are in the habit of engaging in intimate relations with someone you don't trust, but I am not. I—"

"I am gratified to hear that you trust me."

"Cease interrupting and let me finish!" Vivian's voice shook with rage. "I have obviously made a grave error in judgment."

Whit turned at last. His eyes were terrifying, a piercing icy blue even in the dim glow of the dying embers. "You are not the only one who made an error in judgment, madam. I *did* trust you. And you lied. I believed you, and you played me for a fool. That's fine. I deserved it. And you're right. I got exactly what I wanted out of it. I have to admit that there was a moment when I thought you were different—different from the other women who slept with me for my money or my title and status. And I was right. You *are* different. You are worse. You used your body and your wiles to convince me that you were the innocent in all of this, and then you used me to endanger the lives of the very men I am sworn to protect. If people die because of your duplicity, Vivian, I will never forgive myself, but *you* will hang. I will see to it personally."

"How *dare* you threaten me!"

"Believe me, Vivian. It is no threat."

"You stand there and make your ducal pronouncements and condemn me for unspeakable things when I have no idea what you are even talking about. I am not a spy! My only crime, your grace, is trusting a man who took advantage of me."

Whit caught her arm before her hand could make contact with his face.

"Very convincing, my dear, but this time it will not work. Now I ask you again—who is your contact and how do you get in touch with him? We know you have a rendezvous soon. With whom are you to meet and where? I admit that I'm curious, Vivian. Why must you meet in person this time? What is it that you have to deliver? Is it me, Vivian? Did you think to lure *me* into an ambush and then crow as you delivered a British peer to Napoleon?"

Vivian laughed and pulled her arm away from his grasp. "Why on earth would they want *you*? Why would anyone want you? You arrogant, conceited, *stupid* man. I am not in league with the French. Stop accusing me of working against my country. Get out of my room this instant!" She ran to the bell pull to summon help.

Whit moved quickly to stay her hand. "Who are you thinking to call, Vivian? Estelle? Or Annie?"

"What do you mean? Estelle, of course. Annie is still visiting her family and taking care of her mother. Why would I be calling for her? My aunt let me have Estelle's services for this house party."

"We found her, Vivian. We found Annie gagged and bound in an old abandoned mill."

Vivian's face turned ashen. "What are you talking about?" she whispered. "Annie is at her family home, caring for her mother and running the household for her father and her younger siblings."

"Annie was abducted and has been held in a dank

grain room for two weeks. We rescued her yesterday."

"Oh, my God!" Vivian sat down in the chair behind her. "Was she hurt? Was she assaulted? Oh, Annie!" Tears shone in Vivian's eyes and the hand over her mouth trembled. "Can I see her?" Vivian stood and put her hand on his sleeve. "Please, Whit. Please take me to her now."

Whit took a step back—away from Vivian's touch. "She is well and she is safe, and she is somewhere that you and your friends cannot find her." He narrowed his eyes. "Your distress is touching, my lady. Did you not anticipate that she would be found?"

Vivian sat on the chaise, her face in her hands sobbing in relief. "Oh, thank you, thank you. Thank you for rescuing her, Whit, and thank you for getting her to safety."

"She was frightened, but she is unharmed and safe, and so is her family. She was concerned about you. She obviously cares a great deal about you."

Vivian's sobs were the only sound in the room. Whit waited until she had finally quieted herself. He could barely hear her when she spoke. "Whit, is this because I created those puzzles?"

"Your cipher is in today's paper, Vivian," he said coldly. "The puzzle you said would not be there has been published for every French spy to use. You told me your last cipher for the *Mail Observer* ran last Thursday, that you had not sent any others, and I believed you. If my friend had not sought to confirm that information this morning, dozens of my men would have walked into an ambush."

"But I *did* deliver my last puzzle to Mr. Davis last Wednesday, and I have been here since Monday afternoon. How could I have delivered anything else to him?"

"Suppose *you* tell me. Here's the damn paper, and there's the puzzle that you say you didn't deliver to Davis."

He threw the newspaper onto the chaise, and she snatched it up. She moved over to the fireplace and, fingers shaking, lit a candle so she could examine the paper. Her heart sank as she recognized her own work at the top of the page. "This *is* one of the puzzles I was working on…"

"So you admit that you lied about delivering the last puzzle?"

"No!" More calmly, she said, "No, I didn't lie. This *is* my puzzle, but I didn't deliver it to Mr. Davis. Why would I? It is incomplete. It makes no sense. There can be no solution. Also, it doesn't have my end mark. Remember I told you I always put a tiny V at the end of the last clue in the puzzle? This puzzle doesn't have one."

Whit peered at the paper over her shoulder and looked to where her finger pointed.

"Someone else must have delivered my unfinished puzzle." She looked up at the duke. "Why would they do that?"

Whit frowned. "I told you someone has been using your puzzles to encode messages for the enemy. We have been unable to decipher them because the codes keep changing—weekly. Every time one of your puzzles is published in the *Mail Observer*, they have a new cipher." He ran a hand through his hair. His instincts were telling him that something was not right. "Who else has access to your puzzles?"

"I don't know... Anyone who wants access, I suppose. I've never worried about anyone taking them, so I've never locked them up. I usually just keep them in a drawer in my room to keep them out of the way."

"Why can I not find any now?"

"Let me look. I know I put them all together..." Vivian sat down at the desk and pulled out each drawer, looking for her bundle of puzzles in progress.

"How long has your new maid been with the Braddocks?"

"Estelle? Surely you don't think Estelle would—"

"When was the last time you saw her? Did she help you dress last evening?"

"No. Lydia from Lady Haversham's staff came to help me. She said no one could find Estelle, and Lady Haversham's housekeeper had asked her to help me dress for dinner."

"Vivian, listen very carefully to me. I want you to stay right here. In your room. Lock the door and don't let anyone in. Right now, you are the only one who has had access to the puzzle that ran in today's paper. Until I can prove otherwise, you must stay here."

"Am I to be a prisoner in my own room, then? Guilty until proven innocent? You still believe I would do this horrible thing?"

"I'm sorry, Vivian, but this is not about my believing you. If you are telling the truth, then you are in great danger yourself. If you are lying... Well, I cannot take that chance. I'll be back shortly and will know more then. Until then, go back to sleep. Read a book. Create more puzzles. I don't care what you do, just lock your door and stay in your room."

Whit paused with his hand on the doorknob. "Do

you understand me?"

"Is that a request or a command, your grace?"

Whit strode back to where she stood and looked down at the flashing eyes defying his every word. He caught her in his arms, pulling her up on her toes, and kissed her soundly. Then he set her down unceremoniously on the cold floor and challenged her mutinous stare with an icy blue one of his own.

"Both."

****

His footsteps in the hall faded quickly. Only then did Vivian quietly open her door. As ready as she was to defy the Ice Duke, she would rather do it behind his back—or at least when he did not look so grim. She had seen the worry and anger on his face. She would not cause him more.

But she also had no intention of staying in her room when there were things she needed to know.

Poking her head out into the corridor, she listened for any signs that the household was stirring. Then she pulled her dressing gown tightly around her and crept down the hall to her cousin's room. With her hand on the doorknob, it momentarily crossed her mind that if her cousin was anything like herself, she might not be alone in her room. Whispering a fervent prayer that Linney's virtue was still intact, Vivian eased open the heavy door and slipped inside. The room was dark, and she could hear the faint purring of Linney's even breathing. Sending her thanks toward heaven, Vivian moved carefully to the edge of the bed.

"Linney," she whispered. She gently shook her cousin's shoulder. "Linney, dear, wake up. I need to talk to you. Linney!"

"Vivian? What is it? Is something wrong? Are you ill?"

Linney was a bear to wake up in the morning, so Vivian was surprised at her wakefulness, unless...

"Linney, when did you go to bed?"

"What time is it?"

"Just after four o'clock."

"About twenty minutes ago. The stars were so beautiful tonight, and Avery and I went for a midnight stroll that...well, it went a bit longer than midnight. Did you know there's a lovely summerhouse on the other side of the lake? We were going to walk around to it, but we ended up in Lady Haversham's rose garden instead. Oh, Vivian, did you know that some roses smell even better at night? They were—"

"Linney, darling, I would love to hear more about your stroll and the stars and the roses, but tomorrow. Right now I need to ask you a question about Estelle."

"Estelle? You mean your maid?"

"Yes. Do you know when your mother hired her? How long had she been in your household before we brought her here?"

"What an odd question, Vivian. Are you quite all right?"

"Linney, dear, please. Just tell me. It's important."

"Very well. I believe it was about a week before Larette's recital. Yes, I think that's right. Mother told Mrs. Jacobs to hire a second maid because Ellen, the other upstairs maid, was in an accident and broke her leg, so she could not climb stairs. Mrs. Jacobs was very excited about finding Estelle and told Mother that she had hired a wonderful maid with excellent references only the day after Ellen's accident. Of course, Mother was thrilled. She detests not having enough help upstairs. She always says that it makes the whole house feel out of order. She was very pleased with Mrs. Jacobs for finding someone so quickly."

"Thank you, Linney. That is exactly what I needed to know. Now go back to sleep and have sweet dreams about your Lord Hammond and roses and stars."

Vivian kissed her cousin's cheek and tucked in the bedclothes before slipping back into the hallway.

Chapter 25

The duke was almost to the stables when one of the night shadows transformed into Edgewood.

"Whit?"

"You're lucky you spoke up when you did, my friend. My pistol, like my patience, is on a hair trigger."

"The news came back soon after you departed. I thought it best that you know the entirety of what we are dealing with as soon as possible. Have you spoken with Lady Rowden?"

"Spoken, threatened, accused. All of these, and more. And I'm no further along in understanding what has happened than I was when the evening began."

"Well, I've one or two more twigs to throw onto the fire. Davis sent word back that a lady did indeed deliver the puzzle just after luncheon yesterday. Davis is as confused as you. He said he had not expected any more puzzles at all because—as he put it—Miss Burningham had given him an ultimatum of either doing business with *her* or not doing business at all. He said that he had been delighted to receive the puzzle yesterday, and didn't think it wise to look a gift horse in the mouth. He published it straightaway with the hope of working something out with Burningham himself later on."

"Well, I know for a fact that it was not Lady Rowden delivering the puzzle at that time yesterday because she and I were…occupied at about that time. Stranded by a thunderstorm."

"That matches, then. Davis said that his clerk did say it was not the same lady who had delivered the puzzles before. This one had red hair and—according to the clerk—a bit of a French accent."

"So Vivian is telling the truth."

"I don't know that I would go that far, Whit. The other piece of news is that Edwards had someone watching the abandoned mill where we found Lady Rowden's maid. Sure enough, a woman entered the place with food and water—I guess we should be glad they didn't leave their captive to die of hunger or thirst. Edwards' man took the woman into custody. She gave her name as Estelle and, coincidentally, she has red hair and a bit of an accent. She said she was Lady Rowden's maid and that the lady had given her the puzzle to deliver to Mr. Davis at the *Mail Observer*. I'm on my way to speak to the maid now."

Edgewood shifted uncomfortably, but continued, "For what it's worth, Whit, in my experience, it's always the maids and the footmen who end up holding the bag for the nobility. My money is still on Lady Rowden as our spy. I'll go ahead and send someone to Haversham House to escort her to London so we can start the questioning. Maybe then we can get some answers. Will you speak with Lord and Lady Haversham and let them know what's going on?"

"An escort won't be necessary, and I don't want her under arrest. I will handle Lady Rowden personally."

"I don't think that's a good idea, Whit. The woman could easily disappear into the night. You cannot watch her the entire time, and we can't have her warning the French about *Masquerade*. Let me send someone."

Edgewood was right. The evidence against Vivian was more than compelling, and the chances were great that, after interrogating Estelle, he would return with even more damning information. Whit could not afford to make the same mistake twice.

"I said I will handle it."

Edgewood glared at his friend. "Is that an order, your grace?"

"Yes, Lord Edgewood, you may take it as such."

Edgewood inclined his head. "Very well. Will there be anything else, your grace?"

"When will you return?"

"Assuming the maid is cooperative? Late this evening. You'll be here?"

"Yes. Unfortunately. If you recall, it is the night of the Grecian Ball. I will be in costume unless I can figure out how to blend in amongst scores of toga-wearing guests without wearing one myself."

"You've been in Scotland during the rains. Think of it as a plaid without the pattern. Wrap it round your waist, throw it over your shoulder, and tie a belt. Just don't forget your dirk."

"Easy enough for you—your ancestors hail from the Highlands. My ancestors preferred buttons."

Edgewood shrugged. "To each his own. Just be careful. I'll have news for you before you go to bed— assuming the lady doesn't have other plans for you before then."

Whit's laugh was more ironic than real. "I never assume anything, Edgewood."

"Of course, your grace."

****

"I'm quite sure I told you to stay in your room."

Vivian yelped at the voice from the shadows. Drat the man. She had been gone less than an hour.

On her way back from Linney's room, she had encountered several in-progress assignations and ended up having to take the servant's staircase all the way down to the kitchen before she realized it was actually this back staircase that the guests were using to avoid each other during their nocturnal ramblings. She crept back out to the front entry hall and returned to her room by way of the main staircase, encountering no one along the way.

Except now, as she slipped back into her own room.

"Yes, your grace. I believe you did."

"And may I ask why you disobeyed me? Do you not comprehend the King's English? Was there a fire that roused you from your room against my orders? Perhaps an injured child desperately needed your attention?"

"It is my recollection that you issued an *edict*, your grace. And since you are not my father, my husband, nor my king, I chose to ignore it."

"You are under house arrest, madam."

"By whose authority, your grace? You have—for the second time in a single evening—come into my room uninvited and accused me of all measure of things with only the flimsiest of circumstantial evidence and no proof at all. I tell you that I did not deliver one of my puzzles to a London paper this week and because one of my puzzles does, in fact, appear in said newspaper, you conclude that I somehow sprouted wings and flew to

London to deliver an unfinished cipher to a paper whose editor refuses to do business with me because I am female. Perhaps the question you should be asking is, 'Who has stolen Lady Rowden's cipher and how is she to get it back?'"

"I was invited the first time."

"I beg your pardon?"

"You invited me to your room the first time."

Vivian had no ready answer. She *had* invited him to her room when she thought he would bring back word of how her puzzles could be used to help in the work of the Crown. "Perhaps I did, but it was not to ransack my possessions and accuse me of treason."

"I'm afraid that is the state of things at the moment, my lady. And while we now know that you did not deliver the puzzle yourself, there is reason to believe that you paid your maid to deliver it for you. At least that is what she is claiming."

"Would it help prove my innocence if you knew that Estelle was hired because one of the Braddock's other maids was involved in an accident and broke her leg? And that Estelle coincidentally approached my aunt's housekeeper about employment the very next day?"

Whit narrowed his eyes. "When did you find *that* out?"

"When I disregarded your ducal command and left my room to talk with my cousin."

Whit sighed. "Vivian, you don't seem to grasp how serious this is. If you are found guilty of treason during wartime, the penalty is death. If the French find out that you know…what you know, then *they* will torture you to try and extract more information and then have you killed—if you are lucky. You are in danger no matter which side finds you."

"Do you think I am guilty?"

"My friend thinks he will have significant evidence against you after he interviews Estelle. I can only—"

"I did not make love with your friend, your grace. Do *you* think I am guilty?"

Whit looked at Vivian. In her robe and white nightgown with her hair in a loose braid down her back, she looked very young and very vulnerable. "I don't want to believe it…" he began.

"But *do* you?"

Whit studied her face. He was a man who trusted his instincts, and they had served him well. Why would he choose now to ignore those same instincts—every one of which was telling him that she was not guilty of the heinous crimes laid at her feet? With Estelle's allegations, the evidence against her was strong, too strong. And, according to Edgewood, Estelle claimed to have even more evidence that pointed to Vivian's guilt.

But what if it was Estelle who was the French operative? Wouldn't she be a more skilled liar than Vivian? Wouldn't she have a better story and more compelling evidence? Vivian's defense was thin. Sketchy at best. According to her, she could not have delivered the puzzle because it was incomplete, and that would be wrong. Also, she claimed she would not have sent a puzzle to a man who refused to work with her as a woman because of her principles. And—the only iron-clad piece of information he possessed—she couldn't have delivered the puzzle in person because, at the time of the delivery, he was making love with her.

Instincts triumphed.

"No, I don't believe you are guilty. God knows why, but I don't." He grimaced at Vivian smiling up at him. "Don't get cocky, my lady. Maybe I think you don't possess the intelligence to be a French spy."

She raised her eyebrows.

He sighed. "I am almost certain to regret this at some point, but for whatever reason, I simply don't think you have what it takes to betray your country."

Vivian laughed. "You are the only person I know who can make *not* committing treason seem like a shortcoming."

Whit smiled, but his face betrayed his fatigue. "The problem we face now is figuring out who *would* have the wherewithal to provide ciphers to the enemy. They would need to have at least a passing understanding of how a cipher works, and we are almost certain that the person we seek is English. Recent intelligence has suggested that the person is female, which is why you were under suspicion. But now I think we need to re-examine what we know. The problem is that time is running out. We have less than a week to find and neutralize our leak."

Vivian listened intently to the pieces of the equation that Whit laid out. A part of her brain was already working on a solution while another part was registering how much information Whit had about the situation and how much he was sharing with her. His role in this was evidently much more than that of a simple spy who reported on the comings and goings of suspicious individuals. She had no idea what the organizational structure of the Home Office looked like, but she felt very sure that Whit was not at the bottom of the hierarchy.

"Vivian, didn't you say the cipher published today by the *Mail Observer* would not give them a complete code? And that, ultimately, they would not be able to use it to encode their messages?"

"Yes. It has only one vowel. I was still working on it and I always do the vowels last."

"So when they try to use the new one, they'll see that it doesn't work and go back to using the old cipher—the one you actually did deliver to Davis last week. The one that ran in last Thursday's paper."

"Yes."

"Then I think we're back to where we were."

Vivian's eyes widened. "You're right. Once they try to use this latest cipher, they'll soon realize it's incomplete, and they will have to use the previous cipher. It's as if this cipher were never published at all!"

"Exactly. We still have a chance to pull a red herring across their path and send them straight into our trap. Do you have a copy of the last cipher you delivered to the *Mail Observer*?"

"Yes. I always make copies of all the puzzles to keep. It should be there in that last drawer." Watching Whit search through the drawer to retrieve the cipher gave Vivian a sense of *déjà vu*. The status of his operation might be back to where it was twelve hours ago, but she would never forget those hours—the happiness she had felt working with Whit to help his cause and the despair she had experienced when he thought the worst of her. Those feelings were a part of her now—they could not be erased, and they could not be denied.

"I believe it is this one, is it not? How long would

it take you to encode something using this cipher? We need to send out a message that says, 'The Masquerade will be held this Friday evening at midnight.' "

Vivian smiled innocently up at him. "As someone who is not intelligent enough to be a French spy, I will do my best. Let us hope I have enough intelligence to be an English spy."

The corners of the Ice Duke's cornflower-blue eyes crinkled when he laughed outright.

Chapter 26

"…And then she gave me a package and told me to go to the offices of the *London Mail Observer* and hand over the package to the clerk at the front desk. She said to tell the clerk to give it to Mr. Davis for the Thursday morning paper."

"And what did you do after that?"

Edgewood watched the subject of his questioning as she answered each question. Her answers were damning, but not too polished—just exactly what he would expect from a professional operative. And yet she was a little too eager to play her part. He had questioned many suspects, and they generally showed a great deal more apprehension than Estelle was showing. It was as if she were eager to provide him with information—information that would point to Lady Rowden as the instigator.

"I took a basket of food out to the old abandoned mill like she asked me to—that's where you had your gents and where I was apprehended."

Did most maids use the word *apprehended* as readily as Estelle did? Or did she use it because it was so similar to the French word?

"And who is the 'she' you refer to?"

"Lady Rowden—just like I told you before."

"Did you have another task to do after delivering the basket?"

"No. I was to go back to Haversham House and help Lady Rowden dress for the evening."

"Did you ever do errands for Viscount Rowden or any of his friends?"

"Lots of the errands Lady Rowden gave me to do were actually for the viscount—at least that's what she told me. I never talked with him myself. He wasn't at home a lot of the time. He liked to spend time with his friends."

That was an odd observation for a lady's maid. How did she know what he liked and disliked?

"And the viscount never made any unwelcome advances toward you?"

"Oh, no, sir. He was always a gentleman to me."

Interesting, thought Edgewood, to say that someone you never talked to was always a gentleman to you. How would you know? Plus the fact that this directly contradicted the information they had received from a number of other servants. It was, in fact, the only piece of intelligence that all the servants agreed on. Rowden had been a pig—pursuing anything in skirts. The only reason for him to skip over a pretty girl like Estelle was if he already had access to her charms or if he knew she was being protected by someone else.

"Did you ever do errands for anyone in the household other than Lady Rowden?"

"Oh, no, sir. Only Lady Rowden, but sometimes she asked me to do things that…" Estelle paused as if for effect.

"What is it?" asked Edgewood.

"Well, it's just that sometimes when Lady Rowden asked me to deliver packages…"

"What of it?"

"Well, sometimes I was supposed to deliver the packages to strangers in the park. That just didn't seem like something a nice girl should do." Estelle sniffed dramatically and dabbed her handkerchief at her eyes as if to stop the tears.

"Do you know what was in the packages?"

"Papers, I think, but I don't know. They didn't weigh much."

"So you didn't look inside?"

"Oh, no, sir. I would never do that. Only…"

"What?"

"Once when I delivered one of Lady Rowden's packages to a man in the park, he sat right down on the bench beside me and opened it."

"And did you see what was inside it?"

"Just papers—they looked like letters to me, but I…ah…I couldn't read them because they were in French. There was also one of Lady Rowden's puzzles. Oh, and I saw Napoleon's name. And then the man saw that I was looking, and he smiled at me and asked me if I was French—because of my accent, you know—and I told him that my mum was French, but I was as English as a cup of tea."

"What did he say then?"

"Nothing. He just smiled. But he gave me a gold sovereign."

"Did he tell you his name?"

"No."

"How did you address him?"

"He told me just to call him Monsieur—with no other name. He laughed when he said it, like it was a great joke."

It was a joke, thought Edgewood bitterly, because

the man was British and working for the French—a traitor to his country. The seasoned interrogator showed no reaction to Estelle's enlightening comment.

"How long had you been employed in the household of the viscount at the time of his death?"

"I started working there right before the wedding. I helped with all the preparations."

"Have you ever been to France, Estelle?"

"No, sir. Like I said, my mum was French, but we never went there. My da' was Irish. They've both passed on."

"And you have no other family? Brothers? Sisters? Aunts or uncles?"

"No, sir."

"When did you leave the viscount's household?"

"After he died, most of the servants left or were dismissed. I went to Bath for a while and found work with a family there. I stayed for about a year, but I missed London, so I went back up to town right before Easter. A friend of mine worked for the Braddock household, and she told me they were looking to have more help upstairs because one of the maids had broken her leg. The housekeeper hired me on the spot."

"What is the name of your friend that works for the Braddock family?"

"Oh…uh, she's no longer in their service."

"That doesn't matter. What was her name?"

"I…ah, I called her Rosie because she liked to wear rose water. But I don't know what everyone else called her. She left right after I started."

Edgewood continued as if Estelle had not just put another crack in her testimony. "Where in Ireland is your father from, Estelle?"

"Near Dublin, sir."

"Who taught you to read?"

"Uh…it were my…my mum. She taught me."

"So, she spoke English as well as French?"

"No…I mean, yes. Yes, she did."

"And do you understand French?"

"No."

"Not even a little bit that you picked up from your mother?"

"Well maybe I speak it a bit, but I can't read French writing."

"So your French-speaking mother taught you to read in English but not in French. And the letters in the package that you gave to the gentleman in the park—were they in English or French?"

"I could read them, so they must have been in English."

"Were you surprised when you found out that Lady Rowden had come to visit the Braddocks?"

"I'll say—you could have knocked me over with a feather. I never thought to see her again, and there she was."

"Did she seem surprised to see you?"

"Oh, yes, but happy like. She said I could be a big help to her since her maid was away."

"Do you understand why you are being held, Estelle? Do you know why you are under arrest?"

"Because I took food to the mill, and it was for that girl what was kidnapped. Except that I didn't know she was kidnapped, sir. I was just doing what Lady Rowden told me to do."

"We are going to keep you under our protection until we find out more about Lady Rowden. The guard will see to it that you have enough food and water and other comforts, but you must not try to leave, or we will not be able to protect you. Do you understand?"

"Yes, I understand, sir. Thank you, sir."

"Very good, then. Guard?"

Edgewood stood and took a final assessing look at Estelle. He didn't believe a word she said, but she *had* given them several new leads to follow.

Chapter 27

The evening of the Grecian-themed fancy dress ball at Haversham House was nothing short of perfect, giving ammunition to those who actually believed Lady Haversham could control the weather. Whether that was true or just wishful thinking on someone's part, tonight was exactly the sort of evening one would create if one did possess such a power.

A warm zephyr breeze blew, keeping away the biting mosquitoes and fluttering the gauzy togas of the ladies. Luckily—or unluckily, depending on one's appreciation of men in knee-length tunics, sandals, and little else—the men's rather shorter garments were made from sterner stuff and not as susceptible to the flirty breezes.

The indoor ballroom was beautiful and quite cleverly decorated with assorted faux ruins and ivy twining around columns, but the *pièce de résistance* lay beyond the French doors, which had all been thrown open to the evening. Terrace topiaries twinkled with candles that imitated fireflies, and colored lanterns strung on wires and in trees provided all colors of light to delight the costumed guests who strolled beneath them. Candles shaped like water lilies floated in trickling fountains, and carved ice sculptures mimicked the marble statues of Greek gods and goddesses. At nine o'clock, the full moon rose on cue, giving the entire landscape a luminescence and an otherworldly effect that could not have been duplicated by any mortal hostess, no matter how talented.

Vivian strolled slowly around the perimeter of the ballroom, smiling, but with an uneasiness that contrasted with her pleasant expression. Something inside her cringed at the size of the crowd and how everyone stood so closely together. She had to remind herself to breathe…slowly and deeply. Perhaps if she went out to the terrace the closed-in feeling would pass. The problem was getting to those doors without unleashing the budding panic that she knew lingered right beneath the surface. She had learned to recognize the signs of her panic attacks, but she was not always able to quash the cause—as was evidenced by her fainting at Lady Calloway's ball just last week. And although that particular episode had ended quite nicely—she blushed at her own boldness as she let her thoughts momentarily return to that memorable carriage ride home with the Duke of Whitley—she had no desire to repeat the experience.

At least not the fainting part.

"One deep breath," she whispered to herself, "then walk directly to the door."

As if she had spoken the words out loud, a break in the crowd allowed her to see the open doors that led to the spacious terrace beyond the crowded ballroom. Just a few more steps… Finally! The cool, fresh air congratulated her, and the smooth surface of the stone beneath her slippers soothed her. She took a deep, thankful breath and relaxed enough to take a sip from her glass of sparkling wine.

"You look lovely this evening, Lady Rowden."

The voice behind her was neither unfamiliar nor unanticipated. Vivian knew she could not avoid Lord Blount forever. This time, however, she was ready to do battle with the toad. She pasted a serene smile on her lips and turned to her nemesis.

"Lord Blount. You seem to have tracked me down again. Is there a reason you are asserting a claim on my time? If not, I have friends to find—friends whom I actually enjoy spending time with."

"You have a sharp tongue, my lady. May I hope that you have used it to procure payment for your late husband's…peccadilloes?"

"So you do admit that the debt was a ruse. You admit that this is simply blackmail?"

"If you don't need a ploy to get the money from your uncle, then I am happy to dispense with all euphemisms."

"As I told you before, Lord Blount, I am unwilling and unable to advance your extremely dubious claim. Now if you will excuse me, I—"

Lord Blount continued smiling as he gripped her elbow and turned her bodily toward the relatively isolated rose garden. "Lady Rowden," he said under his breath, "if you do not wish to cause a distressing scene that will certainly embarrass your cousin, you will appear to walk with me willingly."

Vivian acquiesced, momentarily going along with the man so she could hear his whole plan.

"It has been my observation," he continued, "that compromising situations—such as those involving you and your late husband—are much more likely to have detrimental consequences for the lady involved than for the gentleman." He chuckled. "And for such as I, the consequences are almost positive—manifested by an elevated status among our peers who wink and nod at our roguish behavior and also by a heightened interest from ladies who secretly imagine what it would be like to be the object of such compromise. Unfortunately, it is the innocents—such as your lovely cousin—who pay most dearly for the indiscretions of their family members. I beseech you to think of your cousin. Linney, isn't it? Think of Linney, Vivian, before you so hastily refuse my very reasonable request."

Vivian shook free of the bully at her side. "Lord Blount, I have spoken with my cousin, as well as with my uncle, who, it should be noted, is a highly respected solicitor. I have also spoken with the Duke of Whitley."

That was certainly true. She had, at one time or another, spoken to them all—just not about Lord Blount's scandalous accusations and untenable demands. She boldly continued her bluff.

"I feel confident in saying that should you choose to pursue this completely false claim against myself or against the estate of the late viscount, you will find yourself not only on the outside of polite society looking in but also a target of an intense, very expensive, and quite expansive investigation into your private life and financial considerations. As my uncle explained to me, one consequence of such an investigation is that no shops or tradespeople will offer you credit for any transactions. You will be forced to pay all accounts immediately, and, because of your criminal actions, you will not be shown the accommodations normally due a peer of the realm."

Vivian held her breath while Lord Blount absorbed the implications of what she had just outlined. If he decided to call her bluff, there was nothing but scandal awaiting her and Linney. However, if, as with so many bullies, he folded when someone stood up to him, then she could finally spend an evening not looking over her shoulder.

As she watched, the face of the handsome man turned dark with rage. She was already terrified of the baron, and when he moved his hand as if to strike her, she instinctively put up a hand to deflect the blow. In the space of a second, he regained his control and instead took her hand and raised it to his lips. She almost questioned whether what she had seen was anger or an innocent gesture, but all doubt disappeared with the words he spoke in a low voice, for her ears alone.

"I regret that we could not reach an accord this evening, my lady. But rest assured you have not heard the last from me." Executing a perfect bow, he dropped her hand unceremoniously and disappeared into the shadows.

"Like the devil incarnate," Vivian said to herself. She marveled at her close call and then shivered.

"Have you taken a chill, my lady? I would agree that it *is* a bit on the cool side for a Greek marketplace in midsummer."

This time Vivian's smile was genuine. She turned and extended her hand to Whit. "Good evening, your grace. How dashing you look as a common citizen. Do you plan to enlighten us all this evening with your oratory skills? Or are you perhaps one of the gods descended from Mount Olympus to walk incognito among us lesser mortals?"

"I had thought to assist you in banishing that blond bully from your presence, but I see you have taken care of that yourself, my lady. Are you, by chance, the brave and beautiful Athena, goddess of wisdom and war?"

Vivian laughed and drew her first carefree breath of the evening. She unfurled her ostrich fan—a party favor from their thoughtful hostess—and moved the air directly in front of her face as she looked proudly at Whit. "I feel as though I might be." She smiled but then shivered again. "I hope he heeds my advice and takes himself far away from me and mine."

"And are you still determined to keep his threats to yourself?"

"I am, but with thanks to you for your offer of assistance. I promise that if the viper emerges again from his nest, I will seek your help."

"I will hold you to that, Vivian," said Whit. He had seen the small movement by Blount, and only a dowager's insistent greeting had saved the baron from a broken nose and a dawn appointment. Whit was not finished with the man, no matter what Vivian said. He was a spy, for God's sake, and he planned to get to the bottom of Blount's unhealthy interest in the lady.

"As you said, Athena is the goddess of war *and* wisdom. I do think that if the baron comes around again it would be most unwise for me to attempt to handle him alone."

"I shall have to be satisfied with your pledge—at least for the moment. May I interest you in some baklava? I understand it is a favorite of yours."

Vivian laughed. "So Lord Hammond has sold me out, has he? It took all my powers of will to limit myself to one serving the other afternoon. They say baklava is a food of the gods. One hopes those gods shared nicely with their goddesses and were as generous as Lady Haversham's staff has been."

"I'm sure they understood the benefits of bringing sweets to their ladies just as much as any man does," replied Whit, smiling and offering his arm to guide Vivian to where Linney stood conversing with Lord Hammond.

"Good evening, your grace," said Avery, inclining his head. "And Lady Rowden, may I say that the Grecian style suits you immensely." Lord Hammond raised Vivian's hand to his lips.

Whit inclined his head graciously to his half-brother and took Linney's hand in his. "Miss Braddock, surely you are the goddess of beauty and grace. May I call you Aphrodite?"

Vivian rolled her eyes, but Linney giggled and said, "You may, your grace. And may I say you look very...ducal in your ensemble." She frowned. "Actually there doesn't seem to be that much of a difference between you in a toga or you in formal evening attire. In both you look like exactly who you are."

"And who might that be, Miss Braddock?" asked Whit haughtily. "The Ice Duke?"

Linney looked shocked for a moment before she burst into laughter at the twinkle in his eye. "I don't know what led you to mention that particular moniker, your grace, but I assure you that *I* would never—"

"Be careful, Linney," said Vivian. "I believe we are in the presence of Zeus and his brother Poseidon, and I am certain there is some severe penalty for telling falsehoods to the residents of Mount Olympus."

The duke and the earl struck godlike poses while Vivian rolled her eyes. Linney chuckled. "If you are waiting to be sculpted, it could take a while," she warned. "You might want to take some refreshment."

"Yes," said Vivian, "do come along, then, your... Goodness, what *is* the proper address for an inhabitant of Mount Olympus? My god? Your godliness? Your omnificence?"

"I couldn't say, Athena," said Linney, linking arms with her cousin. "Shall we discuss it over some ambrosia?"

"An excellent suggestion, Aphrodite. Let us leave the gentlemen to their marbles. Perhaps we might share some hair-styling secrets with Medusa?"

****

The tiny cottage in the middle of the forest was accessible by only one rather overgrown path which led, after several miles, through a pasture and then to the main road. From the main road, the path was undetectable. It was a point of pride that his hideaway was literally in the middle of the English spies who continued to search for his whereabouts.

"Are you sure no one followed you?"

Estelle's musical laughter—normally so enticing when she was on her back beneath him—grated on his nerves this evening. "Oh, *cheri*," she trilled, "of course I am sure. The guard is asleep and will not wake for a long time. And when he does, I don't think he will want to tell the others how it happened that I was not locked up at the time of my escape. At least he went to sleep with a smile on his face."

"Were you able to learn anything more about the man who questioned you?" Would she never stop that endless tittering?

"The Earl of Edgewood? Only that he and all the others seemed to accept my confession and everything else I said as the sworn truth. If the viscountess is able to weasel her way out of this, then you should add her to your stable of spies, for she will have proven herself without equal."

He turned toward the cold fireplace. "I *would* like to add her to my stable, but not for spying."

Estelle poked out her lip in a pout. "Do not tell me any more how beautiful she is. I am quite tired of hearing it. Some things are more desirable than beauty, *n'est-ce pas?*" She slinked up behind him and slipped her arms around his waist, dipping one hand to cup the bulge in his trousers. His body responded immediately, and she laughed softly, massaging his aching groin none too gently. "Let me show you some of those things, *cheri,*" she whispered in his ear.

"There is no time, Estelle," he snapped, removing her hand and pushing her away. "Tell me what else you found out about Edgewood."

"Bah, he is a stupid aristocrat who should be separated from his head, like all aristocrats. He pretends to know what is going on, but it is clear that he knows nothing and is one of the lower operatives. He is forever asking questions of others."

"Did he ask questions of you, Estelle?"

"*Certainement.* But I told him only what you told me to say. That Lady Rowden had given me packages to deliver—sometimes to strangers in the park, which didn't seem like something a nice girl would do. I cried quite pitifully when I told him that."

Estelle started toward him again with a sly look on her face. "I wanted to tell him about all the *other* things I had done that nice girls did not do, but I thought he might want to know more or experience those things for himself, *peut-être*. In truth, I wouldn't have minded showing him—he was very attractive. And he had hands that looked like they could bring much pleasure to a woman."

Was the stupid chit trying to make him jealous? She had become unbearably annoying. "What else did you tell him?"

"Oh, I don't know. I told him I saw one of Lady Rowden's puzzles when one of the gentlemen opened his package, and I told him that Viscount Rowden was always a gentleman toward me. I almost laughed when I was telling that part of the story."

"Did he ask you about Henri's death at all?"

"No, nothing."

"About your family?"

"Yes, but I made something up. I told him my father was Irish but my mother was French which is why I have an accent. I told him that several times. He seemed to forget that he had already asked me about it."

"You idiot! He was testing you. Are you sure you told the same story each time?"

"Yes, of course. I know what I am doing. Why do you ask me so many questions? I told him nothing but lies."

Estelle was acting strangely and was not treating him with the proper respect. "Is that all you told him, Estelle? Did you tell him anything about me?"

"Of course not." Estelle did not meet his eyes as she answered, looking instead at her hand as it smoothed her skirt and pleated the folds of her gown— one of her many "tells."

"If I had told him all that I know about you, *cheri*," she purred, "they would have been here to arrest you long before I ever arrived."

"You have proven yourself most useful, Estelle, as well as entertaining. I will miss you."

An echo of the shot rang through the forest, followed soon after by the sound of hooves galloping down the path and away from the tiny cottage.

Chapter 28

"Excuse me, your grace," whispered a footman to the duke, "but a gentleman has asked to have a word with you in the library. He is not in costume, but he says it is about the masquerade."

Whit nodded and said to Vivian and Linney, "Please excuse me. Lord Hammond, I trust I may leave the ladies in your care? Lady Rowden, may I have the honor of sharing the next set with you upon my return?"

"I shall take it under consideration, your grace, and have an answer for you at that time."

Whit raised his eyebrows at her, as did his brother. No one said "no" to the Duke of Whitley. He looked amused and then followed the footman back inside the house.

Lord Hammond looked after his departing brother and shook his head. "I don't know what it is that you ladies do to mollify his grace, but I do wish you would share your secrets with me. First Miss Braddock charms him at the Evenstone's musicale—an event that I know for a fact he did not want to attend—and now Lady Rowden has him practically begging for the honor of a dance. The duke almost *never* dances. In fact, the last time I saw him on the dance floor—"

Having all of a sudden recalled the circumstances surrounding his grace's last public dance, Avery stopped abruptly and, desperate to change the subject, said, "Was that lightning? I hope a thunderstorm doesn't take the party inside. Although I have to admit that a bright flash or two would add a striking atmospheric ambiance to the assembly."

"Oh, my lord," said Linney with a sigh, "there are so many things to dissemble in your poor attempt at a pun. I fear I will be all night untangling them."

Vivian laughed and added, "I can't help but observe the coincidence that cued the lightning as soon as our Zeus was called away. Do you suppose he lost something up on Mount Olympus and has called for the lightning to help him in his search?"

"His grace *is* rather bad at finding things—at least that is the impression he always gave when I tormented him into playing hide-and-seek as a child. I could never understand why he always failed to find me. Only when I began playing the same game with the Furies did I fully comprehend Whit's strategy. Those girls think I am the very worst 'seeker' there is."

Vivian and Linney laughed at the picture of the duke and the earl playing a very poor game of hide-and-seek with their younger siblings.

"Hold a minute, cousin," said Linney, narrowing her eyes. "I seem to recall that *you* were not a very good seeker yourself. What's more, every time it was your turn to hide, you always hid in the library. I must have a word with the Furies sometime soon, so we can plot stratagems."

"I would never allow for the merger of two such forces," said Lord Hammond, only half joking. "In the meantime, I put a question to the two brightest lights of the evening: If Zeus had lightning bolts and Poseidon had the trident, what did Hades have?"

"Oh, that *is* a good question, my lord," said Linney. "In the ancient Greek, Hades means 'invisible,' so maybe he had no accessory—or at least none that we could *see*."

"He must have had *something*," mused Vivian. "All of the gods and goddesses had some symbol associated with them, didn't they?"

"I thought they did," said Linney. "Surely it would not be fair for his brothers to have such splendid accessories and poor Hades to have none. I believe I read somewhere that Hades was actually the eldest of the three brothers."

"Perhaps we have erred in our character assignments, then," said Avery. "If Hades was the elder brother, wouldn't that make his grace the Lord of the Underworld? Then I could be Zeus...or Poseidon."

"Well, whichever you are, you must escort me to the floor," said Linney, tapping Avery's sleeve with her ostrich fan. "The sets are forming for the next dance, and you have promised it to me."

"The two of you go along. Since the duke is not back, I am going to take the opportunity to look up Hades in Lord Haversham's library. If he returns while I am away, please tell him that I will, in fact, bestow upon him the honor of the next set. I have never before been led out onto the floor by a god. It's all very exciting."

"Oh, my lady," groaned Avery, "please do not encourage his already inflated sense of importance. The next thing, he will be renaming his country home to Mount Olympus."

Laughing, Vivian headed off toward the library as Linney and Avery joined the other dancers. With her head already in the clouds, she sailed up the main staircase and down the hall to the library and really shouldn't have been at all surprised when she ran straight into the Duke of Whitley.

"Oh, I do beg your pardon, your grace," said Vivian. "I seem to be running into you quite a bit of late."

"You do indeed, my lady," said Whit gripping her shoulders to steady her in what was becoming a rather familiar ritual. "I blame you entirely, and, for the record, I would like to say that I was not skulking about but merely having a conversation with Lord Edgewood here. The library has become rather crowded—" He frowned. "Something about it being a place of refuge from a lady whose name I did not catch, so Edgewood and I adjourned to the hallway. I thought we were out of the path of most revelers, but I had not counted on your unerring ability to find and run into me at every opportunity. Lady Rowden, may I make known to you the Earl of Edgewood? Edgewood, the Viscountess Rowden."

Vivian curtsied and held out her hand to Edgewood. He brought her fingertips to his lips and murmured, "Delighted, my lady," and then continued to hold her hand in his. "And may I say that I also seem to run into his grace quite often. He does skulk quite a bit." Edgewood smiled down at Vivian—he was almost as tall as Whit. His intense scrutiny of her made her blush, and she could feel a flush creeping up the one bare shoulder of her flowing toga. With another bow, Edgewood released her hand.

"Will you be attending the Grecian Ball this evening, my lord?" As handsome as Edgewood was with his russet brown hair and trim physique, Vivian couldn't help comparing him with the duke, who was looking every inch the part of a full-bodied Greek god this evening.

"Yes, Edgewood," echoed the duke, "won't you join us? I'm sure Cooper can help you with a costume. It's not unlike wearing a Scots plaid, except of course without the pattern."

"Oh, do join us, my lord." Vivian took a step closer to Edgewood, and whispered loudly in his ear as Whit looked on with a scowl, "I have it on good authority that there is baklava. Have you ever eaten baklava, my lord? It is a pleasure not to be missed."

Edgewood laughed. "I do not doubt that eating baklava with you would indeed be one of life's great pleasures, my lady. But, alas, as tempting an offer as it is, I am afraid I must decline your kind invitation. I was in need of a moment of his grace's time, but we have concluded our business, so I return him to your company. I feel sure we will meet again—either here on earth or perhaps at your home in the clouds."

"You are welcome on Olympus any time, my lord," said Vivian. She executed a perfect curtsy to Edgewood, and when he raised her from her bow, she said, "I am off to the library then, to settle a wager with Lord Hammond as to the nature of Hades' weapon of choice."

"It is a helmet, my lady," said Edgewood.

Vivian turned back quickly and inadvertently tripped Edgewood, who had taken a step forward. Off balance, he steadied himself on her arm. "I do beg your pardon, m'lady."

"The fault was mine entirely, my lord. How do you

know that about Hades?"

"I had an older brother who decided one summer that we were all to be gods and defend our Mount Olympus home from enemies both foreign—meaning the villagers—and domestic—meaning the servants. Like his grace here, my brother was rather used to being in charge of all he surveyed. He decided that, as the eldest, he would be Hades and that my younger brother and I could choose between Zeus and Poseidon. Of course, he also decreed that, as Zeus and Poseidon, we had to carry our lightning bolt and trident everywhere we went. We had made them as big as we possibly could, and they became quite the clumsy encumbrance. He, on the other hand, being Hades, had a helmet of invisibility and nothing to carry. He was always sneaking up on us as we dragged our great weapons about with us. To this day, there is a lightning bolt made from wood lodged in one of the trees at my country home."

Vivian laughed delightedly. "I do hope to see you again, Lord Edgewood. With or without your lightning bolt."

"A pleasure I look forward to with great anticipation. Your servant, ma'am."

"I will see Edgewood out and then join you in the library, my lady."

"Of course, your grace. Good evening, Lord Edgewood."

The men watched Vivian enter the library and heard her greet several of the gentlemen there. Whit smiled after her and then led Edgewood toward the door, his hands clasped behind his back.

"I'd say you have your hands full with that one,

Whit. And if you don't, you should." Edgewood spoke with uncharacteristic admiration.

Whit paused and without making eye contact with his friend, said in the quiet, level voice of the Ice Duke, "I will overlook such crude remarks this once because we are friends, Edgewood, just as I will, this once, overlook your putting your hands on Lady Rowden. But let me be clear that if you do either again, you will find yourself looking down the wrong end of my pistol."

Edgewood raised his eyebrows at the interesting direction the conversation had just taken and chuckled. "And to whom would you turn as your second, your grace, as that is a position I normally enjoy?"

Whit turned to look directly at his best friend. "I'm sure Hammond could be imposed upon to help me show you the error of your ways."

Edgewood bowed his head in concession. "I meant no insult, your grace. To the contrary, considering this new intelligence, I have nothing but respect for the lady, and I look forward with great anticipation to watching you navigate a relationship with her. She is quite beautiful and a formidable adversary for you. What a lucky chap you are. Were I a betting man, I would be at White's even now making a wager about a date for your nuptials."

"Was there anything else you wanted to tell me, Edgewood? Before I toss you out into the night?"

"So you don't believe anything that we learned from Estelle?"

"Do you?"

"No," Edgewood admitted reluctantly. "I think her plan all along was to spread stories that implicated Lady Rowden—although I don't think being shot in the head was part of her plan."

"That is a troubling revelation, although frankly I am more concerned about the location of what appears to be an enemy hideout in the middle of Haversham's hunting forest and just a few miles away from here."

"And the note in the fireplace?"

"Rather too convenient, don't you think? A half-burned note in a lady's handwriting—presumably Lady Rowden's—with only the words 'silence Estelle' legible? Most likely another red herring."

"I agree."

"However, the note and the defiant location tell us much about the person we're dealing with, as does Estelle's execution. He is ruthless and he leaves no loose ends. He has made secondary plans as a precaution. And he seems to have set his sights on Vivian. Either she is to be made the scapegoat in all of this by our own forces, or, as your new intelligence suggests, she is to be abducted and taken to France. What I don't understand is why her and why now? What is it that necessitates her removal? Or is it simply that our interest in her has sparked an equal interest on their part?"

"Perhaps it is *your* particular interest in her, Whit. Maybe that's the catalyst. As long as she was tucked away in Somerset, everything was fine. But her appearance in London and her name linked with yours in the gossip columns—maybe they just don't want to lose control of what has been a valuable, albeit unwitting, asset for them. I would also wager that it has something to do with the untimely death of the viscount, but I have nothing yet to back that up. None of it seems to fit together."

"I thought you were not a betting man, Edgewood."

"I'm not," said Edgewood, sighing. "If I were, I daresay I would not be standing here now." He bowed. "Good night, your grace."

Chapter 29

It was half past three in the morning when Vivian and Whit finally made their way up to her room. The midnight fireworks display had been the highlight of the evening, but instead of signaling an end to Lady Haversham's *Greek to Me* fancy dress ball, it gave rise to several more hours of frivolity, followed by an unusually long time for guests to settle in their beds— or at least in the beds they had chosen to occupy for that evening.

Whit sprawled in an overstuffed chair in front of the fire, his toga draped discreetly as he watched Vivian slip out of her Grecian gown and begin her nighttime preparations. His original plan had been to take her to bed and, in keeping with the theme of the evening, introduce her to some of the more sensual pleasures of ancient Greece. However, Edgewood's impromptu visit had made that impossible.

The intelligence Edgewood had collected—the reason his friend had defied all established protocols to visit Haversham House that evening and speak directly with Whit—was from several sources. In each case, the word was that "the codemaker" would soon be in France and, because of that, Napoleon's victory was assured. None of Edgewood's sources had an actual name, but several of them included references to "the lady" who would soon be rescued from the clutches of the British.

As Edgewood had pointed out, "It is obviously some sort of kidnapping plot on the part of the French, but the devil of it is that, right now, Vivian is in just as much danger from the Crown. Until we spring the trap and *Masquerade* is over, she could be seen as a traitor who is planning to betray her country, and could be arrested—or worse—by the British."

The only thing Edgewood's sources seemed to agree upon was that the "rescue" would take place in two days' time. The day after tomorrow. Whit had until then to make sure Vivian would be safe from all enemies—both foreign and domestic.

Edgewood had called in what additional forces he could, but most of their men were already deployed to carry out *Masquerade*. "You have Hammond, of course," he told Whit, "and by Sunday evening we can have enough men here to surround Haversham House. Until then, I suggest you keep her in your sight at all times."

"I'll do my best," replied Whit with a grimace, "but enticing as that sounds, it's going to be difficult. She has not exhibited a penchant for doing what I tell her to do."

Now, from beneath almost-closed eyelids, he watched as Vivian took down her hair from the stylish upsweep and brushed it out. His mind was busy reviewing the facts that troubled him most. First, Vivian already had scandal attached to her name. If things went wrong with *Masquerade*, the Crown would need someone to blame, and she would be a most convenient suspect. Second, he was the only person—other than the Prince Regent—who had the authority to ensure her safety. Third, if something happened to him, Vivian would have no champion and would most likely be arrested immediately and found guilty of treason, with only the barest mockery of a trial. Even Edgewood would not be able to stop the onslaught of lies and half-truths.

His heart stopped at the thought of it—Vivian in prison awaiting a trial or Vivian convicted for a crime he knew she had not committed. Given enough time, of course, she would be completely exonerated and absolved of all charges, but in the meantime, she was both the probable subject of a French kidnapping scheme and the unwitting bait in a carefully orchestrated British stratagem to identify the traitors responsible for the ongoing sale of arms and munitions to the enemy.

Granted, it wasn't his idea for her to create her ciphers and sell them to the newspapers and so become embroiled in this whole business—which is exactly what she would say to him if she were privy to the conversations going on in his head. However, he *was* the one who had initially suspected and accused her. It was he who had involved her even more by divulging his association with the Home Office, and it was he who had...entangled her in other ways as well.

And so, while a part of him—and right now a very insistent part of him—would like nothing more than to spend the rest of the night practicing the Grecian art of making love with Vivian, the rest of him was trying to figure out how to successfully protect her from his enemies—and from his friends.

Whit watched in fascination as Vivian loosely braided her long hair. She was sitting in her shift and nothing else. Physically, he was certainly ready for a night of passion, but he simply could not turn his mind from the fact that she was in danger. She finished with her hair and looked over at him. And then, without a word, she crossed the room and knelt in front of him, between his knees. Her breasts brushed his thighs as she leaned in. She raised one hand and traced the furrow on his brow with her fingertip as she wrinkled her own.

"What are you thinking about so intently?" she asked softly, still trying to erase the worried crease.

He did not answer. He could not—which was part of what distressed him so greatly. He mirrored her actions by tracing the line on her forehead. Then he leaned forward to kiss the same place. "It is not something for you to worry about," he answered. "I will not have you getting wrinkles just because I cannot figure out the solution."

"Is there something I can…"

He moved his fingertip to her lips. "Shhhh," he murmured. "Let us think of something else. In fact, I have several suggestions we should consider."

Vivian laughed and stood up. She reseated herself on his lap, straddling his legs and wiggling her bottom until his arousal fit snugly between her thighs. "I believe I can guess at least one of those suggestions," she whispered in his ear, "but I fear I would be sharing my bed not just with you but also with these thoughts that plague you. Would it not help to talk it through? Perhaps a solution would present itself if you looked at the problem from a different angle."

"Finding a solution is not the problem, my dear. I know the solution. The problem is in convincing others that my solution is the one that should be followed."

"How so? Are you not the great and powerful Duke of Whitley? Do you not command a great duchy as well as lesser lands? Can you not use your colossal arrogance and pompousness to manipulate any mere mortals who would dare to disagree with you? And failing that, can you not just glare at the uncooperative individuals with the cold, blue eyes of the Ice Duke until they do your bidding?"

Throughout her soliloquy, Whit's smile had grown bigger and bigger. At the mention of the Ice Duke, he laughed. "How wise you are, my dear. I shall take your advice from this minute forward."

He rose and pulled her into a passionate kiss that left her breathless, and then he stood her back on her feet, still a bit wobbly. Holding her shoulders, he looked down into her eyes. "Listen to me, Vivian. I do need your help, but you must do as I say without question. We must work quickly. I need you to get dressed again—*not* your toga—just a simple day dress will do, but hurry. I will be back as soon as I can, and I will tell you everything then. Lock the door after me and stay here. Do not open it for anyone but me."

He started toward the door and then another thought occurred to him. "And Vivian, I mean it this time. Do not leave this room, or I swear I will take you over my knee."

He pulled open the door, smiling slightly at the stunned silence behind him that was Vivian's only response. He had a couple of favors to call in. Luckily the bishop was an early riser.

Chapter 30

Her east-facing window was showing a pale pink sky as dawn approached. Vivian sat in front of the looking glass in her room, fully dressed. Whit had been gone for almost an hour now, and she was beginning to imagine all manner of things to have delayed him. Her most dire thoughts were punctuated with visions of Annie being taken prisoner and held captive alone and frightened, and of Lord Blount warning she had not heard the last from him.

She jumped at the knock on her door and hurried across the room. She unlocked the door and pulled it open. The duke stood on the other side.

He stepped into her room and quietly closed the door behind him. "Please explain to me the point of locking your door if you unlock it to anyone who knocks? Did you not think to ask who it was?"

"Are you here just to berate me, or are you going to tell me what is going on?"

"We need to go. Now. And be quiet." Whit took her arm and all but pushed her out the door and down the hallway.

"If you wouldn't walk so quickly, I could keep up," hissed Vivian. "Where are we going?"

Whit didn't reply but took her hand and continued his long strides down the stairs with Vivian trailing behind him like a kite. Out on the terrace, she jerked her hand from his grasp and planted her feet firmly on the stone. She crossed her arms over her bosom and scowled at him. "I am not taking another step until you tell me our destination."

Whit glared back at her. Then he sighed.

"To the country home of Bishop Wren. He is a neighbor of Lady Haversham's and an old friend of mine." He grabbed her hand again and pulled her down the path toward the stables. "Come on."

"Whit, listen to me. I've been thinking about another way to—why are we going to see the bishop?"

"We are going to be married."

Vivian stopped dead in her tracks and shook her hand free of his. "Married? What are you talking about? Have you been injured in the head?"

Whit reached for her hand again, but she stepped back, just out of his reach.

"I have not been injured—at least not yet. But if I am, I'll be damned if I'll let you be tried for treason. Come *on*."

Vivian allowed herself to be propelled forward. "I don't understand what you're saying, Whit. What makes you think you're going to be injured? And why do you think we are going to be married?"

"Would it be possible for you just to trust me? I will explain once we are on our way." By now they had reached the stables. As he had directed, a dog cart was hitched up and ready to go. He handed her up to the narrow seat and climbed in after her. Taking the ribbons from the groom, he chirruped to the bay mare and they started off.

As they rode, Whit explained. "You are currently the prime suspect in a spy ring that is providing ciphers to the French. At the moment, the evidence against you is overwhelming and will get worse. If something goes wrong, without my protection you will most likely be put in prison to await a trial for treason, which could take years. I am well connected at the Home Office. I know they would afford my family all due consideration—especially the Duchess of Whitley, which you will be as my wife."

"And if I refuse?"

"Refuse what?"

"Refuse to marry you."

"I have just told you that you will be my duchess."

"Yes, thank you. I heard that. The part I did *not* hear was the part where you *ask* me. And the part where you tell me what happens if I refuse."

Whit was silent as he considered her words. "If I *asked* you to marry me, what would you say?"

"I would refuse, of course."

"Then you don't give me much incentive for asking, do you, my lady?"

"This whole conversation is ludicrous."

"I couldn't agree more. When we get to the home of Bishop Wren, however, he will insist upon asking if you will take me to be your husband. I will then insist that you say 'yes.' You had better get used to the idea. Otherwise this is going to be a very long day."

"Is that a threat, your grace?"

"I like to think of it more as an observation."

Vivian was silent. Her frustration with this man was proving to be very wearing. "Why will you insist that I say 'yes'?"

"I believe I just explained it all to you. The evidence against you is overwhelming, and until everything gets sorted out—"

"You make it all sound so logical."

"Thank you. I tried to examine all the possibilities and come up with the best solution."

"It wasn't a compliment, your grace." Another few moments of silence. "May I ask *you* a question?"

"Certainly."

"Do *you* think I'm a spy for the French? Do you think I am a traitor?"

"That was two questions, but 'no' on both counts."

Vivian smiled, then frowned as she mulled over his answers, trying to see if they contained any hint of a reason to marry him. "So…as I understand it, we are to be married because you believe that I am neither a spy nor a traitor?"

"That is one way to look at it."

"Is there another way to look at it, your grace? Because I must tell you, if you think that I am going to marry you and, for the smallest of reasons, trade my independent life for the privilege of becoming the property of any man—much less the property of an arrogant, pompous, infuriating duke with a heart of ice—until death do us part, then you are sadly mistaken. And you and your bishop will be waiting until hell freezes over to hear me say 'yes'!"

Vivian crossed her arms and stared straight ahead. For the first time in her life she regretted not wearing a bonnet—it would have blocked her view of the lunatic man beside her. After all the things he had accused her of…after all the things he had said to her…and all the things she had said to him. Now he wanted to marry her?

The silence between them was heavy, but the duke

broke it a few moments later.

"May I ask *you* a question, my lady?"

"Certainly."

"Why would you *not* accept an offer of marriage from me? Do you *want* to go to prison? Do you want to be accused of betraying your country?"

"That was three questions, not one," said Vivian tartly.

"The second and third were rhetorical. It is the first that matters."

Vivian sighed. "Obviously I do not want to go to prison or be accused of something I have not done. But that is not a basis for marriage, your grace. Certainly, not for me. I was married once, so I no longer have to worry about being a spinster." Her tone softened. "And because of you, I will not go to my grave without knowing the wonderful pleasures that can be shared between a man and a woman. But the truth is I know very little about you. I don't know if we could be happy together or even if you think happiness is important in a marriage. Do you realize that we were formally introduced less than two weeks ago?"

"Many *ton* marriages are based on much less, Vivian. My own mother and father first met on their wedding day."

"And were they happy, your grace? Is theirs a model you want to emulate?"

"No, but their lack of happiness had nothing to do with how long they had known each other when they were wed. It had more to do with the fact that my father was a mean, insufferable tyrant. He was interested in my mother only for her ability to provide him with an acceptable heir. Once I was born, he went back to his previous life with his mistress and had nothing more to do with us. I want you to marry me so I can protect you. So you will be free to do the things that make you happy."

Vivian listened to the sound of the horse's hooves on the dirt road. He was right. Most *ton* marriages were about property and heirs and had little to do with happiness…or love. But was she willing to do without those things in her own marriage?

Her heart told her the answer before she could even finish forming the question. She could not—she *would* not—settle. She had made a poor first choice with Henry, and she would not make another mistake. Not now, not when she knew how unpredictable life could be and how fragile. She had seen how things could change in an instant—for better or for worse. She could not—she *would* not—gamble so much on a chance that she and he would be happy. Having his protection was a huge asset and a great honor, but it was not enough. She wanted his love.

And, she admitted sadly to herself, that was something he would not—or *could* not—offer.

"I am honored, your grace, but if your protection is the only reason for this decision, then I must regretfully decline your very kind offer. I will not marry you."

"It would not be the only reason, Vivian. I—"

A gunshot cracked in the quiet morning, tearing through Whit's words as well as his flesh. Vivian could see a dark red patch on his left shoulder growing larger and larger as, with his right hand, he pulled a pistol from beneath the seat. She screamed as three masked men on horseback surrounded their cart. Whit managed to settle the bay, and leaned over to shield Vivian with his body.

"Get her!" said the big man who had shot Whit.

Two men came up on Vivian's side of the cart. The one in the lead lunged at her, but she fought back, struggling and kicking and making contact more than once. Whit stood and fired his pistol. The first man tumbled from his horse, dead before he hit the ground.

The second man slapped the hindquarters of the mare, causing her to rear and throw Whit to the ground. The horse ran only a few yards before the man pulled on the harness to halt the beast. He then aimed his pistol back at the still figure of Whit on the ground, but Vivian grabbed at his arm and the shot went wild, missing its mark. Cursing, the man reached over and caught Vivian by the waist, pulling her onto his mount in front of him. She bit the arm that held her and kicked at his horse.

"Bitch!" The man hit her hard across the face. Momentarily stunned, she slumped back, grabbing and pulling at his coat as she tried to unseat him. She heard someone yell and looked up to see the big man with his reloaded pistol aimed at Whit's still form on the ground.

Vivian froze.

"Stop!" she cried. "Don't shoot. Please. Leave him alone and I will go with you quietly, I promise. If you shoot him, you will also have to kill me, for I will never stop fighting."

Breathing heavily, she waited for a decision from the big man. She craned her neck to see if Whit had moved, but he was still motionless on the ground.

The man looked from Vivian to Whit and then lowered his pistol. "Let's go," he called to the man holding Vivian in front of him. "We were only paid to bring the woman. Come on. We have a boat to catch."

The whole incident had taken less than five minutes.

Chapter 31

"Whit, where are you?"

Lord Hammond called out again in the silence of the still morning. Like the other men riding beside him, he continuously scanned the path ahead, the trees, the bushes—everywhere for any sign of the missing duke.

Behind him, Edgewood's voice was louder. "Damn it, Whit, answer! Where are you?" He turned to Avery. "Are you sure they came this way?"

Lord Hammond shrugged. "The only thing the groom could tell me was that the two of them set out around dawn. When the horse came back with the empty dog cart, they sent word to me."

Edgewood called out to the side riders, "The newest tracks lead this way. Two of you come with us. The rest of you stay on the main road. We'll meet where the two paths join back up, near Bishop Wren's house."

"What the devil was he thinking, Edgewood?" said Avery. "Why did he not tell me, you—anyone—of his plans? That's not like Whit. He's usually more deliberate than this."

"I think we have to face the possibility that he was taken against his will."

"But who would…?" Lord Hammond glanced over at Edgewood and then snorted. "Surely you don't think… Edgewood, do you expect me to believe that

Lady Rowden has kidnapped the Duke of Whitley? Are you quite mad?"

"That's not what I'm saying. But if someone kidnapped Lady Rowden, wouldn't Whit follow without waiting to tell anyone? He thinks he's invincible, so he'd assume he could handle everything himself—even though he says he never assumes anything."

"I could see him doing that," said Hammond. "That sounds like my pig-headed brother, thinking he can do something that twenty of his men could not."

"Or maybe someone abducted them both."

"Also a possibility," agreed Hammond.

"We should also consider that it's possible he doesn't *want* to be tracked," said Edgewood.

"What are you talking about? Why on earth would he *not* want to be tracked?"

"Maybe he had something other than work on his mind."

Avery snorted again. "Whit? Having something other than work on his mind?"

"Have you not been paying attention these past few days, my lord? Your brother has developed quite a *tendre* for the lady."

Hammond furrowed his forehead. "You mean Lady Rowden?"

"My God, is there another? The man could not possibly have time for *two* affairs."

"No, no. I had not realized things had gone that far, but you're right. He has seemed overly agreeable for several days now."

"Perhaps you didn't notice because you were so busy with your own romance?"

"Whit told you about that, did he?"

Lord Hammond's embarrassed grin lasted only a few seconds. "Oh, my God! Whit!"

Edgewood had already dismounted and was kneeling beside the body of his best friend.

"Edgewood, is he…?"

"He's still breathing, but he's unconscious, and there's a lot of blood. His arm looks broken."

Avery had dismounted to examine the second body on the ground, still masked. He pulled off the mask as he called out, "This one is dead."

On the ground, Whit moved his lips slightly.

"Take it easy, old chap," said Edgewood as he bent closer to hear his friend.

"Not unconscious. Conserving strength. Th' hell have you been?"

In a matter of just half an hour, the bandages that Edgewood always carried in his pack had been put to good use. His experience as a medic in the early part of the wars helped him splint and immobilize Whit's broken arm. The injured spymaster now sat upright against a tree, his bloodstained shirt in tatters, as most of it had been used to stem the flow of blood and bandage the wound.

"That's the best I can do until we get the bullet out. It will continue to ooze until then. How does your arm feel?"

"It hurts like the devil," snapped Whit. "How do you think it feels? Can we go now? Do you have another shirt in that pack of yours? And I'll need to borrow a cloak to cover the blood on my breeches."

"What difference does that make? You can change when we get back to Haversham House."

"We're not going back to Haversham House. At least, not yet."

"I'm sorry—is there a social call you need to make?"

Whit leveled an icy glare at his rescuers. "We are going after Lady Rowden."

"Whit, you are in no condition to—"

"I do beg your pardon, Avery, but I have not asked a question and am in no need of a discussion."

"Hammond is right, Whit. You need medical attention. You need a physician to get the bullet out, and you need someone to set that arm properly."

"And I have every intention of doing all of that just as soon as we find and rescue Lady Rowden. Now, will one of you gentlemen help me up, or shall I do it myself? Undoubtedly such an effort on my part would restart the bleeding and undo all of your hard work, Edgewood. A hand, if you please?"

"Do you think you can ride?"

"Do you have a horse?"

"Yes."

"Then I can ride."

"Whit, this—"

"The sooner Lady Rowden is rescued, the sooner I can get the medical help you crave on my behalf. The lady saved my life—twice. A rescue is the least that I owe her."

"Whit, tell us where she was taken. We'll take you back to the house and then set out to—"

Whit sighed. He then looked up at his brother and his friend with his best icy blue glare and one raised eyebrow. His low voice was pleasant which made it all the more menacing. "In what way have I been unclear?"

Edgewood looked over at Avery and shrugged his shoulders. He then reached under Whit's good right arm and helped him to his feet. He kept hold of Whit's elbow until the duke had steadied himself, and then he called orders to the other men.

"Perry, you and Jessup come with us. Stratton, give the duke your horse. You and Evans double up and get back to the house. Tell Lady Haversham to have a physician ready."

"And the bishop," added Whit.

"The bishop?" said Avery. "Don't worry, Whit. You'll make it. Only let me take you back while Edgewood goes on to find Lady Rowden."

"Not for me, you dolt. When I return to Haversham House, I intend to marry the lady."

Avery, his eyebrows at new heights, again traded looks with Edgewood, who, after glancing at Whit, amended his orders to his men. "And tell Lady Haversham to call Bishop Wren with a special license to await the return of the Duke of Whitley."

"And then follow us to Selsey with a carriage, supplies, and two more men," said Whit, walking over to where Stratton held his mount. "Now, help me up on this damned horse."

Chapter 32

Vivian kept her word. They traveled hard and they traveled fast, and she was forced to hold on tightly to the man who had struck her. She lived in fear of falling off and being trampled, and she lived in fear of what lay ahead, but her greatest fear was what she had left behind.

Whit was dead. If his neck had not been broken when he fell, there was always the bullet in his chest. The two of them had left Haversham House early— before even the servants had begun to stir. It would be hours before anyone realized they were gone, and hours more before anyone would be able to track their route and find Whit, who, if he hadn't died from the bullet or the fall was surely dead from loss of blood.

Vivian closed her eyes tightly, knowing she was right, praying she was wrong, and hoping against hope that the man who had literally laid down his life for her still lived. Tears rolled down her face as she remembered Whit protecting her to the end—even as his life's blood spilled out from his wound.

The infuriating man had found his way into her walled-up heart, he had warmed that heart with passion and caring, and he had offered to protect her with his name and his position.

And the last thing she had said to him was that she did not want to marry him.

If only he might survive. If only she could tell him how very much she cared for him. If only she could tell him that she loved him and would do anything he asked of her.

****

They traveled south, toward the ocean. Vivian could smell the change in the air, and she saw the fields and hedgerows eventually replaced by coniferous forests and sandy hills. Her two captors spoke little, and when they did, their words were lost in the wind.

When they finally rode into the village that had grown up around the busy harbor, Vivian felt a sense of dread. There were so many people. How would anyone be able to find her here? How long would her captors keep her here? What was their final destination?

She had heard the men whispering about France, and one of them spoke English with a heavy French accent. Is that where they would go from here? What were they planning to do with her? What were they planning to do *to* her?

Eventually the horses stopped in front of a cottage that was set a little apart from the other houses, and the two men dismounted. Although they had long since removed their masks, Vivian still had not seen their faces. The first man—the big man who had shot Whit—turned to give the reins of his horse to his partner and Vivian gasped. At her sudden intake of breath, Lord Blount raised his eyebrows and smiled.

"Lady Rowden. I trust you enjoyed the ride? My friend will lead you around back, where you may refresh yourself before I present you to my employer. He is most eager to meet you."

She'd ridden astride, and her skirts were rucked up

to above her knees. The man who rode in front of her on the long trip ran his hand up her leg. She kicked him in the arm, and he laughed, reaching up to pull her from the saddle into his arms. The moment her feet touched the ground, she jerked away from him, putting as much distance as possible between them. The man laughed again at her pitiful attempts to avoid his touch. He grabbed her by the arm and led her around to the back of the cottage.

Vivian used the hem of her dress and water from the pump to wash most of the dust from her face and hands. After a few moments, Lord Blount reappeared and offered Vivian his arm. She raised her chin contemptuously and looked the other way. Blount laughed at her defiance, grabbed her by the elbow, and pushed her ahead of him as he stepped inside the cottage.

****

"Vivian, may I present your host, Monsieur…ah… Jones. Monsieur Jones, Lady Rowden."

Jones took Vivian's hand and raised it to his lips. She shuddered at the touch of his soft hand. When he spoke, there was no trace of a French accent—just the King's English as might have been spoken by any member of the *ton*.

"I am delighted to meet you at last, Lady Rowden. I have heard so much about you, and I am, of course, familiar with your work. Please sit down."

Vivian sat on the edge of the only chair in the room and stared at her captor. "What is it that you want of me? Why have you brought me here?"

"Excellent. I like getting right to the business of things," said Monsieur Jones. His voice was low and mesmerizing, almost soothing. "Your presence has been requested by the Emperor himself, so it has been my very great honor to pave the way for your meeting with him. Our ship sails with the turning tide—about three hours from now. The trip is quite short, actually—just across the Channel. Once in France, you will be conducted to the place where the Emperor now resides. You will be welcomed because of your skills, and I will be the hero who brought you there."

Monsieur Jones touched a fingertip to the cut on her cheek. "If you do not struggle and fight, you will not be hurt. If you do..." He shrugged his shoulders. "The level of comfort you enjoy during our time together is entirely up to you. If you behave, we will not be forced to bind your hands and feet or put a gag in your mouth."

The man turned to Blount. "Did you take her from her room as we discussed? Did Estelle's key work in the lock?"

"There was no need. Lady Rowden came to us." Blount was beaming with pride. "On our way to the house, we encountered Lady Rowden and her beau out for an early morning ride. She put up a bit of a fight— kicking and screaming and biting—but I managed to get her out of the cart and up behind Harvey."

"Did you give her this mark on her face?" Monsieur Jones caressed Vivian's cheek again.

Blount frowned. "That was Harvey. She fights like a spitfire. When Harvey pulled her up on his horse, she bit him and kicked the horse, so he hit her."

"What of our other friend?"

"Dead. Felled by the great Ice Duke himself with a single shot. Of course, that was the last thing the duke did after I put a bullet in his chest. I made a deal with the lady that if she came with us peacefully and stopped her screaming, I wouldn't put a bullet through his head."

Monsieur Jones' face turned pale. "The Ice Duke? Do you mean the Duke of Whitley? You had the Duke of Whitley literally at your feet and you left him there? You idiot! Do you know how much money we could have made on his ransom? Plus we had the perfect way to make him give us information."

Blount looked confused.

"*Her*, you imbecile! We apply a knife creatively to the lady in his presence, and he is desperate to save her from pain and mutilation by giving us any information he has. But, no. In your great wisdom, you left him there."

"Harvey said he was already dead." Blount's weak explanation sounded whiny. "Besides, we got her to come peacefully by telling her we wouldn't kill him. If she saw that he was already dead, she wouldn't have come so easily, and we might have lost her too."

Vivian spoke quietly. "Are you sure he was dead?"

"If the bullet didn't kill him, then the fall did." Blount chuckled at his own cleverness.

"My lord," said Jones, "might I have a word?" He led the way into the next room. Vivian heard what sounded like a brief struggle and then the sound of something heavy falling to the floor. A few minutes later, Jones re-entered the room.

"I do apologize, my lady. I have taken care of that loose end. The baron will not be bothering you anymore. We will now proceed to the tavern near the dock. I have taken a room there for myself. You and my man can wait in the public room. They have an area there that is suitable for ladies with their escorts. When the tide turns, we will be ferried out to the ship and on our way. We will be in France well before sundown."

Vivian stared up at the man. She would not give him the satisfaction of seeing her tears. She sat straight, her back stiff, never touching the back of the chair. Thoughts of Whit whirled in her head. Would she know, she wondered, would she know in her heart if he were dead? She alternated between fervent prayers and agonizing fears. If only he had survived the shooting. If only someone had found him. Please, she begged whomever was listening. Please let him be alive. Please let him be safe. All of her prayers and promises boiled down to a single, heartfelt plea that she whispered over and over.

"Please."

Chapter 33

Monsieur Jones went to the door to summon Harvey. "We will proceed to the tavern," he said, and then grinned at Vivian. "I am anxious for you to show your skills to the Emperor, my dear."

"What skills are you talking about?" said Vivian. "I still don't understand why I am here and why you have gone to all the trouble of kidnapping me. For what? What skill is it that I am supposed to possess?"

"Come now, Lady Rowden," said Monsieur Jones. "You are famous for your puzzles and ciphers. Your work is published in one of the leading papers in London. It is those skills that have impressed the Emperor."

"Puzzles? Oh, yes, I do like to solve the puzzles that are published in the papers—or maybe I should say I like to *try* to solve them. I almost never finish any of them. Some of them are quite difficult."

"My sources have told me of your skills, madam, so there is no need to deny it. Estelle was quite complimentary about your ability to create ciphers quickly, which was quite unusual for her. She almost never has anything pleasant to say about other women."

"I have not known Estelle long, but even she can tell you that she has never seen me create a—what did you call it? A cipher? I just call them all puzzles." Vivian laughed. "But I wouldn't know how to go about creating one. I'm afraid you have made a rather significant mistake, monsieur. If you are planning to impress someone with my puzzle-making skills, you will be very embarrassed when it becomes clear I have none—although I did copy out the puzzles that Henry created. Just ask Estelle."

"Unfortunately, that is not possible. According to my sources, when she was questioned by your government spies, she told them more than she should have. She betrayed me, and by her own admission, she knew too much. I dealt with her betrayal so that she will spill no more secrets."

"Another loose end?"

"Precisely. Not that it matters. It is you the Emperor wants. It has been you since Henri discovered your unusual abilities after your marriage."

Vivian laughed. "Oh, my goodness. What on earth did Henry tell you?" She could see that she had the man's attention. "The puzzles were not *mine*. In fact, Henry liked to tease me about how badly I did when I tried to solve the ones from the paper. No, *he* was the brilliant creator of all the puzzles. And the ones that I sold to the paper? He created all of those right before he died. I thought they would last me forever—pin money, you know—but I delivered the last one to the *Mail Observer* last week." She sighed. "Oh, how I *wish* I knew how to make those puzzles like Henry did."

There was silence as Vivian waited to see how the man would react to her story. Would he rethink his plan to take her to France? Even if her story caused him to delay until the next turning of the tide, it would be worth it. Maybe by then she could bribe one of the guards or find an ally in the harbor town. The longer she could put off their departure, the better her chances of finding a way to escape. Once aboard the ship, all hope was lost.

"You would have me believe that it was your drunken, whoring, idiot husband who was the brilliant codemaker? That I killed the wrong person?" Jones laughed. "Do you think me a fool, Lady Rowden?"

"Do you mean to say that when you killed Henry, you did it because you thought *I* created all of those puzzles? Don't tell me that my idiot husband, as you call him, fooled Napoleon's great network of spies! You truly did not know it was *he*? I just assumed that you eliminated him so he would not sell his secret talent to the British and create ciphers and puzzles for *them*. Oh, how he would laugh if he could see this."

Jones struck Vivian across the face. "You will learn not to play games with me, my lady. I play to win, and I do not like to lose."

Vivian covered her cheek with her hand. "You can believe what you want, monsieur, but that does not change how things are. My only contribution was that I wrote a better hand than Henry. I copied all of his puzzles so they were legible—otherwise no one could read them. So perhaps I did play an important part. But, as I said, without Henry creating new ones, there are no more puzzles. I don't know what your Emperor wants from me, but all I can offer is a neat hand."

Monsieur Jones studied Vivian for a moment or two before he smiled and gave a half laugh. "You are an exceptional liar, Lady Rowden. You almost had me believing you. But you forget that I knew your husband, my lady. I talked with him. He and I spent a great deal of time together. And I know that he was intellectually incapable of producing even one of the ciphers published by the *Mail Observer*—much less providing them on a weekly basis. Come now. It is time we go to the tavern. Once I have delivered you to the Emperor, you will find out what he requires of you. And never fear, my lady, the Emperor's men have ways to get what they want."

He nodded at Harvey, who pushed Vivian outside to the waiting carriage. Another man was already inside. After the short ride to town, they stopped in front of a tavern beside the docks. Harvey and the other man escorted Vivian inside to sit at a table in the back. A few minutes later, Monsieur Jones entered the tavern, ordered an ale, and took a seat in the shadows near the stairs where he could keep an eye on the codemaker.

Chapter 34

It was a ragtag collection of men that regrouped on the hill above the bustling fishing village of Selsey. The busy harbor was filled with ships of all sizes—all waiting for the tide to turn before they could sail through the harbor entrance and continue on to their various destinations. Flags from all over the world flew from the vessels, confirming that this was indeed an international port. Taverns along the waterfront were doing a booming business while passengers and off-duty sailors waited for the next turning of the tide. The harbor was congested with small rowboats and dinghies ferrying all manner of passengers and freight to the larger ships. Out on the ships, captains and first mates plotted their courses and oversaw the longshoremen who loaded and unloaded cargo of all kinds—most of it legal, some not.

"We need to find out where they have her," said the duke. "Two men brought her here. There is at least one other man, possibly more."

"I'll send young Jessup to reconnoiter and report back here," said Edgewood. "If we're lucky, they will be keeping her near the docks. The tide turns in just over two hours, which is when all of these ships will set sail. We have to find her by then."

While Jessup canvassed the waterfront, Edgewood and Avery did their best to make Whit presentable. He insisted on being part of the rescue party and, as his exasperated brother finally proclaimed, if he ended up dead, he had no one to blame but himself.

Not everyone could afford to while away the time in a room or private parlor at the exorbitant prices the taverns charged, but the most respectable-looking of the three taverns did boast a somewhat secluded area of the common room where ladies could sit with their escorts. When Jessup visited this establishment, he saw two women who matched Lady Rowden's description. He ordered an ale and chatted nonchalantly with the barkeep. After finishing the last of his pint, he returned to the hill and reported back that he believed Lady Rowden was in the third tavern, guarded by two men.

Edgewood laid out his plan. Jessup would stay back with the horses. Avery would go into the tavern to confirm that Vivian was there and establish a stronghold at a table to the side. Next, Whit and his valet, Cooper, would go in together. Edgewood would go in last. Upon a signal from Edgewood, they would neutralize the men around Vivian and get her out of the tavern. They would then ride on horseback back to the top of the hill where the duke's carriage waited.

What could possibly go wrong?

Chapter 35

The key to it all was, and had been from the beginning, patience. And he could be very patient. He caught the eye of the barmaid and signaled for another ale.

The waiting must be endured. It was simply a part of the game. They waited to board the boat that would take them to the anchored ship. Once on the ship, they waited for the tide to reverse itself so they could depart the harbor. When they were clear of the harbor, they waited while the ship made the short voyage across the Channel to the continent. After docking in France, they waited for the short trip to the Emperor's headquarters.

And then, the waiting would be over, and his triumphant homecoming would begin.

Monsieur Jones was already dressed in his most elegant attire. Only a few hours more and he would be a hero. The Emperor himself would offer his congratulations. The generals would put the codemaker to work immediately, and victory would be in their grasp.

He signaled for another ale.

Jones briefly regretted the death of Lord Blount. It would have been satisfying to share the anticipation of this victory with someone who appreciated the importance of the moment—especially a fellow countryman. Blount had proven to be an adequate replacement for Henri after the viscount's demise, but Estelle had reported that Blount was threatening Lady Rowden with blackmail. His greedy actions could have endangered the entire plan. What's more, his careless handling of the kidnapping could not be forgiven. He had squandered the opportunity to capture the Duke of Whitley. The value of such a high-ranking peer was immeasurable and could have led to a very fruitful prisoner exchange.

Instead, Blount had left the man in the middle of the road without even knowing for certain he was dead. Such a lapse was unpardonable. Blount had no vision and no initiative. He followed orders and looked out for himself, but as far as seizing an opportunity or improvising—well, that had turned out to be his fatal flaw.

Monsieur Jones had directed his men to sit with Lady Rowden at the most secluded table for security, but also for his amusement. He enjoyed watching her. She was uncommonly beautiful even in that filthy gown. It was in the current style that did much to show off a lady's assets, and she had plenty to show off. He had a wager of sorts with himself that at least one of his men would steal a kiss from the lady before their ship sailed. Of course that meant he would have to kill or at least severely injure the perpetrator. He grinned. A *kiss* from her might not be worth dying for, but bedding her? That would definitely be worth the risk—just as the late viscount had always intimated.

Just imagining her in his bed made him hard. He nodded when the barmaid asked if he wanted another ale.

He thought back to Lady Rowden's claim that she

was not the codemaker. The thought that he had almost fallen for her little ploy infuriated him. She had thought she could outsmart him—make him doubt himself. It was a clever ruse, but she had severely underestimated who he was. He should teach her a lesson. Show her who was smarter. Punish her for lying to him. He shifted as the ache in his loins grew.

Bedding the codemaker was an excellent idea. With her beneath him, he would show her that he was her superior in every way. Why shouldn't he sample the favors of the codemaker before handing her over to his Emperor? Who knew how many would have her after that, but he would be first. He would go up to the room he had reserved and then have one of the men bring her up under some pretense. There was plenty of time before the tide turned, and it would certainly make the waiting more pleasurable.

He rose and left money on the table for his bill. He stopped briefly at the table where Vivian sat with her captors and spoke softly to the man on her right. The man grinned widely and nodded. He left a gold sovereign for each man, held up a splayed hand to indicate five minutes, and climbed the stairs to his room.

Ale, lust, and visions of grandeur had dazzled him and dulled his normally finely honed senses. He had not noticed the subtle change in the occupants of the tavern.

But then, almost no one did.

****

The idea was to get all four of them into the tavern, one or two at a time. It helped them that she was not hidden in a private room; it hurt them that they still had no clear description of the leader and didn't know which one he was or how many men in the tavern were working for him. They didn't know exactly which men would fight and which men would run at the first sign of trouble.

It was a smart strategy, Whit admitted to himself, hiding her in plain sight. But then, he'd expect nothing less from the man in charge of Napoleon's intelligence gathering.

The other thing that Whit knew about the leader was that he was a killer. The bodies of Estelle and Baron Blount confirmed what Whit already suspected of the man's *modus operandi*. He never left loose ends. Edgewood's intelligence reported that Estelle had been the man's mistress for many years and yet she had been summarily executed. There had been no attempt to bury or even hide her body. Likewise with Blount.

While the duke appreciated the fact that there would be no messy trial for the baron, the death of a peer was yet another item on the list. Whit had no doubt that the person responsible for garroting his associate, murdering his mistress, shooting a duke, and kidnapping a vicountess would not hesitate to kill everyone in the tavern in order to make his escape.

If they were to come out of this with no further bloodshed, they would need a perfectly executed plan and all sorts of good luck.

Avery went into the tavern first. He was to get a table, order food, and then ask directions to the necessary so he could report back to Edgewood. After just a few minutes, he reappeared back outside.

"She's in there. In the back left corner, between two men. Both have pistols. I think her hands are tied, but I can't be certain. She looks tired. She has a black eye and her cheek is cut, but other than that, I think she fares well enough."

Whit tensed at the mention of Vivian's injuries, but Edgewood glared up at him. "Please remember, your grace, that I am in charge of this operation and you are here—in spite of my better judgment—under my command."

Whit took a deep breath and nodded once.

Edgewood softened for just a moment. "We'll get her out, Whit. We all have a great deal at stake, but none as much as you. Have faith that you've trained us well."

"I'm going back in," said Avery.

Edgewood nodded.

Five minutes later, Whit's valet began a slow advance into the tavern with his employer leaning heavily on his arm. The bandages on Whit's chest and arm were real, but the bandage around his head as well as the limp and the cane added another dimension to his perceived infirmity. Cooper hovered over him like a worried mother hen and established him at a table in the corner opposite Vivian and her captors. Once they had ordered from the serving maid, the two men sat in silence, looking straight ahead and speaking to no one.

With everyone in place, Edgewood entered the tavern himself. He took a chair at an empty table, near the back exit, with a view of the whole common room. He ordered his breakfast and then lazily watched the actions of a man who was dressed much too formally for the morning. The man seemed to be on his way out. He paid his bill, but then made his way over to the table where Vivian sat. Edgewood hoped Whit did not see how this man stroked Vivian's bare arm or notice the bulge in his tight pantaloons. Was this dandy the leader of the spy ring they had been battling for more than two years? It was hard to believe that he could kill a man as big and strong as Lord Blount, and yet remembering the surprised look on Blount's corpse, Edgewood thought it quite possible. His familiarity with Vivian was a bad sign.

Edgewood watched as the man left a sovereign for each of Lady Rowden's escorts. He held up five fingers—perhaps indicating five minutes?—and then turned and made his way up the stairs.

****

Sure enough, approximately five minutes later, one of Vivian's captors stood up and urged her to rise, nodding toward the stairs. Vivian's eyes showed her fear and, as understanding dawned about what was planned for her in the room upstairs, she struggled against her captor. He jerked her to her feet and said something in her ear. Her eyes showed hope, and she let the man pull her out from behind the table and lead her toward the stairs. Edgewood could see now that her hands were bound in front of her, covered clumsily by her cloak.

Before Whit could move, Edgewood was on his feet, also headed toward the stairs. With a seemingly clumsy gait, he bumped into Vivian and inadvertently stepped on her foot.

"I do beg your pardon, m'lady," said Edgewood, looking Vivian directly in the eye. "Vertigo…from the boat, you see. I meant no disrespect." He doffed his hat and bowed unsteadily. "Just making my way out to the… Oh, beg pardon again, ma'am, for mentioning such a thing in front of a lady."

By this time, Vivian had recognized Edgewood. "The fault was mine entirely, my lord," she replied.

With a minimum of fuss, Whit's valet crept up behind the man still seated at Vivian's table and held a pistol to his back as he whispered words in his ear. The man stood up quietly and preceded Cooper out the back.

In the meantime, Whit had come up behind Vivian, his limp miraculously gone. He held a pistol to the back of the man holding Vivian's elbow. The man released Vivian. Coming up from behind Whit, Avery took Vivian's arm and started for the front door, while Whit turned his captive toward the back.

Edgewood nodded at Whit and started up the stairs. At the top, he drew his own pistol and opened the first door. The room was empty, as were the second and third rooms. In the fourth room, a window that faced the rear courtyard was open, the white curtains floating in the breeze. The bed had been creased as if someone had lain on top of the covers.

Looking out the window, Edgewood saw that a daring—or desperate—man could have climbed out onto the roof and easily dropped behind the bushes that grew up against the building. Muttering a curse, he hurried back down the steps and out the back. He shook his head at Whit who, with Cooper, had bound Vivian's two captors. The men raced around the tavern toward the docks. Rounding the corner, they saw Avery on the ground and saw the well-dressed man from inside the tavern put a cloth over Vivian's nose and mouth. Like a flower, she wilted immediately, and the man picked her up and carried her toward a rowboat at the end of the dock.

Leaving Cooper to minister to Avery, who was already sitting up, Edgewood and Whit ran down the path to the dock. Two burly sailors stood in their way. Employing his cane to his advantage, Whit pushed one of the men into the water and had engaged with the other man when he saw that, farther out on the dock, the man from the tavern was almost at the rowboat.

"Get Vivian!" he called to Edgewood.

Struggling under Vivian's dead weight, the well-dressed man suddenly realized that his burden would prevent his escape. He moved to the edge of the dock and dropped Vivian's drugged, lifeless body into the deep water. Free of his burden, he jumped into the waiting boat and called to the captain to push off.

Edgewood made his choice in an instant. As he jumped into the water after Vivian, he saw the well-dressed man grin and raise his hand in salute.

Chapter 36

Monsieur Jones had chosen this particular port for a reason. Its deep waters made it a popular destination for ships of all sizes, from all around the world. And when the tide flowed out of the harbor to the sea—as it would in a matter of minutes—the harbor came to life.

Just today, more than sixty vessels would weigh anchor and proceed out to sea. In this morass of ships, finding someone who wanted to be found would be difficult; finding someone who did *not* want to be found was next to impossible.

The craft that currently carried him out to the ship he had hired—a merchant ship flying the American flag—would eventually return to shore for another fare, but the captain would have conveniently forgotten everything about this particular passenger.

He signaled to the captain to detour around a fishing vessel. When the smaller boat was eclipsed by the larger one, Jones lay down on the bottom of the boat and covered himself with a tarp so he could not be seen from the shore or even from other boats. To anyone watching, it would seem that he had boarded the fishing boat. His captain then navigated to several other vessels—each time momentarily disappearing behind the ship, and then re-emerging on the other side. During one of these detours, Monsieur Jones actually climbed aboard the merchant ship that was carrying soft cotton from the new world up to Ireland. Anyone trying to follow him would be without a clue about which ship he boarded.

Once aboard, he changed into the clothes of a sailor and went up on deck. His help was not needed, so his main contribution was staying out of the way. On a whim, he took a spyglass and climbed to the crow's nest. He was curious to see if anyone was looking for him, and curious to see if there was still activity on the dock near the tavern. For all he knew, some of his men were still undercover and might have avoided the British net.

Chapter 37

The first darkness was different from this new darkness. The smell of ether was gone, but she was still floating. This darkness was cold, and while part of her mind told her to breathe, another part told her she could not. She was still surrounded by danger, but it was not the same danger as before.

Vivian slowly realized she was in the water—no, under the water. Cold water. Fear penetrated her brain and told her to struggle. Her arms would not move—they were tangled together. She tried to move her legs as she had in the lake with Whit, but her water-logged cloak wrapped around her like seaweed and pulled her down…down.

Fully awake now, Vivian was terrified, and could not tell in which direction lay the water's surface. When she finally detected a lighter section, she aimed her struggles in that direction, her lungs bursting.

A huge splash disoriented her again, and she fought against the waves that seemed determined to push her deeper. The darkness lurking around the edges of her consciousness began to close in again. Her lungs burned.

She heard voices—one of them calling her name and telling her to lean back and float. Float? Now? But it was a voice she knew she could trust, and floating seemed much easier than fighting. She relaxed onto her back and let her body's natural buoyancy take over as the darkness covered everything. She felt a push on her back and chest and heard another voice saying, "Breathe, Vivian. He needs you. Breathe."

All of a sudden she felt weightless, as if she were flying in the air, and then the first voice was back, hard and demanding.

"Take a breath, Vivian! Breathe...breathe! You're safe, sweetheart. Breathe."

Struggling against the pressure on her chest, Vivian took a big gulp of air. Coughing replaced the darkness. She took another breath. And another. Someone was pounding on her back.

When she finally opened her eyes, she saw piercing cornflower-blue eyes looking worriedly into hers and saw Whit kneeling beside her, holding her hand in his own.

"Ah," he said, smiling. "The lady returns."

****

So, the codemaker lived.

His spyglass confirmed that—although chaos still reigned at the edge of the dock—the person of one Lady Rowden seemed to have been rescued. Encircled by men from the tavern, the lady was sitting up and talking—even smiling.

Was the tall man with the injured arm the Duke of Whitley? And was that the Earl of Edgewood who had chosen to rescue a woman rather than capture an enemy he had pursued for more than two years? He owed the man a debt. One he intended to pay back as soon as possible.

He couldn't really blame the duke for saving Lady Rowden. Under the same circumstances, he might have done the same. The lady was beautiful and very clever—she had certainly played him. If he had not been so tormented by her claim that she was not the codemaker, he might have succeeded in his plan. Anger, doubt, and lust had made him careless and had lost him several good men, to boot. He would not allow that to happen again.

The ship was picking up speed as the sails caught the wind. The only thing that mattered now was his escape. He would be more careful next time.

Chapter 38

Vivian and Whit strolled silently in Aunt Thea's butterfly garden. Growing up, Vivian had always sought out this garden to bolster her spirits. It was one of her very favorite places, but today it brought her no joy. She did not want to do what she knew she must, and she was fairly certain it would break her heart in two.

Whit was alive and would be completely recovered in another week or two. She pasted on a smile to remind herself of that—even though her association with him must now come to an end.

"You know, my lady, the Crown's spymaster could make good use of your skills once we are married," remarked Whit, taking her hand with his good one.

Vivian replied lightly, "Have you not heard? The only skill I have is a neat hand for copying out ciphers. Besides, I've already met one spymaster, and if that man's British counterpart is anything like him, I am happy to decline the honor."

"I happen to know that Britain's spymaster is a top-notch fellow. All the ladies like him, and he is the life of any gathering. His friends and family sing his praises."

Vivian snorted. "He sounds unbearably pompous and quite arrogant. I wonder what his wife thinks of him."

"He is not married, but has plans to wed a rather cantankerous woman. From what I understand, he also hopes to involve her in increasing his domain."

"She must be a saint to put up with him, and a very unique lady if the spymaster is thinking about using her as a spy."

"Not as a spy, *per se…*"

"And why would he need to increase his domain? Napoleon has been captured and sent to Saint Helena. Does this man anticipate another escape? Is there another threat to the Crown?"

"There are always threats—both real and imagined—to the Crown, but I don't think that is the domain he seeks to increase."

"You sound as if you know the man quite well, Whit. What sort of increasing does he plan?"

"The sort that involves a new wife and quite a bit of kissing," said Whit, illustrating his point with several well-placed kisses on Vivian's nape.

Vivian blushed. "And he discussed this…this increasing with *you*? You should tell him he might be met with more promising results if he discussed it first with his wife, preferably *after* they were married."

"Why don't *you* tell him, Vivian?"

Vivian turned to look at him in confusion. Whit cocked his head as he tried to gauge her reaction.

"Whit, are…are you telling me that *you* are the Crown's spymaster?"

"As part of my oath, I can neither confirm nor deny that information, my love."

Vivian put her hands over her mouth, stunned. Finally, she whispered, "The Ice Duke a spymaster! Who would have guessed it?"

"Hopefully, no one. Only those who need to know are told. I decided you needed to know. Especially since, in addition to that special sort of increasing I crave, there are others who want to make use of your more mundane talents of creating and solving ciphers. Is that something you might be interested in doing, my dear? Your country—specifically your country's spymaster—needs you."

He frowned when he saw a troubled look in the dark brown eyes that were bright with tears. "Vivian, you don't have to do the ciphers. I only thought it to be something you enjoyed."

"Oh, I do, and I would be very pleased to help in any way I can."

"Then what is troubling you, my love?"

Vivian turned away from those piercing blue eyes that seemed to see inside her soul. She bowed her head and after a moment whispered, "You forget that I am barren, Whit, and there will be none of that special increasing." She looked up at him, love shining in her eyes even as the rest of her face showed her sadness, and then she quickly looked away.

"So I release you from your promise to marry me, your grace, and advise you to find another to be your duchess. I cannot provide you with an heir, and you must make the decision that is right for you, your family, and the title. I promise to accept your decision with all the grace I can muster and leave you to your life, never asking anything again from you except your kind regard."

"So it is entirely my decision? And were I to choose another, more suitable lady to be my duchess, you would accept my decision without question?"

"Yes."

He could barely hear her whisper.

"And you would also accept my decision should I choose to ask *you* to marry me again?"

"Yes. God forgive me for my selfishness. I would say 'yes' and I would love you with all my heart for the rest of my days. But Whit, I will tell you here and now that it may not be enough, and I think one day you will regret not having your own sons and daughters."

Whit still held Vivian's hand in his. He toyed with each finger and marveled once more at how perfectly they all fit in his and how complete it made him feel. He brought that hand to his lips and lightly kissed her fingertips, looking directly into her eyes as if trying to read what was there. Then he let their hands—still joined—fall to his side, and started walking again.

"As a rule I don't enjoy gambling, Vivian. That's something you should know about me, were you to become my duchess. I don't enjoy the long odds that some gentlemen find addicting, but what I do enjoy is winning—succeeding. I enjoy identifying and arranging things that give me the best prospect of succeeding. And, when I feel I have a good chance of winning, I admit that I do enjoy wagering on my own success."

Vivian looked up at him in confusion. "Very well, your grace. Thank you for telling me that, although I don't know why it is something I need to know now."

"I do think I might regret not having my own sons and daughters."

Vivian bit her lip, determined to delay her tears until later, when she was all alone.

Whit continued, "Did you know that some physicians believe when a woman does not conceive, it is not necessarily that the wife is barren? These physicians believe it is possible that the husband is unable to provide the proper seed. I am willing to bet that was the case with the late viscount."

"Why would you think that?"

"He drank a great deal, did he not? That can affect a man's ability to father children. He also had...pardon my bluntness...numerous mistresses, did he not?"

"Yes. More than I was ever aware of, I'm sure."

"Did you ever hear any rumors or stories of any of his mistresses bearing his child?"

"No, but I am told there are ways to prevent such things, and as I said, I did not know of all his liaisons."

"I did."

"You knew of his mistresses?"

"Every single one of them. He was the subject of our investigations for quite some time, Vivian. We found out everything we could about him, and there was never any evidence of any children by him. That is the first circumstance of my gamble."

"I understand and appreciate what you say, Whit, but you forget that you and I...I mean *you* also..."

"Are you trying to remind me that you and I also made love on several occasions and that I was not at all careful about preventing unintended consequences?"

Vivian blushed. "Yes."

"My lady, making love with you is something I would never forget, so I need no reminder. May I ask if you have had your courses this month?"

At this incredibly intimate question, Vivian blushed an even deeper shade of pink and snapped her answer. "No, your grace, I have not—not that it is any of your business. I have never experienced the regularity that other women enjoy."

"That is certainly something for me to keep in mind for the next time."

"What next time? Whit, what are you talking about, and why are you asking me all these questions?"

"Vivian, for such a very intelligent woman, you are something of an innocent. Even *I* have noticed that you are often unwell in the mornings. Even *I* have observed that your bodices seem tighter. And the last few times when we…kissed, I noticed that your breasts are tender to my touch. And that, my love, is the second circumstance of the gamble that has me once again asking you to marry me."

Vivian narrowed her eyes and stared at him. Then she whispered, "Do you mean to say you think I am…with child? That cannot be. It's not… I never…"

Her eyes grew wide as Whit, still holding her hand, got down on one knee.

"Lady Rowden. Vivian. Would you do me the very great honor of accepting my hand in marriage? I can offer you riches and status…"

"Oh, Whit, you know I don't want all of that…"

Whit sighed. "Madam, you have interrupted what was going to be quite a lovely proposal. I must insist that you allow me to finish. I will not have you telling our grandchildren stories about how their grandfather managed to bungle the only real proposal of marriage he ever made."

Vivian clamped her other hand over her mouth and nodded.

"My lady, will you do me the great honor of accepting my hand in marriage and all my love forever?"

The cornflower-blue eyes that had stolen her heart from the very first time she saw them were intense, as always.

"Please, Vivian?"

She smiled and bent down to her duke. And before she kissed him, she said, "Yes."

The Dukes in Danger series continues with
Linea's story…

The Duke's Dilemma

by

Carolina Prescott

Dukes in Danger:
A Haversham House Romance

Chapter 1

Haversham House, late August 1815

"Oh, for heaven's sake, Vivian, stop fussing!"

Miss Linea Braddock, cousin, confidante, and maid of honor to the soon-to-be Duchess of Whitley, batted at her cousin's hand and continued to adjust the silk underskirt.

"You look beautiful, but I must say it's a good thing the current fashion is for high waists, short bodices, and gathered skirts. No one can tell your condition just from looking at you, although…"

"What?" The almost-duchess narrowed her eyes at her cousin.

"Well, with the way you look at your duke and the way he looks at you, I doubt anyone will be surprised when your little one makes an early appearance."

Linney twitched the train of the exquisite gown of *Poussiere de Paris* satin the exact color of *café au lait* encrusted with patterns of seed pearls on the bodice and around the hem.

"There. That's perfect. You have the glow of a bride with just the slightest undercurrent of being in anticipation of a happy event." She stifled a chuckle as the bride tugged once more at the snug bodice.

"Stop laughing," said Vivian crossly. "You and I have always been blessed with an abundance when it comes to our *décolletage*, and I knew I would become more…abundant, but I had no idea it would happen so quickly. Madame Augustine let out the bodice just this week at my final fitting. How can it already be so tight?"

"It's penance for anticipating your vows," proclaimed Linney, in a decidedly superior tone.

"I didn't anticipate them all by myself," muttered Vivian. "I don't see Whit suffering any consequences. In fact, it's just the opposite. He's embarrassingly ecstatic about what he calls my 'blossoming' figure."

"Of course he is. He's a man. He has eyes, and he is fond of using them to enjoy the female form—especially yours. I think it's sweet."

Turning away from her cousin's answering glare, Linney picked up the bridal bouquet of bachelor buttons, Queen Anne's lace, and honeysuckle and tightened the blue ribbon holding the flowers.

The spacious dressing room looked out over the famous formal gardens at Haversham House. The estate—just outside London—was the location for many of the most talked about *ton* gatherings, most notably the infamous house parties given by the effervescent Lady Haversham. Today it had the happy honor of being the site of the most unexpected and most romantic wedding of the London season as the eleventh Duke of Whitley was joined in holy matrimony with Lady Vivian Rowden.

As Linney observed, whispers ran rampant about the source of the bride's glow and the groom's uncharacteristic but decidedly dear manner toward his fiancée. And although the official reason given for a special license and hasty nuptials was the duke's required presence in Paris to help negotiate the peace after Napoleon's defeat at Waterloo, many a dowager would be counting the months until the appearance of the duke's first offspring with a knowing smile.

"You can tell me how sweet it is when *your* breasts are overflowing your stays and tender to touch," said Vivian, continuing her grumble. "I all but snapped Whit's head off when he…"

Vivian stopped abruptly. "Never mind. That's probably something I shouldn't be discussing with you." She glanced over at Linney, but then smiled broadly at the rosy blush coloring her cousin's cheeks. "Oh, I see. Has Avery spoken to Uncle Will yet?"

"No." Linney poked out her bottom lip. "Actually, he hasn't even spoken to me. It is the *most* annoying thing in the world. I do hope he's not waiting to ask me until after he speaks to Papa. Avery can be rather stubborn and old-fashioned at times. This whole marriage business puts me in the mind of two farmers bartering over a milk cow."

"Don't say milk. Or cow. Or… Just use some other analogy, please."

With another tug at her bodice, Vivian studied her reflection in the looking glass, turning and looking over her shoulder to see a back view of the gown.

"They do get a bit medieval when talking about their women, don't they?" she mused. "Perhaps they think about it as a rather large transaction that needs all sorts of contractual safeguards. Truly, I don't know what comes over them."

"I love Avery," said Linney, "and I was under the impression that he loves me, but now I'm starting to wonder. Why doesn't he just ask me? Do you think it's because I have no title and he's an earl and will someday be a duke?" She held out the pearl-and-diamond earrings that were a wedding present to the bride from her duke.

"What I *think* is that you are *overthinking* it. Just be patient. Men can sometimes make very simple things quite complicated—much more complicated than they need to be."

"Maybe…but what else could it be? I don't have a huge dowry or property to negotiate. And even if I did, the undeniable fact is that everything I have—up to and including my very person—becomes his when we marry."

"It *is* rather antiquated," agreed Vivian. "Although Whit did insist that my widow's portion and all the income from V. I. Burningham's puzzles be set aside in a separate account of my own. I thought that very forward thinking of him."

Linney groaned and leaned back against the bed post. "Oh, you're right. If I think too much about it, I become terribly insulted, so I'll just bury my head in the sand like the proverbial ostrich. But really, what is he waiting for? Did you talk to the duke about your vows? What did he say?"

Vivian smiled. "When I told him I would not promise to obey him unless he promised to obey *me*, he just closed his eyes and shook his head. But later he told me he talked Bishop Wren into leaving it out of my vows."

"Good for you! Now I can use you as my example when it's my turn—if it ever is."

"Avery is reportedly not on good terms with his father. Perhaps that's the issue," offered Vivian.

"I suppose...but if that were the case, wouldn't it make sense for him to just say so?" Linney fluffed Vivian's skirt one last time and took a step back. She sighed at the picture her cousin and best friend made in her wedding gown.

"Perfect. You look exquisite, Vivian. Truly, you do."

Linney carefully hugged the woman who had been like an older sister to her since an early age, hoping to forestall the tears that threatened. "Shall we go down? Papa is waiting, and you're already late—such a trial to a man like the Duke of Whitley."

Laughing, the two linked arms and made their way to the top of the grand staircase. With a final kiss to Vivian's cheek, Linney took a deep breath and started down the stairs toward the waiting crowd.

****

Most of the thoughts swirling in Linney's head as she descended the curved marble staircase that morning were about wishing Vivian and Whit a lifetime of happiness together, but at least one or two were spent wondering if she would ever be making that same bridal journey herself.

As she reached the last step, her eyes met those of Avery, sixth Earl of Hammond and heir to the Duke of Easton. Her heart skipped a beat as he held her eyes and slowly smiled that slightly dangerous, velvety smile that brought color to her cheeks and a tingling warmth to other parts of her body.

And while everyone else watched the Duke of Whitley's lovely bride process to the altar, Lord Hammond only had eyes for her.

A word about the author...

Carolina Prescott loves writing historical romances almost as much as she enjoys reading them. The first "real" historical novel she read was Victoria Holt's *Mistress of Mellyn*. One spunky governess, one spooky castle, and one dark, brooding hero later, it was true love at first sight.

As a child, Ms. Prescott loved reading fairy tales with their happily-ever-after endings, and now she's writing her own happy endings for grown-ups.

Ms. Prescott divides her time between an apartment in the trees (and a block from Starbucks) in Northern California and her native North Carolina, where she has lots of room for family, friends, and a very understanding Brittany spaniel.

Visit her at:
http://www.carolinaprescott.com